Sara Dowse was born in Chicago in 1938. She lived as a child in New York and then Los Angeles. In 1958 she came to Australia, settling first in Sydney, and ten years later moved to Canberra where she still lives. She worked in publishing and as a journalist and in 1974 joined the Prime Minister's department to head its newly created women's affairs section, which under her leadership became the Office of Women's Affairs, now the Office of the Status of Women. She resigned this position to become a full-time writer. Her work has appeared in a wide range of publications. In 1983 Penguin published her first novel, *West Block*, and in 1984 *Silver City*. She contributed to Seven Writers' *Canberra Tales*, published in 1988, and another novel, *Schemetime*, appeared in 1990. She is currently working on a biography of her great aunt, who disappeared in Stalin's purges.

also in Penguin

West Block
Schemetime

Sapphires

Sara Dowse

Penguin Books

For my mother, Anna Louise Fitch

Penguin Books Australia Ltd
487 Maroondah Highway, PO Box 257
Ringwood, Victoria 3134, Australia
Penguin Books Ltd
Harmondsworth, Middlesex, England
Viking Penguin, A Division of Penguin Books USA Inc.
375 Hudson Street, New York, New York 10014, USA
Penguin Books Canada Limited
10 Alcorn Avenue, Toronto, Ontario, Canada M4V 3B2
Penguin Books (N.Z.) Ltd
182–190 Wairau Road, Auckland 10, New Zealand

First published by Penguin Books Australia, 1994
2 4 6 8 10 9 7 5 3 1

Typeset in 10/12 pt Garamond Euro by Midland Typesetters, Maryborough, Victoria
Made and printed in Australia by Australian Print Group

National Library of Australia
Cataloguing-in-Publication data:

Dowse, Sara.
Sapphires.

ISBN 0 14 014629 6.

1. Title.

A823.3

My life is a page ripped out of a holy book
and part of the first line is missing.

Kadia Molodowsky

Acknowledgements

Parts of this book have appeared in slightly different versions in various places: 'Sapphires' in *Island* and the Fremantle Arts Centre Press anthology *Readings From the Left* edited by Wendy Jenkins; 'Dough' in *Island* and the Heinemann anthology *Amnesty* edited by Dee Mitchell; 'Naked' in *Voices*; 'The Googol and the Tripwire' in *Southerly*; and 'Paris' in *Blast*. A short version of 'Safar: To Count' appeared in *Redoubt*. I would like to thank the editors for their encouragement.

My thanks also go to my friends in Seven Writers, whose criticism has been so important, and to the Literature Board of the Australia Council for its financial support, to Margaret Connolly for her persistence, Bruce Sims for his patience and Bryony Cosgrove for her judicious and sensitive editing.

Contents

Sapphires

Long ago my grandmother told me a story. Like most grandmothers, she often told stories, but in other respects she seemed very different, not quite a proper grandmother. She was neither plump and round, like the white-haired grandmothers I saw on the labels of ketchup bottles, nor withered, like the ancient grandmothers of some of my friends. She was small, with a straight little figure that made her seem more a child or a doll than a woman, as if she had never traversed adulthood on her way to old age. Her hair was still black, so black that it gave off blue sparks in the light. She wore it bobbed, with a straight fringe clinging to her brow, which made her look vaguely Chinese. She wore grey crepe dresses with deep, white lace collars.

Sigmund Freud once wrote that only those who knew their grandparents can believe in God, but I don't know. My grandmother didn't seem venerable. She was too small, too doll-like, too sedentary to inspire much awe. She had black eyes and her lambent cheeks glowed pink through a waxen skin. My grandmother had a bad heart. When she was really a child she contracted rheumatic fever, and childbirth ruptured an already weakened valve.

For this reason, my grandmother led a careful life. She read a great deal so at least her imagination could roam. (The wire-rimmed reading glasses perched on the end of her nose were the only thing about her that suggested she might be old.) She read books in English but felt more comfortable with Yiddish. She taught me to write Yiddish, of a sort. I could neither speak nor understand it, apart from the odd word here and there, but she taught me anyway, a strange transliteration from the English in which Hebrew letters, those spirals, squiggles and curlicues that looked like a series of tightly coiled springs bouncing right to left across the page, were substituted for the Roman ones. Now I know how unorthodox this method was, but perhaps she was leading me to the next stage, where the words and the letters and the meaning would all match.

Think of it. A language evolved from medieval German, transcribed in the letters of an altogether different alphabet, the letters of which as they are written by hand are different again from the way they are printed, in the Haggadah, for example, that the family used on Passover. Another thing to consider: my grandmother never knew the language of the letters she used. She had never learned Hebrew. My sweet, patient, doll-like grandmother – Miriam, a name with its roots in the Hebrew word for rebellion – had never learned Hebrew because it was not allowed. And this was not because she was sickly, or unlettered (she was, as I've indicated, well-read, and blessed, though this I was not so quick to see, with a penetrating intelligence), but because she was a woman.

My grandmother, like all the mothers and grandmothers before her, was taught to read the language she was permitted to speak – the mama-loshen, the mother's tongue. She learned the scriptures not from the holy texts themselves, (her black eyes were too tempting, her long shiny hair and succinct girlish body too distracting for her to learn the Torah and the commentaries alongside her brothers in a cheder), but from the woman's book, the book that gave the game away in the vernacular, the book that out of his loving kindness a Polish rabbi in the late sixteenth century had written for the people. *Tse'ena-Ure'ena*. 'Come and see.'

Come and see. Or sometimes translated as 'go out and see'. Go forth, O ye daughters of Zion. A ragbag of stories, homilies, allegory, legend and commentary woven around a Yiddish telling of the Pentateuch, the Prophets, the Book of Esther and the Book of Ruth, the whole concoction flavoured by insights from the Kabbala. My grandmother treasured her copy, which had been her mother's and her mother's mother's. She kept it in the drawer of her dressing table wrapped in a piece of old linen. When she removed it and slowly unwound it from the cloth it smelled of old leather and orrisroot. It felt like her skin to touch. *Tse'ena Ure'ena*. Pronounced as one word – tse'en-eh-re'en-eh – it had a happy, beckoning, hurdy-gurdy lilt. But just as the original Hebrew had been fenced off from my grandmother, its Yiddish was closed to me.

'Let me tell you a story I made up instead,' she said.

And this is the story I remember, out of the many that Miriam, the rebel, my grandmother, told:

Long, long ago a young woman married a very rich man, old enough to be her father. The woman had loved a younger man, a boy with thick chestnut curls and cheeks like apples from rushing to her through the cold, but he was a poor boy, a tailor's apprentice, and this was not to be. This was not the way it was in those days. The young woman's heart had skipped on seeing the tailor's apprentice and pounded when they spoke in the street, but she was not sad for not marrying him. Her loveliness had attracted a merchant who sold grain and timber from the big estates to people in faraway kingdoms, and marrying him would provide her parents with comfort in their old age. She was a pious, obedient daughter and was happy to do this for them. And the merchant, as it happened, was not disagreeable, but a handsome man in his prime. He treated his young wife kindly. Her bed was soft down and covered in beautiful linen, the cupboard where she kept this fine cloth was made of inlaid mahogany. Her table was filled with food, and graced with a pair of golden candlesticks that he had brought from his travels.

But, sadly, the marriage bore no fruit. The merchant was patient, but as the months went by he grew more and more worried about his lack of a son. The young wife grieved, too, and as the months became years and the years passed like leaves in the wind, her barrenness weighed upon her. She felt she had betrayed the good faith of her parents, she felt her husband's sorrow. Like Sarah of old she lamented, but still she had no children.

As he grew older, the merchant gave up all hope that his beautiful wife would give him an heir. To comfort himself, he befriended a young man from the yeshiva, a promising scholar, a candidate for the rabbinate, destined one day to head a school of his own. He persuaded this young man to accompany him on his travels. The student had a thirst for knowledge, and so it was natural for him to want to learn about the world, more than he could know from the Mishnah or Gemara. He developed a taste for the fine things the merchant could give him, the clothes, the food, the exotic places, and soon, as the merchant had hoped, they were as father and son.

Now the merchant's beard was white. He felt himself gnarl and bend. He was weary. He went on his last expedition and, to mark this, brought back for his wife a bracelet of splendid sapphires, an old piece of jewellery that he had spied in a bazaar. Its stones were so brilliant they could not escape his notice, it was as if the blue light within them winked even more brightly so that he might not pass them by. He slipped the beautiful bracelet on his wife's wrist and gently closed his fingers around it. 'For you, my dear wife,' he said. Soon after the kind merchant died.

The merchant left his chattels to the student, to his wife he left the house and its effects. But the student had no head for business. His head was turned by the high life he led on his travels and all too often he came back empty-handed. He gave no more thought to the Torah, to the Mishnah or the Gemara, to the honour of the man who had behaved to him as a father, or to the widow who had been entrusted to his care. The widow, for her part, was too proud to ask him for much, and after a time saw that he was not worth asking.

She became poor, her fine dresses shabby, till one by one they were hardly fit to wear. She lived on the potatoes she sowed in her garden, but she had no goosefat to fry them in. She sold the gold candlesticks and the linen. But she could not bear to part with the bracelet. All that she had to recall her former splendour was the brilliance of its smooth oval stones. On the coldest nights, when her stomach was grumbling and she shivered for lack of fuel, she would light a candle in a saucer, open the door to her cupboard and take out her sapphires. She placed the candle on a table near the window and, with the door of the cupboard positioned so that its mirror reflected the black night in the window and the candlelight flickering before it, the whole room would brighten as if by a miracle from the light of the candle endlessly reflected in the glass.

She would gaze at the bracelet in the light and, thinking of how many chickens she could buy if she sold it, her tongue would swell from the taste of them in her mouth. She would imagine the new gown she would buy, the shoes to replace the ones that were wearing out. But the brilliance of the bracelet held her. She saw herself, her golden hair and green eyes, repeated in each gleaming stone. She held it to her shabby dress and ran her fingers over it for warmth.

One night, when she was fixing the catch, she dropped it. Her hands were too stiff from the cold. The sapphires were strewn like stars on the floor. But she gathered them up, all ten of them, and strung them together in the bright, reflected candlelight, stone by brilliant stone, knotting the string tightly between them. It was late and she was tired but she could not go to sleep until the task was done. Holding the broken bracelet to the light she thought she could see faces in the sapphires, not her own, as she had on every other occasion, but the faces of her father and mother long since dead, and the full-bearded face of her husband, and the faces of her girlhood friends who had married peddlers and butchers, and even the red-cheeked face of the tailor she had loved so many years before. And when she had finished stringing all these together, she wrapped up the bracelet, put it back in the cupboard and went to bed.

During the night snow had fallen. But the woman had not noticed this because she had been so busy repairing the bracelet. In the morning the still, frozen whiteness stretched as far as she could see out her window, and the snow began falling again for days. She was terribly hungry and cold. In desperation she took the axe and drove its head into the mahogany cupboard until it was all in pieces, and out of them she made a fire, except for the door with the mirror which she leaned against the wall. She thought that she would be forced to sell the bracelet at last and was almost relieved that the snow was still whirling and the sky was so bleak that she could not venture out. She looked for a place to hide it, but except for the mirror and the table and her bed the house was now bare. So she removed a loose tile from the hearth, dug a hole in the dirt, buried her treasure and replaced the tile. She knelt by the fire she had made of her cupboard. The flames roared and dwindled and soon sputtered out. A few days later she was found frozen in her bed.

Many, many years later the house was bought by a cigar maker who had moved to the village. The cigar maker, a widower with two sons, had married the daughter of the rabbi. By the time the cigar maker's new wife had borne him a child, his grown sons had gone away. The baby girl was a joy to her father but he missed the company of his sons. She grew into a sturdy, solitary child who spent hours by herself playing with her doll on the rug before the fire. Or sometimes she lay flat on her stomach reading, with one leg up in the air and her forehead perspiring slightly from the heat from the flames. One day as she was reading she raised her eyes from her book and looked thoughtfully ahead into the fire. And something caught her eye that she hadn't noticed before. The hearth was uneven. One of the tiles was higher than the others, like a crooked tooth, or ivory lifting off a piano key. The child got up on her knees and crawled over her book to the hearth. The tile was hot but after a while her fingers got used to it and she was able to prise it off. It came away easily and she quickly laid it aside. It surprised her to see the exposed earth. Earth was what she played with out of doors, and even then it wasn't often allowed. Her fingernails scratched at the dirt: it was soft and warm, not at all like the cold mud outside. It was like having summer in the middle of the long dark winter. She dragged her fingers through it, breaking it into a powder and sifting it through her fist until suddenly she felt something hard. She dug deeper, scraping away, and held her breath and dropped back on her heels when the gleam of the first sapphire revealed itself under her fingers. She plucked out the stone, dragging the others with it. The flames from the fire danced back and forth along the bracelet, which she saw as a beautiful necklace for her doll.

The little girl never told anyone of her discovery. On winter afternoons she would remove the loose tile, scrabble around in the dirt for the jewels, shake the dirt off in the fire and carefully clasp them around the smooth, white, porcelain neck of her doll. Or she would wind them around the doll's head in a crown, telling herself stories of princesses and princes. And when she was finished she would bury them again so nobody else could see them.

One day soldiers came through the village, smashing windows and throwing old men to the ground. They set fire to the factory so the cigar maker had to move. He took his family far away, and the house stood empty for a time until a new family came. But no one found the sapphire bracelet, though it was buried there, under the hearth tile, and is there still.

'So,' my grandmother said when she had finished. 'What do you suppose it all means?'

'It is like a fairy story, Grandma. Only the ending isn't very happy.'

'Yes, perhaps. But what does it tell you?'

'You mean the moral?'

I thought a while. No clear moral would come, but I felt safe enough with my grandmother to hazard a guess. 'You must marry the man you love, no matter what,' I said.

My grandmother watched me with a rueful expression. I could see that she wasn't satisfied. 'Tell me what you heard,' she said.

'A beautiful girl married an old man because that's what her parents wanted.' Even as I was speaking the husband seemed repulsive, in spite of what she had said about his being handsome and kind. I could smell his strong breath and feel it on the back of my neck; he reminded me of the men who came to eat pickles and play poker with my stepfather. 'He wanted a son but she couldn't give him one so he kind of adopted one instead and when the husband died he was very mean to her and she was very poor and froze to death.'

'And this was the story?'

'Yes, Grandma,' I said.

'What about the little girl?'

'Well, it was good that she found the sapphires but she must have had a pretty boring life, alone in that room all winter. And anyway, she had to move.'

'Do you think the woman would have been better off if she had sold her sapphires?'

'Certainly,' I said. In real life, I knew, she would have had to, and she wouldn't have wasted any time. 'But then,' I reconsidered, 'the little girl wouldn't have found them.'

'Do you suppose the little girl had any idea of their worth?'

I puzzled over this. 'Well, no. They must have just looked like pretty beads. Only she must have thought they were special because they were hidden . . . But no, they were just a game.'

'Every story has a meaning, Evelyn. Don't feel too bad if you don't understand it right away. You have to keep digging, like the little girl did. And the more you dig, the more you will find.'

'I'm not sure I want to keep digging. It's so sad.'

'Not at all. The sapphires are there, and someday someone will find them.'

She saw I was not convinced. She folded her hands in her lap.

'A story is not only a story,' my grandmother said. 'A story that is only a story is, at best, a parable, with a moral that is easy to grasp. Everyone feels happy with a parable. But a story that is more than a story, my child, is a text!'

Now I remember how her dark eyes blazed that day. I see that my sweet, gentle grandmother was angry, though as patient with me as she always was. Intent on the narrative, I had missed the sapphires. I wouldn't have mentioned them at all if she hadn't prodded me about the little girl, and asked whether the woman should have sold them. Think of it. I had overlooked them, as I had the splendour of the mirrored light. But now I see that this was the story she told me to show me what had happened to stories, how they had been used. The homilies, allegories, and parables of the lovely *Tse'ena-Ure'ena* were not texts. Only the men had texts, which is not to say that these weren't also stories, but refers to the manner in which they were read. It was all the same, the same five books of Moses, the same five scrolls of Esther and Ruth, the same endings from the Prophets, but one was read in Yiddish, as examples and correctives, and the other, in Hebrew, was combed like fleece in search of hidden jewels.

Council Bluffs

The man stands beside a truck, an old brewery truck. It has splintered sides and a worn wooden tray. The truck is parked in front of a warehouse; well, a dark brick garage converted to a warehouse. The warehouse is in Council Bluffs. Across from Council Bluffs, over the Missouri, lies Omaha, a bigger city. Omaha, Missouri, Council Bluffs: Indian names or, rather, names that acknowledge a presence, a bustling, fiery presence now departed, a breath on the prairie. In its place are the brewery truck, the crates of oddly assorted bottles, and countless illegal stills hidden away in barns and in the fields, although here it takes skill to hide things. The land is flat: prairie land, stirring once with buffalo herds, grain land now, corn land, fields of rattling green as far as the horizon. The bluffs, sandstone cliffs overlooking the wide muddy river, are a relief from the flatness. But from the top of them the land is as open as the sky.

In certain light, at dawn in summer, or when the sun descends over the river and the cornfields in autumn, these bluffs seem to rise from the waving grain in a mysterious silver shroud. Mirage-like, they offer the illusion of security and power. The Omaha elders met there in times of impending war. They could see for miles in all directions, they could see the Oto and the Pawnee galloping across the flatlands, and no enemy, they thought, could take them by surprise.

Is the man scratching his beard beside the brewery truck an enemy? One would have to think about this. The man is a peace-loving man, the descendant of ancient warriors, yes, but himself a peaceful man, a mensch. He has crossed nearly half the breadth of the planet to stand on that one spot next to the brewery truck, the very spot perhaps where the Omaha chiefs watched for the Pawnee, or beat clouds of fine dust from the ground, bruising it with their feet while offering incantations to the sun.

The Omaha were fond of ceremony. The cries of their sun dance echoed from the sandy cliffs, over the river and the grasses, the smoke from their fires rose in the blue night air. The Omaha so loved their ritual that they lost all stomach for warfare. They suffered raids: their squaws and their horses were stolen, their finest braves were scalped. They watched the wagon trains trundling westward, and the iron horse steaming after; they heard the ring of rifle shot, the boom of the cannons, they felt the burning of the firewater in their guts; and they looked more than ever for intercession from the spirits in the sky. They became a melancholy people, known for their beautiful laments.

How is it then that this man, of all men, is the enemy? He the victor, they the vanquished, when he himself has heard lamentation enough?

The man is a short man of middle age, short but powerfully built. He has massive shoulders and his chest is so large that one is conscious of the heart and lungs inside. His legs under the black serge trousers are, by contrast, thin. He wears a black coat, a black waistcoat, a platinum fob watch and a skullcap. Beneath the yarmulke his balding head is round, and the hair that remains hangs in scruffy wisps to the tops of his ears. His beard, however, is thick and neatly trimmed, forming a bold square around his chin. It is early autumn; the fierce summer heat has lifted and the cold has not set in, so the man is content. His narrow eyes, set deep above the high bones in his cheeks, reflect a gentle sun.

He is counting. His mind is in perfect concentration. He counts the bottles as the men haul the crates off the truck. They work quickly: the man on the tray bending and swinging towards the man on the ground, who grabs the crates and stacks them inside the warehouse, running past the man in the baggy black suit with the fob watch. Sunlight glitters on the glass – green, blue, brown, but mostly clear and iridescent, the rainbows escaping from the smooth bubbled textures and glowing softly in the shade of the iron-roofed garage.

The man counts in his head. He has never been known to be wrong. A glance at a crate as it comes off the truck is all that he needs to gauge exactly how many bottles are in it, and he takes this number and adds it to the total number of bottles in the crates that have come off the truck already, and there are fifty, sixty, seventy crates in each truckload. These numbers of his work magic, though he fears a shameful magic, akin to the Indian shaman's, or the gematria of the kabbalist, and the men work swiftly, anxious to finish before sundown, and the man keeps juggling the numbers in his head, as if his life depends on them, which it does.

But Lev Kozminsky is a scholar, a talmid chachem. He would devote his life to the study of the Torah, but the Talmud discourages this. If a pious man can earn his bread and provide for his family, then applying himself to his work he performs a holy act. Besides, he is good at this business. His mind, sharpened by the years of diligent study, is useful for other purposes as well. Good or bad? This he cannot say. It is forbidden of course to break the laws of the lands of residence, but he is not breaking the law. The men who run the stills break the law, but is he not their neighbour, their friend? They need the bottles and he, who has made a living out of collecting things, can supply them. Is the only one who can supply them.

He doesn't think about this now but when the men have finished unloading the truck and he can stop counting, and he has written the final number in the small calfskin notebook he keeps in his lapel, he sighs. The men mop their cheeks with their handkerchiefs and drive away in the truck.

The garage is at the edge of the yard. He hears the children playing. He sees them in the patchy grass, riding in the goat cart and climbing the apple tree. He hears the bell on the cart and the children's cries. The setting sun is still warm and shimmers on the flywire on the porch. He moves towards the house. Suddenly the sky grows dark and the house and the children and the shaggy white goat pulling the cart seem to spin off the ground. A cold rain falls – he can feel it on the nape of his neck – bringing mud and pebbles from the hills. The house floats up from its wooden foundations and when it settles, a foot or so still off the ground, the dark logs are crooked and the goat prances in the mud. Terror grips Lev Kozminsky's chest. The children perch like angels on the roof.

He takes another step and the scene sets itself right again. The two-storey white frame house is solid on its foundations. Red apples glow between the leaves of the tree and roll in the grass where the children have shaken them down; the goat is pulling the cart and the child inside is squealing with delight. On the way to the house he passes the chicken run, where the big Rhode Island Red paces the silky dust behind the wire.

The schul that Lev Kozminsky attends is on Nineteenth Street, a block from his house. Until they established the synagogue he used to worship at home, and often still does. But they are building a congregation, what with all that has been happening in Europe, and now his prayers seem more appropriate in the schul. From the outside, in any case, the weatherboard cottage is almost indistinguishable from his house, and most of the other houses in the neighbourhood.

It is Shabbes eve. They are thirteen, three above the quorum as set out in Leviticus and Numbers; thirteen men, middle-aged like Lev or beyond, clasping their shaking siddurs and nodding as they intone, like frail old Shmuel Beber with his rheumy eyes and skin so transparent you can see the fine blue veins on his temples and the backs of his hands. The rabbi, Plaut, is a young man, and Lev watches as he lifts the Torah from its ark, mouthing the words with him, as though he doesn't quite believe that a man so young can be pious enough to lead them. He watches the tassels on Plaut's shawl that looks too new, too white. All through the shemoneh-esreh, Lev observes Plaut.

The violin is an instrument whose music can be beautiful or abominable, depending on the player, but Lev Kozminsky has cast out music: even in its divine, liturgical mode it can be a lure, away from the texts, the words. Sometimes on his rounds in the brewery truck he hears music pour from shop radios, the tinny, thumping sounds called jazz. He remembers the pianos in the nearby brothels, in the neighbourhoods where he lived when he first came from Russia, and the whores singing, drying their hair in the midday sun, and how he had tried to shut his ears. But now the violin is invading him: the tiny music of a grandchild. He opens the gate in the low picket fence and walks down the path to his door. The music is neither divine nor execrable but small, tentative, moving by steps, and he finds himself moving in time with it, counting the notes. And he stops, and he listens, arching his back to gaze at the stars that swirl in the prairie sky.

From the doorway he sees her with the instrument in the parlour, by one of the open sash windows, next to Miriam, her mother, who rests in a chair. She is a plump child, Bernice, with dimpled cheeks and pale brown curls, bobbed according to the fashion; she wears white stockings and a blue lace dress. Lev shakes his head – they are turning her into a shiksa. Spying him, she lowers the bow before glancing towards Miriam, but Lev smiles and raises his hand.

Miriam laughs and touches her daughter's elbow. 'Play, bubele, play.'

The child lifts the bow and sets it on the strings again. The dimples deepen as she bites her lower lip. They listen attentively: Miriam and Morris, Carl and Fritzi, Chava, Zipporah, even the children. Lev has things to discuss with Morris, but this must wait until after the music, and he hears a sadness in the notes, despite the laughter and applause that erupt moments after. The little girl curtsies and runs through the room, the violin bouncing against her thigh. Still at the door, Lev rubs his back, above his left kidney. The child blushes as she races past. Ruchel catches her in the hallway and bends to squeeze her granddaughter, and the child wriggles free but stops at a chair to put the violin in its case.

The Talmud says that on Shabbes eve a good angel and a bad angel hover over each man who returns from the synagogue to his home. If the man finds the candles lit, the table set, the bed made, the good angel is pleased. In Lev Kozminsky's house the candles are lit, the table is set and there are so many beds that even he could lose track. In the six years it took him to persuade Ruchel to leave Russia – from 1892, the culmination, so it seemed, of a decade of pogroms and official repression, to 1898, when things had got no better – they had had four children, one for each time he returned from America to try to take her away. So that when she did come she surprised him, and though she was disappointed that he hadn't settled in New York with his brother Meyer, when she saw the prairie she knew why. ('It's just like the steppe!' 'The steppe without the Cossacks,' he said.) And then there were four others, now three, because of the one who died. Then the older ones married and began to have children themselves, and Ruchel, who had once owned the bakery in Kapulya, loved to feed them all.

She has blessed the candles. The house is filled with the aroma of burning wax, spices and Ruchel's bread. Lev leans over his soup bowl and raises his eyes towards Miriam and her husband Morris. The children are obedient – silent – and Miriam seems content, though her pallor is still disturbing. Morris, does he see this? His cool eyes shine in the candlelight, like agates, or that thick bottle-glass that Lev collects from the farmers. As Lev watches, his son-in-law looks at each of his children, at Bernice and her two little brothers and this, Lev sees, is how he keeps them subdued, as if he were saying: Yes, it is fun at your zaydeh's, but you must behave yourself, you must be on your best behavior. Lifting his spoon to his lips, Lev fights hard to conduct himself in the manner that seems to be expected of him. He feels stiff with the responsibility. Morris turns again to Miriam and it is then that Lev remembers how handsome he is, with his fine straight nose and the cool green eyes and the thick brown hair brushed off his forehead. Too handsome, Lev thinks. He thinks of the fiddlers and the bandits of the Moldavanka and how Odessa Jews sprinkle rosewater in their hair. He glances back at his daughter and then his wife. Slowly, Ruchel nods. And then Lev realises that everyone is silent because he is.

On weekdays it is different. The nights especially. Lev comes with a crate through the door, his slippers sliding on the floral linoleum, his ears ringing with the noise. It rattles through the wooden frame of the house, down the carpet runner on the stairs, and when he follows it to its source and leans against the cool tiles after setting down this additional crate on the floor, he smiles through the racket, watching the kneeling children pour the pellets of gunshot into the bottles. They shake them and the noise is so deafening they can't stop laughing and this makes the bottles shake more. Then the first of them stands – Harry, Miriam's boy – and upends his bottle, and the beebees come clattering down into the bathtub, ricocheting like hailstones against the zinc sides and all the other bottles and Harry holds his up, shining and clean for the bootleggers, to the light beaming from the bulb swinging overhead, so that its iridescence shivers and glows, down on the heads of his brothers and uncles and cousins.

Lev sees their reflection in the bathroom mirror. He sees his own. To him, glass is a wondrous substance and mirrors all the more mysteriously so. He scans his features – are they his features, or the features of the reflection, the eidolon? He ponders this through the clatter. Perhaps it is not so simple to judge a man by what one sees. He takes comfort in this: he would like to be a better man than he seems.

Autumn sets in and Miriam is better. Her cheeks are tinged with pink again and the muddy patches around her dark eyes have gone. Morris comes to take her home. Ruchel gives Morris a tray of food for their dinner, which he will balance on his knees on the streetcar. Morris and Lev talk in low voices, suspending a mutual distrust. Morris needs him, Lev sees.

After she's been gone a week Lev decides it is time, a duty he can put off no longer. Instead of the truck he also takes the streetcar, which delights him with its bell and the scrape of its wheels along the track. He alights on Decatur Street, walks a block in the biting autumn air, diverting himself with memories of Kapulya and the warm smells of Ruchel's bakery. And how she looked coming away from the oven, with her curls falling loose on her forehead and along her temples and her expression of stern concentration, until she saw him and soon, for whatever reason, she would explode into laughter. Perhaps it was him. Not his wit, which was known to be dry, understated, typically Litvak – a man from Vilna was no wild prankster. But he could be impetuous, her bookish admirer, and would come to her shop on the slightest pretext, and maybe that is what she liked about him, what made her laugh: his measured solemnity clashing with the abrupt, somewhat jerky spontaneity. As though she was pleased that he was meeting her more than halfway. But in the give and take that makes a marriage, who had given, who had taken? There was a balance, one he would dare to measure. Marriage had made her stern, had clipped her hair, hiding it primly under a starched white kerchief, so when she took it off at night it clung to her skull like folded wings. Until America. Yes, he'd been right after all about America.

Morris has his shop on a street bordering the coloured people's neighbourhood. Morris Lavan, General Store. He sells ice-cream, mousetraps, saddlery and ploughs for the farmers, cloth for their wives. The boys are playing baseball on the road, Harry and Abe and the shvartser children from the next block. Harry is at bat; he rests it like a caveman's club across his shoulder as the dark boy with long thin legs winds up his arm for the pitch. Harry holds the bat out and the ball whizzes past; the catcher yells 'foul'.

Lev sees Bernice on the steps leading to the store. She has wrapped her arms around her knees, her loose, plump girl's smock covers her like a tent and the shadow from the overhanging roof deepens the tones of her hair. The boys are absorbed in their game but she has been waiting, and when she sees him she jumps up and runs. 'Zaydeh,' she cries, and flashes her dimples and Lev senses as he embraces her that there is something too sad about this greeting, that she is welcoming him with too much relief.

'How are they?' he asks.

The child shrugs. 'Very quiet,' she says. 'They still won't go out.'

'Do you play your music?'

'Oh yes,' she says. 'They like that. But I don't think they like to hear us talk.'

A door at the back of Morris's shop leads to the dining room of the house. Bernice takes her grandfather past the solid oak table bathed in the slanting light; he catches their reflections in the silver menorah, he looking stout and worldly, she like a cherub in her angel's smock. She takes him into the parlour, smaller and barer than his own, except for the grand Victrola on its cherrywood case, with the fluted speaker that reminds him of a shofar.

Morris is already there. He has removed his shop apron, his collar is buttoned but he has no tie. He extends his hand and when Lev takes it, he covers Lev's with his free one. 'Thank you. Thank you, Lev Kozminsky.'

'I only hope I can make a difference.'

'If you can't . . .' Morris says.

Lev is struck by the silence. It occurs to him that Miriam may be sick again, that they are keeping it from him, and he feels a wave of panic that ripples up his arms and breaks in a froth of sweat at his neck. But no, she must be working in the shop, or Morris could not be at his side leading him down the hallway, so she must be much better, and the child has gone to join her. Lev feels his breath relax. But the silence is still unnerving. It makes the shouts of the baseball players and the caws of the crows as remote as they would be in a memory, or a dream. So that when Morris opens the door it is like waking, and the first thing Lev sees is the man seated by the window, so still he might have been frozen there. And though Lev stares, after a moment it becomes painful, and that's when he sees the woman, and she looks even sadder than her husband.

'It's not such a bad place,' Lev says. 'Sometimes it even reminds me of Russia.'

'It certainly gets cold enough,' says Morris.

Isaac Lavan is stiff, impenetrable. His hair and beard are white and his features are starker than his son's, not quite as elegant or refined. He is past the age when one might call him a dandy, but Lev wonders if once he had been less stern, his manner softer; he can't imagine this but he can't dismiss it either.

'In early summer,' Lev continues, 'the prairie is covered with wildflowers, and then I can hardly believe I am gone. Poppies, cornflowers, sunflowers. It can be very beautiful.'

Isaac Lavan says nothing, though his wife's eyes are rimmed with red. She is a stout woman with kinky grey frizz stretched into a bun, so that it forms a series of ridges on her crown. The light from the window plays over the jet beads of her necklace, against her sallow skin.

'And there is no sight more wonderful than the corn. Miles of green, tall as a man, growing as you watch. When the wind comes it makes waves, as in the sea, and you can hear it – a noise like hundreds of birds flapping their wings. Of course, it's been harvested now . . .'

Lev glances up at Morris who stands with his arms folded against the door. He seems troubled yet at ease, with the look of a man who has done as much as he can and has handed over his burden. Lev rubs his back. If it is a mitzvah to give comfort, he is sure that it wasn't meant to be as hard as this. He tries again. 'We have a schul,' he says.

'Hah!' says Isaac Lavan, so suddenly and with such force that Lev looks over to his son-in-law again.

'It's true, the schul is small, and the rabbi is a little wet behind the ears . . .'

Lavan has composed himself. His manicured hands with the pearl-pink fingernails rest on the knob of his cane.

'Think of your son,' Lev says. 'Think of Morris. He has worked and saved to bring you here.'

'You are a kind man, Lev Kozminsky. But can't you see that we are in mourning?'

'It is past the time for that.'

'For you, maybe.'

Lev can hear his voice rising. 'You are alive. So are your children.'

'In a manner of speaking,' Lavan says. Today he has children in Latvia, in Palestine, in Argentina – places like this, Lev supposes, that he has no more than snapshots of, places he can scarcely imagine. Lev's eyes roam over the bare walls of the room, and now he remembers the silver menorah on the table in the dining room. He glimpses Lavan's fingers and the glowing white of his collar and the black beads around his wife's neck; and it is though he is staring at the mirror again, through the tarnished glass, at an image that could or could not be his own. But he wonders if Isaac Lavan could stoop to deal with the bootleggers, or if he would even know how.

'I was once in Odessa,' Lev says. 'I remember the sparkle on the water and the smell of the sea, the great ships at anchor. And the acacias, and the bookstores, and the Bessarabian wine they served in the cafes. And Deribasovak Street . . . so elegant . . .'

'Please,' says Isaac Lavan.

'And the mud – it was autumn . . .' And here Lev pauses, before bellowing out in a voice he hardly knows as his own, 'And the way that the Jews stayed on one side of the street!'

Lavan stands up, glaring at Lev. He brushes his dark coat and fingers the point of his beard; he takes a step towards the door but seeing Morris there, he stops. Then his pupils cloud, his shoulders sag, and he sits down.

'Tell me,' he says. 'How long is it since you have been in Russia?'

'Twenty-six years. Twenty-six years and seven months, precisely. I have counted every day.'

'It has changed.'

'When? How? When was it different?' Lev is feeling ashamed, he is losing all patience. But the man is a fool. They made rich fools in Odessa. 'I was glad to leave, I couldn't wait for the chance. A young man with a head on his shoulders, why would I want to stay in a place where whatever I had would be taken, if the army didn't get to me first? Get out and about a little, Lavan. Look around you, this is a house, not a grave!'

It is the most passionate speech that Lev has made for a time. Though he can be eloquent he is normally a taciturn man, slow to anger, sparing with words. Only Ruchel can make him so angry, stubborn Ruchel who stuck to her shop through the Cossacks and the rampaging peasants, the taxes, the quotas. Only when he had given her children and she could see no future for them in Kapulya would she come. And Lavan, the clod, did he think that he could have escaped all that?

'We should give thanks!'

Suddenly, Hannah Lavan moans, a deep, tremulous cry that sends her son to her side and Lev's glance moving swiftly towards her, and he realises that he had forgotten she was there.

Miriam and the children walk him to the streetcar. She is dressed in Ruchel's warm coat and her cheeks are bright in the tingling air. So, she is really better. He squeezes her hand. With Miriam time is precious. This makes Lev grateful; his heart is full. He looks at the sky: the pinks, the purples, the clouds' wondrous shapes, animals and castles, he points them out to the children. Abe sees a pig with a cap on, Bernice sees a duck, Harry dreams about shut-outs and goose eggs. Miriam laughs, and Lev sees tears in her eyes. 'It's so good to laugh, Pa,' she says. 'You have no idea.'

'They will get over it. One day.'

He climbs on the streetcar, the one on which Morris has carried so many meals. The bell rings and he waves to Miriam and the children who stand in the descending dusk. Yet he can't chase Isaac Lavan from his mind. If a man stops believing, it is because he thinks too much of the world; he is bound to be disappointed when the world offers little but evil, pain and loss. For Lev there are no surprises, and so he is always surprised. And that's when he hears the music, above the scrape of the metal wheels as the streetcar lurches on its tracks. He hears voices rising from one of the mean wooden houses: a low ululation that rises in a tumultuous shout and dies down again, the voices of the coloured people singing their version of the Torah. They rise in a crescendo and die down again, like the waves on the windswept prairie.

Dough

In the shtetl where Ruchel Kozminsky lived and worked and waited for her husband, there was a clock. It had been installed in the sixteenth century, when the province was still a part of Poland, and it stood in its carved wooden tower in the centre of the town's market square. The town had prospered under the benevolent rule of the local noble, who had pressed the peasants into producing grain and cattle for export, and he himself had commissioned the tower. Carpenters built it from thick planks of oak, and the clock, with its cast-iron bell that struck the hour, was imported from England. The town, too, was constructed entirely of native timbers, and as such was subject to frequent fires; and in the middle of the following century Cossacks led by the infamous Bohdan Chmielnicki burned it down. But wood was plentiful in the region and such was the shtetl's spirit that within two years it was rebuilt completely, including the synagogue and the nobleman's clock.

It was the first thing that Ruchel saw when she came at dawn to set up her stall. The tower, with its straight sides and pointed, pyramid shape at the top, would be licked by a rosy, golden light that reminded Ruchel of flames, and it seemed as though the clock had indeed stopped and was at that very moment being consumed by Chmielnicki's fire. She would give a little shudder, adjust her kerchief and set to work, balancing the timber slab on the trestles, snapping out the starched white cloth and letting it drift down onto her table, unwrapping her hot braided breads and placing them in artful piles on the cloth.

Through the day, as the sun grew hotter, and her mind grew tired of the chatter of the marketplace, she would find herself staring at the clock again. At midday, when the bell gave out twelve deep, clanging reverberations, the shadowless tower seemed as squat and smug as the local nobleman, the drunken descendant of the man who had commissioned its original. It was as if time itself had lost its soul, that Keteb, the noonday devil, had stolen it; and, as if to confirm this, the face of the clock, too, seemed to have lost all expression. Ruchel blinked, she was losing her mind with loneliness: it was all superstition, Lev had told her so.

And yet. And yet. There were many things she did not understand. When she was younger she thought that time was like the day, the early sunlight climbing over the horizon like honey pouring onto the land and then the sun rising higher and burning brighter in the sky and falling at last like a molten ball singeing the boughs of the pine trees on the hills. And the days became years, circular in their seasons; the hard frosts of winter melting into the muddy slush of the thaw, the sudden thrust of mountain springs and the joyful babble of the birds. Then came the flocks of new rabbits chasing through the thickets and next the tall bending grasses of summer and autumn's blanket of leaves. And she saw all the ages since creation spiralling, uncoiling, circles within circles tumbling towards her, time like the spinning spokes of wheels, or the hands of the clock in the tower before her, slowly extending its shadow across the square.

The year was marked also by the feasts, the grand cyclical procession of holy days. And thus it had been, for centuries, until one year there was a tumult, far away in France, and time shot forth like an comet, and everything, forever, was changed.

As a rule, girls and women were not to know of this. As a matter of fact, for many of the old people the Haskalah, the Enlightenment, was a curse, a blight, a plague, for men and women alike, to be stamped out as the worst form of trayf. But only the most pious were immune. All men are born, and remain, free and equal, the Frenchmen said, and this was to include the Jews. Into every far-flung ghetto and shtetl this notion crept, to some like a stealthy demon. What Ruchel had learned she had learned from Lev Kozminsky, the quiet, fervent scholar from Vilna. Litvaks were known to be sceptics, but this one seemed to gobble up uncritically everything he read. It was not that he would abandon the Torah, he told her, but that things from now on would be different – in the wider world a Jew could command respect. And she had thought that though he was naive and foolish, for even in the marketplace it was easy enough to see the respect that Christians had for Jews, his words stirred something inside her, something like a dim ancient memory whose precise delineations she could not yet grasp, and which frightened her for that very reason. But she went ahead and married him, in spite of her fears and the knowledge that though he would want her to leave with him she would not go, and even then she was fearful, not that he was wrong but that he might be right. So who was the more stubborn? He or she?

At the end of the day Ruchel shook out the crumbs from her tablecloth, folded it into a square, slipped it into the basket with the money she had earned, dismantled her trestle table and began the slow, weary, market-day trundle home. Her youngest daughter, Zipporah, was there to greet her when she got to the gate of the house, and Ruchel propped the table and the trestles against the gateposts and embraced her, worrying as she did that her thoughts were making her absent and aloof. For it seemed sometimes that she was all alone in the town when in fact not a day went by when she was not surrounded by people. Her mother, her father, her sisters, her friends, were all dear to her, so much so that she couldn't imagine a life without them, but for all her resisting it was clear that her marriage to the stubborn Vilna chachem had set her apart. And even as she was thinking this Zipporah was telling her of the letter that had arrived, was dancing about her, begging her to hurry inside and open it so they all would hear the news.

Dearest Ruchele, Lev Kozminsky wrote. *Last week I bought a horse, a little spotted mare, not young but in reasonable condition, and a cart in which I am able to transport many more items than before. Out here in the west there are not many landsmen but the farmers are good customers. Pots, pans, boxes, bottles and cloth are popular – I get bolts of flannels and a tough-wearing denim from Des Moines. The farmers give me a bed but tonight I am lying in the cart, reading and writing under the stars with the help of a kerosene lantern. It is better for studying this way. The sky seems very low and bright with stars, this is what I notice, the vast expanse of it, that is at the same time close . . .*

It was then that the eldest, Miriam, cried, 'Oy, there are Red Indians out there!'

Her brother, Carl, kicked her and laughed. 'Stupid! Des Moines is the capital, a city.'

'It is only at night that he studies?' asked Ruchel's mother.

When she had finished reading, Ruchel laid the pages in her lap. She shook her head. 'Does he need to work, with me as provider?'

'He's saving for us, Mama,' Zipporah said. 'To take us to America.'

'How much does a yeshiva bucher save?' grumbled Ruchel's father.

Ruchel lifted her burning gaze from her lap. 'I will write at once and tell him to come back.'

All this running, scurrying over the globe. She looked around her, at her two frail parents and the dirty faces of her children and felt secure. This was home, where she could feed her family, bless the candles, bake her bread. If part of her knew it for a dream, that it all could go up in a moment's rush of flames, and whispered like Lev's voice in the night that she must flee, then this is the part that most frightened her, and she would pay it no heed.

The good thing was that everyone needed bread. Not only the fine white challah for Shabbes but the coarser, weekday varieties, the pumpernickels and ryes. In theory, every woman could bake her own, but not everyone did when Ruchel was around. Some had too many children, some had too many clothes to sew, another might have had too much work in her dairy. Others were too old, or too poor, and in summer perhaps the fear of fire kept some from running their stoves throughout the day. Only Ruchel could have told me for sure. Of course, I didn't know her well, and didn't think to ask her when I did. But one thing is clear. It was not at all unusual for a woman to earn money in a shtetl. It was needed, it was expected; it was tradition.

So, with the children scrambling around her and the old people grumbling in the corner, Ruchel tended her oven and kneaded her dough, except in the summer months when she would work when they were sleeping and it was cool. In the deep silent dark of the morning she would wake with the chimes of the nobleman's clock, creep with her candle into the kitchen where Zipporah was still fast asleep, arrange the pile of kindling in the stove, setting larger, slower-burning chunks on top of that, set the mass of it alight, and begin the expert process of sifting, mixing, kneading and shaping for which she was praised far and wide.

If you have done it yourself you would know that there is something deeply soothing in the simple, humble act of making bread. You take the flour and shake it through the sifter or a sieve, you take the yeast, dry or caked, and crumble it into the tepid water, mixing it with the sugar or molasses and salt and oil, now you add some flour (no need to be exact), then some more, you beat the dough, add more flour and then, when by touch you sense that it all has reached the requisite pitch of elasticity, you begin the marvellous business of kneading. An ancient art, it can have the same effect as gazing at the moon and stars, a sensation of having transcended the boundaries of space and time. I have known people to take up breadmaking suddenly, unexpectedly, at crucial moments in their lives: a man who started after breaking up with his wife, a bank teller who taught herself to make croissants on receiving a promotion. I suspect it is due largely to the kneading. They say, in the utilitarian, instrumental fashion peculiar to Sunday supplements, that it's a means of releasing tension, all the wrapping and squeezing and folding and punching, and the man who'd divorced his wife claimed that he was only doing to the dough what he had regularly done to her breasts. But now that I know Ruchel's story I believe that dough can be more than just a device for assuaging hungers, sexual as well as visceral, although with Lev away for such long stretches at a time, there could have been something of that for her too. But still, there was more, definitely more; deeper, and different.

This particular summer night was in the middle of the week, so Ruchel was not making the light, slippery, oily dough for challah. Her recipe called for a thick grainy dough that required a good deal more kneading – at least fifteen minutes, and probably two or three extra spurts of five minutes each. Moreover, this dough was a sticky dough, which made the kneading that much harder again. In the winter she welcomed the labour and, besides, the children would often pitch in, to fold, push and turn and fold, push and turn, and their squabbling over who would do it next and for how long at least gave her muscles a rest and broke the the monotony, and if Lev was home he would sometimes take over. But here, in the dark, aside from the sleeping Zipporah, Ruchel was alone, and as she worked her fingers and the heels of her hands into the tacky dough, her thoughts circled aimlessly, like the gnats bobbing and spinning in the waving air above the candle, and she began to think of time again, and space, because I suppose of the very great distance that lay between her and her husband. She pictured the stars above him in the farmers' fields, and the warm steady glow of his lamp, and the greater her concentration on these the more she sensed that the distance was really nothing, if time, as her thoughts, could stop circling, to move straight and clean like a silvery comet through the sky. And she imagined him, her sweet yeshiva bucher, her luftmensch, lying with the Torah in his cart, and it was as if she were actually there, lying in the straw beside him. She pressed the heels of her floury hands harder into the dough, then, relaxing the muscles of her arms, lifted the furthest end of it and folded it once more into the middle, rocking with such force she might have been davening as she did. And after several more minutes of this the world seemed plunged in silence, out of which a low, humming, buzzing noise began to slowly gather strength, blotting out any visual register of her surroundings: the rough, smoke-darkened walls, the packed earth of the floor, the black flaking iron of the stove, her sleeping child, the worn, scrubbed wood of the trough where she worked. Ruchel squeezed the dough, gripping it now in her sweating palms as the trance seemed to grip her soul. The buzzing got louder, a shriek that bounced off the bones of her skull. Was she being possessed? Had a demon – a dybbuk – jumped inside her? But no, she was neither agitated nor raving. She was calm, peaceful – the only disturbing thing was the noise. And that, too, Gott zu danken, was fading now. She was only vaguely aware of her hands on the dough and the yeasty fragrance rising up from it. Ahead was a swirl of stars; it was as though they were spinning through a tunnel, or perhaps it was she who was spinning; it was hard to know. But after a second or so, maybe less, the dizziness stopped, and ahead she could see a wide, green land, green everywhere, with tall leafy plants coated with silvery drops of dew, and all this under a bright hard sky a dense, vibrant shade of blue. She could feel herself enter, the broad leaves sprinkling moisture in her face as she brushed against them in passing, the soles of her boots sinking deep into the black, spongy earth. The buzzing that assaulted her before was now the singing of pearly-winged insects, and the warmth of the sun high in the blue overhead caressed her as she walked. She saw, in the near distance, what appeared to be the skyline of an enormous city, a city of ziggurats and onion domes, which glittered and shimmered in the sunlight cascading from the sky; and it seemed like no time at all before she had entered the gates and was surrounded by these fabulous golden constructions. And at her feet were cobblestones, so smooth and so clean that they glowed, and when she looked again she saw that they too were gold, just as she had heard from the storytellers who visited the village. So this was what Lev has been drawn to, she whispered, sucking in her breath – America, El Dorado, the goldena medina! So beautiful, so foreign that she was more afraid than she'd ever been. But then, her eyes at first quizzical, then wide with a grateful wonder, as if she were relieved that in all this beautiful strangeness there was still something familiar, something that she, a humble woman, might understand, she saw a clock. A clock like the nobleman's clock and yet, not like it, different in one or two arresting respects, but similar enough to make her feel, well, at least partially at ease. The clock had its tower, though needless to say this tower of solid gold had a dazzle altogether different from the dawn-kissed oak of the tower in the market square. And her heart gave a kick when she saw that the clockface had no hands – yet the crenellated tower cast a shadow, odd, she thought, with a noonday sun so high in the gleaming sky. And her eye, following the line of this shadow, laid like a dark velvet cloth over the phosphorescent ripples of the cobblestones, almost overlooked what was central to the picture. A woman, an astonishingly beautiful woman, whose beauty Ruchel was unable to compare with anything she had ever seen. Her hair – what can I tell you about her hair? By what means could I describe it? Well, it was the deep, red, tawny colour of the woods in autumn, an intense, lustrous scarlet speckled and streaked with gold, and it spread over her majestic shoulders in a fury of waves and curls. Her lips were the darkest crimson, her skin was as pale and luminous as pearls. She wore a mantle embroidered with them, and lapis lazuli studded here and there, so that the vestment had the sparkle and the deep blue solemnity of the evening sky. Her eyes were a strange, dark, glittering grey, the colour of hematite, glowing as if from some implacable iron strength within. Her white arms peeked out from the billows of her hair; her left hand pressed against her hip and on her right was perched a beautiful mauve-pink bird. She held it out, shoulder high, but from time to time would bring it in close to her face and nuzzle its feathers with her splendid nose. Her legs, in sea-green trousers shot through with threads of gold, were crossed at the ankles, the right over the left, in a curiously jaunty pose, and she leaned back against the tower as if deliberately relaxing her regal bearing for Ruchel's sake, to lessen her awe. And, accordingly, a smile appeared on the crimson lips, gentle and beneficent, but revealing a set of such perfectly shaped, brilliant teeth that the effort to calm her onlooker was almost immediately undone.

For Ruchel was positively shaking now, from fear or excitement she couldn't have said. Shame was mixed up in it, too, for in such company she couldn't help remembering how poor she was, how shabbily she was dressed. But somehow this creature didn't seem to mind, was giving Ruchel her full attention in fact, her manner suggesting that she was waiting for her to speak, to remark on her extraordinary personage perhaps, with a semblance of pluck or wit. But Ruchel, whose tongue could be so sharp that at times she blamed herself for losing a husband, was unable to utter a word. She forced herself to move the muscles of her mouth, but it would only make disgusting little circles like the bubbling mouth of a fish, and her throat would eject no sound. Then the woman, kind and laughing, but nonetheless with impatience in her voice, which seemed to throb like a gong through the boulevards and avenues and piazzas, asked, 'Don't you recognise me, Ruchel? Don't you see who I am?'

Because of the clockface, Ruchel thought of Keteb, then remembered the shadow. Then who? Lilith. Yes, it must be Lilith, the demon, the succubus, robber of infants and men's night fluids. Was this a test? Then how dismally she could fail. She longed to stay, but the teachings commanded her. She might have known: in her loneliness she had been wavering and all this was the test. She must flee this goldena medina, and keep its false, siren beauties safely out of her reach. And she inwardly keened for Lev, for it was clear to her now as it had never been that he wasn't going to leave this place – no mortal man could resist. And she felt a sudden rush of irritation, no, anger, that men were such children, that the most pious and unworldly among them could let their heads be turned.

How long did this take, for Ruchel's emotions to transform themselves from wonder at this awesome woman to a rising scorn, and anger at all the gullible men in the world? A minute, maybe several, maybe only a split second. But it was all she needed to give her back her voice.

'I should have known,' said Ruchel. 'I'm not fooled.'

'Oh really?' the woman said, as though she were half-expecting this. 'But perhaps you are.'

Ruchel continued to looked at her accusingly, but the woman shrugged. 'Oh, I know what you are thinking, Ruchel, and you are wrong. So very, very wrong. I know, you have been told that I am evil, a blasphemy – a witch or worse. This has been my ignominy, an exquisite humiliation designed especially for me. Do you realise how they slander me? Give me bad names, erase my true ones, all to obscure my identity? To quiet me they have strapped me to their pedestals, or cast me down to the depths. And this has gone on for centuries. As long as I'm sweet and docile, like Ruth or Esther, I'm praised, for then I can't do any harm. Either that or I'm lascivious Lilith. Spiteful, the devil. Either way, I am kept in my place. And now even you are tricked into thinking that I am merely a demon. Ach, I've come to expect it. Though, frankly, it has been mortifying – for someone like me.'

'That is pride.'

The woman gave Ruchel a sidelong glance. 'Ooh,' she said, 'how you speak to me, Ruchele! Still, it takes nerve. I was beginning to think you had lost it. Maybe you are not the timid, whimpering soul I've taken you to be.'

'Only about some things,' Ruchel confessed.

'There is too much terror in you, Ruchele.'

Now Ruchel was sarcastic. 'Forgive me, it's been bred in my bones.'

The woman came closer, drawing away from the support of the tower. Its shadow clung to her, accenting the lustre of her skin, of the strange quicksilver eyes. 'I realise that, and it has saddened me. Don't you see? I am doing what I can to help. But you must trust me.'

She held out her hand, and with a flutter of its mauve-pink wings, the bird lifted off in a gliding, looping flight.

'Trust you?' Ruchel cried. 'This is the greatest blasphemy!'

At this the woman drew herself up to full height; with both hands free she pressed them to her hips and stood with her slippered feet firm on the ground and her legs wide apart. 'Oh come, Ruchel Kozminsky. I took you to be much cleverer than this. I thought that with you, for all your shortcomings, there was hope! How can you fill your head with such nonsense?'

'I am a simple woman,' Ruchel said.

'Yes, yes, indeed. Very simple. Tell me, who makes the money in your house? Puts the food on the table? Pays the taxes, cares for the children, applies the medicines, cleans the windowpanes, blacks the stove? In short, organises everything that needs to be done in that miserable place?'

'This is nothing.'

'Nothing. Nothing? Ruchele, it makes me weep to hear what you are saying. Although as you must understand, I am not the weeping kind.'

'No. Nor am I.'

'You see?'

Ruchel was beginning to. She sensed with a sudden prickling in her skin that she was being told things she had known and long forgotten. She nodded, as much to herself as to the imperious female who, with all the suppressed exasperation of a teacher, stood waiting before her. Finally Ruchel stilled herself, looked up and gave her a feeble smile.

'Well. That is more like it. This gives me heart. It seems I was not mistaken after all.'

'No, kayn aynhoreh, you were not.' Then, wishing to show herself capable of casting off old superstitions, Ruchel amended that. 'I mean to say, no, you were not.'

The woman sighed a sigh of great contentment and smiled. She stretched out her arm and, as if from nowhere, the beautiful bird glided towards her and skidded to a rest on her palm. It climbed onto her finger and the woman crossed her arms. For a time she did nothing more, content to observe her acolyte, her silvery gaze moving over her, measuring, assessing. Then she stroked the bird's feathers and tilted her head, indicating the gilded city, its glittering pyramids and tapered domes, the shiny fruit hanging from its trees, the streets paved with gold. 'Beautiful, isn't it?'

'Oh yes, yes it is,' Ruchel agreed.

'But quite strange, wouldn't you say?'

'I found it so, at first sight.'

'Do you know why?'

Ruchel, quite at ease now, permitted herself a laugh. 'Where I come from nothing looks like this.'

'Look again.'

Ruchel did as the woman asked, and saw this time an all too familiar sight: a landscape of muddy streets covered with ash, which floated in curled black flakes through the thinning tendrils of smoke, embers smouldering here and there, the charred, collapsed wall of the prayerhouse, or a store, and over everything a pall of silence. And it was only after she had stared at this scene for some time that Ruchel realised that the silence was the same as the silence of the golden city, for in neither were there any people – not a person, not a body, not a soul.

With her eyes wide with horror and wet with tears, Ruchel looked back at the lady.

'Go, Ruchele, go. For life. You will need all the courage I can give you, and America is no El Dorado, but go.'

There was an awful pain down one side of her neck, and when she lifted her hand to rub it she felt the muscles across her shoulder bunch up in a knot. She wriggled her shoulders and shook her aching arms. Down in the wooden trough lay a perfectly round, springy mound of dough. Ruchel pressed a finger into it and was pleased to see the dent disappear almost as soon as it was made. Well, you know the rest: she put it aside to rise, took another mound that had already risen, swollen like a nursing breast to twice its size, plopped it into the greased pan, slipped it in the oven. All in the comforting, circling rhythm of her ritual. The sun came up, she was setting up her stall, she stared at the clock. Perhaps she expected to see someone there, partly obscured by its shadow. She shook her head, and laid out her wares. A fly came, but she hesitated before shooing it away. The hours passed. She gossiped with friends and the other stall-holders in the square as the sun traced an arc in the sky like the curve on her pumpernickel loaf.

And so it went, day by day, for a number of weeks until one day the word came from a neighbouring town that the tsar had issued another decree and that soldiers were hunting for Jewish boys to conscript them into the army, this time for an extra six years, on top of the standard twenty-five. Ruchel then thought only of her son. She pulled out an old dress from her trunk, shook it and pressed it and thrust it onto Carl, who wriggled and swore and made faces in the darkening windowglass when she tried to fill out his hair with one of her wigs. Angry and frightened and tired, she told him to hush, yanking him by the upper arms and slapping a hollow between his shoulder blades to make him straighten up. And then she too saw the reflection in the glass, the ridiculous, ludicrous sight of him, and of her, yanking and slapping and shoving like some ill-bred peasant; and something snapped in her and tensed her jaw and she saw herself moving her head from side to side, slowly, deliberately: no. No. What was she afraid of? The boy was only seven! Yet her every action had been primed by fear. Ancient fear, crazing fear, over and over, fear. She turned to her mother and father who were already heading for bed to lie cowering under the quilts, blinked, and snapped her head away. She ripped off the dress that hung in folds from Carl's shoulders and told him to put on his clothes. She rammed the dress into the trunk, pulled out a coat and a scarf, and a pair of Lev's old breeches, and threw these all on, stuffing her skirt into the legs of the pants as she hopped to a corner of the kitchen and reached deep into a bag of rye flour, extracting a coin sack and a bundle of notes. She took four of these notes, wetting her finger and counting them out, and placed them with great care under a glass on the table, reconsidered, took another from the bundle and left that, looked wildly about her and, remembering, broke off a bit of her yeast and wrapped it in a cloth, grabbed a valise and some bread, her three little daughters and her son, and that very night left the village, following the route that Lev had taken the four different times she had refused to go with him. They rode in a cart to the nearest town, the children asleep in the straw and the stars so close they seemed to prickle the back of her neck; and there was a succession of carts, lumbering and stumbling, after that, and train carriages after that, and one night spent in a field of tall grass where they hid when they heard the carousing Cossacks trotting past, until they got to a river and Ruchel bribed her way onto a barge; then walking as far as the next train, moving when they could at night, and then at last the blustery port of Danzig and the hold of the cattle ship over rocking northern seas and the five of them arriving hungry but healthy, Gott zu danken and thanks too to the Ellis Island officials, in America; New York.

Heroic? Ruchel thought so, though at times their progress had seemed as plodding and as measured as an ant's over a patch of dirt. Or as slow as scraps skimming a silty puddle in the old market square. Now, of course, we have the language for this: it's relativity, we would say, but even though she hadn't the words for it, I have a feeling in my bones that Ruchel thought of it first. But the point is that when she wasn't thinking she was moving, and every bridge she crossed, every field and sea, made her feel marvellously, exuberantly, thankfully alive. She stood with her four children at the iron gates of the city and was filled with such wonder at the ships and the crowds and the tall buildings on the other side of the bay swamped in a sooty, golden haze that she announced to Lev's brother Meyer, who'd been waiting for them in that swarm of people, that they weren't in a hurry yet to hop on the train out west. 'Meyer, I want to see a real city – just once.' So they took a spanking new ferry boat across the mouth of the Hudson to Manhattan and they saw the streets of people and the peddlers and their barrows and ate ice-cream in biscuity cones. They had fun, oh how they had fun, though Ruchel could see that here too in America the people were poor; but she tried for the moment not to think of that. The most exciting thing of all was to climb on an omnibus, a double-decker one – you know, the small kind pulled by horse – and they sat in the open air at the top, far above the pungent fumes of the city, and rode on the avenues past the fine granite mansions uptown. Ruchel took off Lev's scarf and let her hair that had grown inch by inch throughout the long journey float free and, as the bus lurched and swayed to a halt in some snarl of carriages and horses, she caught a reflection in the shimmering glass of one of a series of tall, ornamental windows on a mock baroque facade. It was that of a woman, an astonishingly beautiful woman, with flaming hair covering her shoulders in a tumult of waves and curls.

The Lake

Tell me this: why do cities draw us? What is their pull? What is it that makes large, smelly, dirty, cacaphonous congregrations of slaughterhouses, pinochle parlours, stock exchanges, water towers, mayonnaise plants and chemical plants, railway yards, grain elevators, diners and steak houses and burlesque houses, gross, grimy, granite cathedrals, balloon stands, ice-cream carts and cheap nickelodeons, butcher stores, department stores, lingerie stores, bakery stores, candy stores, low dives and needle-tipped skyscrapers and *crowds* so exciting, so irresistible; so inevitable?

For a long time now, ever since the first neolithic woman got it into her head that the seed she gathered with such cunning and patience could be planted in the ground and, with water and weeding, made to grow, people have been collecting in ever bigger concentrations; from hamlets to villages to towns to cities to mammoth metropolises like Chicago. It is as if the need for company is so instinctive in this gregarious human animal that it has, over time, run riot, and no amount of inconvenience or discomfort can hold it back. So for Bernice Lavan, a young, talented, brown-haired woman from Iowa, the attraction was no more than predictable. Natural, you might say.

Chicago then was dominated by the stockyards on the south-west side. The big, draughty, rust-coloured freight trains brought the beasts in from Texas, Oklahoma, Kansas and Nebraska; fat hogs and grimy sheep and Texas longhorns; big, red, shaggy animals with rough mournful lowings that wakened the city's newcomers in the night; until they got used to it, as they did to the traffic and the rush of the trains and the shouts coming out of the bars; and then the shrieks of the dying animals became so much a part of the music of the city that they were heard no more.

Not a particularly good setting for a love story – but then, what is? What really mattered was that Bernice was ready.

The first night she spent in Chicago she heard these eerie nocturnal noises, but paid them no mind. She stood at the open window of her room in the boardinghouse, her freshly manicured hand holding back the gritty lace curtain, every inch of her electric with hope. The prairie, transmogrified, rolled out before her: a grand table laid with a feast of lights. The lowing of the cattle was a refrain, in minor key, sounding so like the moans of a shofar, or the tremulous bass of the cantor that it obliterated fear, leaving her only with the sense of having arrived. She could feel it in her fingers, in the roots of her hair, in twinges up her spine, even if she didn't know precisely what it meant. What she did know was that she was free. For five years, since leaving high school and a short, pointless spell at Creighton University, she had been working at station YHWH writing advertising copy, trying to inject life, that is, into otherwise pretty dreary material about corn feed and sheep dip, and occasionally delivering it herself to the farmhands and cowpokes who made up the large part of YHWH's audience. She had been reading out copy promoting the benefits of a local funeral parlour when she stumbled, finally, on the patent futility of her position. It was hard enough getting feeling into her patter without either hamming it up or sounding too cold and matter-of-fact, but the night-shift piano player kept muttering obscenities into her ear, which had the unfortunate effect of making her laugh. She put in her resignation, said goodbye to the family, and headed east for Chicago, where, as she saw it, her talents might be put to better use.

On the second day after her arrival, after she had found the room and a beauty salon and unpacked her clothes, she went with her references from the manager of the station and the director of Omaha Players to look for work. With an excellent eye for business, the networks had opened up studios in Chicago, and radio was going strong even in the Depression. Bernice marched briskly through the crowds on Michigan Avenue and stopped, checking for the third or fourth time the address on the slip of paper in her pocketbook, at a tall granite building with recessed windows and a narrow centre panel inlaid with diamonds of stained glass. She spun herself through the revolving doors into an echoing, marbled interior, took the elevator to the tenth floor, introduced herself, and the next thing she knew she had got herself a job.

It wasn't much of a job, but it had promise. There was to be a big benefit that fall for the unemployed, sponsored by Hanley's, the soft drink manufacturer. Bernice, dressed in a formal red satin gown, with a white satin sash inscribed with the words Miss Hanley, was to be the emcee, introducing the stars who would, in turn, introduce other stars who would actually perform. The producer, the man who dreamed it all up, went with her to a clothing store on Maxwell Street that specialised in theatrical costumes, and waited in the front of the store until she came out of the dressing cubicle wearing what he considered the right gown. It was slinkier than what she might have chosen, but she went along with it – did she have much choice? – and was in fact somewhat pleased; it seemed all of a piece with the new life she was creating for herself. The producer's name was Francis Lytton. He was tall, dark, and moved so quickly that she would have said that he seemed more a presence than a person. Even when sitting on the edge of the customer's chair in the clothing store waiting for Bernice to come out of the dressing cubicle, he would cross and uncross his limbs, light a cigarette with one hand cupped over the operation and the other waving the match as soon as the cigarette was lit, after which he would take a few puffs before jumping to his feet and crushing it out when she emerged, to order her to move this way and that.

The right dress bought and arrangements made for its delivery, Lytton suggested they go for a cup of coffee. He took her to a delicatessen on Rush Street, evidently a show business hangout, but it was in the middle of the afternoon and there weren't too many people about. He occupied her instead with stories about himself, smoking and shifting position in their booth all the while. He was from 'back east', he told her; his father the senior partner in a prominent law firm; the family home in Connecticut; there were stints at prep school and Harvard. At Harvard he developed an interest in student theatricals and spent every free weekend seeing the New York shows. He left Harvard finally to work off-Broadway and then he got a job with CBS and soon after that he was given the brief to set up operations in Chicago.

When he had finished Bernice noticed that he had stopped fidgeting and was focusing all his energy on her.

'You're new here, on your own. Let me give you some tips. Walk quickly, look where you're going. At night, take taxis - don't go near the Loop. Unless you've got company.' Then he moved his big body again, lifting his buttocks and turning his torso so that his coat flapped against the table and he was no longer facing her but the door. He let his gaze linger there but after a few seconds he returned to her. 'Though I can't expect you'll be without company, Miss Hanley.'

Well, the job had promise, so Bernice faced the following morning and all the subsequent mornings with the same frisson she had felt that first night. She went to the office on Michigan Avenue and read short biographies of the stars participating in the benefit and, as the program began to take shape, started rehearsing her speeches. She consulted with the writers who were coming to the office to argue about changes or to bring new routines, and one of them - Danny Goldring - starting taking her out to coffee and occasionally to the pictures. Once he took her to see some friends of his in the Hooverville in Grant Park. This was a city of tents right in the centre of the real city, a city of hopelessness most of the time, but Danny saw something else - a kind of spirit, a camaraderie that he tapped into. He had been born in Chicago and knew his way around better than Francis Lytton did, and despite the misery he saw and the anger it produced in him, he took a quiet joy in the city rather than laying claim to it the way Lytton did. He was funny, too, with the kind of quick, self-deprecating humour that she understood, and which would always assure him work. Her favourite story of his was about his mother, the tsaddik. Why a tsaddik? Aren't all mothers tsaddiks? Well, Danny's mother was extra, extra saintly. So much so that they might have ceased arguing about it in the neighbourhood, if it weren't for the fact that 'that neighbourhood was so full of wonderful mothers,' Danny said, 'that the kids were laying odds.

'Mrs Katz made such strudel that when she lifted the dough from the table you could see right through it, like the sheerest silk. And Mrs Landau made such latkes that the rabbi himself would make excuses to drop by around supper time. And Mrs Solomon, my best friend Arnie's mother, saved every week from her housekeeping to give to the poor, and Michael Feinstein's mother cleaned apartments on Lake Shore Drive when Mr Feinstein lost his job and she cleaned so many apartments and cleaned them so beautifully, not to mention her own – which shone like the tsarina's jewels – that after feeding the Feinstein family, which included Michael and his five good-for-nothing brothers, and paying the rent, she still was able to save and give to the poor. But then there was Sylvia Koppel's mother, who not only cleaned and saved and baked and took in washing but after she finished that she took soup with her own hands to the sick and the poor, and no one could really top that. So Sylvia won that competition. Everyone agreed that Mrs Koppel was the tsaddik among tsaddiks, a pure, shining saint of a mother, about whom any family could be proud, and all the other kids nodded soberly, and without rancour of any serious kind. Except Eddie Lipkowitz who, listening to these accounts, but not saying anything himself and all the time looking rather sad and kicking a tin can and starting to walk away, turned around and said, "That can't be."

' "So what's it to you, Lipkowitz?" the others said, because everybody knew that Eddie Lipkowitz's mother kept a dirty house, and never got out of bed until noon, and after that she never got out of her bathrobe and Mr Lipkowitz had to bring home the dinner from the corner delicatessen and Eddie and his sisters were always dressed in rags. And Eddie himself was stunted from smoking cigarettes and what kind of tsaddik was that?

'But Eddie said that the whole point of being a tsaddik was that no one was supposed to *know* about the good things that you did, so how could Mrs Koppel be a tsaddik when she *advertised* her goodness, exercising no restraint? So the kids thought about this and figured maybe it was true and then they stopped feeling sorry for Eddie and someone suggested that maybe Eddie's mother was only pretending to do nothing so she could perform her mitzvahs in secret.

'So they all marched over to Eddie's apartment, tiptoeing very quietly through the door in case she might be asleep. But she wasn't sleeping, she was in the kitchen smoking and playing solitaire and when she saw all the kids, bug-eyed with surprise at seeing her holey bathrobe and unkempt hair, she screamed at them all to get the hell out of there, and then of course they were convinced. Sylvia Koppel told her mother that Mrs Lipkowitz was a tsaddik and when Mrs Koppel scoffed, Sylvia said it was because she kept it secret and Mrs Koppel thought maybe it was true, and she told Mrs Feinstein who, though reacting with disbelief at first, reconsidered when Mrs Koppel passed on what Sylvia had said to her. And they both went to the rabbi who quoted the appropriate words from the Talmud and these they passed on to Mrs Landau and Mrs Katz and all these good women were filled with such awe and envy over Feiga Lipkowitz's sainthood that they ceased to be saints themselves, and soon all the kids in the neighbourhood were as ragged and neglected as Eddie and his sisters were, until the rabbi himself began to wonder what on earth had happened.'

The first time she heard this Bernice laughed until she thought she would crack a rib. Each step Danny took with it had her doubled up in a fit. Perhaps it was his voice, or his gestures, perhaps it was the manner in which he sent up the cosy, claustrophic world he described, the one they both knew too well not to understand what the envy of the Mrs Feinsteins and Mrs Landaus might mean. Or it could have been that she preferred this explanation for what she saw in the streets to the harder one about money and jobs. The gangs of hungry kids and the gaunt, despairing faces of the adults struck fear in her, and at the same time made her want to cry.

Her own work, however, improved after the benefit; on the strength of it she got a contract with Hanley's for regular commercials, and her picture in the red gown graced a few billboards here and there. Her performance drew the attention of other producers and she landed a couple of ingenue roles in the morning soap operas. Her best part was the teenage daughter in a show about a woman from Tennessee who married an English lord, because although it didn't pay much it provided an excuse for brushing up on her accents. She told Danny that she was keeping her eye out for local productions of Shakespeare and he did some scouting for her. She was reluctant to ask the same thing of Lytton, even though he would of course have been able to find work for her more readily, but she didn't want to be beholden to him. She sensed that she was seen around the place, at Rick's, the delicatessen on Rush Street, for instance, as Lytton's protégé and the whispers she imagined made her want to keep him at a safe distance. But to Danny she grew closer.

Although his looks were unprepossessing, she admired him in every possible way. If his jokes made her laugh he could be serious too. They spent long hours discussing politics, he being a passionate New Dealer, as was she. 'You?' he would kid her, 'a living, breathing, walking, talking advertisement for home-grown capitalism?' She would fall into a semi-pout and he would add, 'Capitalism, let's say, with a friendly face.' And he would have her laughing again, so at ease, because however much time they spent together, he never pressed her for anything more than her company, though she thought at times that he would have liked to. But perhaps that was because she found herself wishing he would; and she worried why he didn't; deep down it hurt her that he was just filling in time. It never occurred to her that he was abysmally shy. (And why wouldn't he be, she being a beautiful young actress courted by producers and he a bum of a writer from the west side?)

The curious thing was that although using words of sentiment and emotion was her business – and she used them everyday in the soaps – she had no possible means for using them in her life. She was forced to rely on subtler measures: looking into his eyes a little longer each time than she dared, subsiding into a sigh after laughing at one of his jokes. But she was too self-conscious to execute any of these ploys for long. She would break her gaze, or compose herself firmly after sighing; yet excruciatingly nervous as she was that her actions were too crude and obvious, they never seemed crude enough. It wasn't as though he was the one to stop staring, or to launch without provocation into a subject as remote from romance as one of his tsaddik jokes, but the meaning of the sighs and the glances seemed to escape him – he would never follow them up.

Sometimes she felt she was dying inside. She wanted to touch him, and drew back. She wanted to lift the golden hairs on the nape of his neck that crept over his threadbare collar, and watch them spring back. She wanted to run a finger over his fullish lips. She pressed her hands in her lap instead, like birds kept from flight, and tried to take refuge in their conversation. There was show business, there were politics, there were jokes.

By that time she was renting on the near north side, on Superior Street: a one-bedroom apartment that, having little in the way of furniture, she filled with green plants. She sent pictures of it that she took with a Brownie flash to her mother and father, pictures of the tiny kitchen with its compact gas stove, of the bedroom with its studio bed, of the living room with the plants and the couch. But there were no pictures of Danny on the couch because that would have only distressed them, although he was often there, coming up for coffee after the movies or a stroll along the lake. One night she really thought something might happen, and she exercised great patience, her fluttering hands coming to rest serenely in her lap while she waited for the kiss that she had seen so many times on the screen and engaged in so often herself on the stage with the Omaha Players that she could scarcely imagine it would elude her, here, when they were alone, with the hushing of a prairie wind stirring the leaves on the shrubs in the quiet street just blocks away from the hubbub on Michigan Avenue. But Danny stretched his arm over the back of the couch and his fingers crept towards her, only to be withdrawn, again and again, and she thought she would go mad.

'Are you hungry?' she said.

'Not really.'

'You must be tired.'

'A little.'

'Is there . . . anything? Anything . . . you want?'

This met with a palpable silence.

'Danny,' she said. 'I can't take this much longer.'

'I know. I'm sorry. I'm a schlemiel, a terrible bore.'

'You aren't!' she said quickly, breathlessly. 'Not a bit.'

More silence.

At last he turned to her and smiled. Such a sad, engaging grin.

A flush of perspiration spread across his cheeks and the bridge of his nose as he started to speak. 'Did you ever hear this one, about the chachem?'

'No, Danny, no!' she cried, jumping up and standing to face him, shaking her hands in the air in an act of unbearable frustration. 'Please, Danny, please, no more jokes!'

Then she gasped, realising what she'd said.

Could it be, that his eyes were filling with tears? He nodded, soberly, just as the wise little kids did in the stories that he told, told so beautifully that she couldn't believe that she, she of all people, had actually begged him to stop. She followed him, in a frenzy of remorse and anxiety, to the door: 'I'm *sorry*, Danny. I didn't mean it like that. It came out all wrong!'

He shook his head. 'It's hopeless. Hopeless,' he whispered, to himself, as if she weren't even there. 'Whatever made me think . . .?'

'Think what, Danny? Think *what*?'

One last time he looked at her, then turned away and went out the door.

She stood there, watching it close, sensing its grim finality as though her breath had stopped. Then she went limp, and slumping against it, felt herself sliding until she reached the floor.

Bernice Lavan, the actress; Bernice Lavan, the actress; Bernice Lavan, the actress. She repeated it over and over, in front of the mirror, in the back seat of cabs. She forced herself to keep working, she had to, she was fortunate to have the work that she did. She knew that the routine of it kept her from going under, that and the thought of returning to Iowa, where she would be rocked in her mother's arms and die a slow death. She was numb enough now, getting up in the morning to do her exercises, flipping mindlessly through the *Tribune*, running over her parts. At first she shunned company but that made her worse, so she persuaded herself that getting out and about would lift the gloom that was swaddling her like a shroud. She cultivated a bright, ready laugh, which rang pretty hollow in her ears, but seemed to convince the people she met. She began seeing more of Lytton again, a move that she recognised as more fatalistic than was wise. But it took all she had in the way of technique and energy and talent to pass herself off as a vibrant, attractive young woman; she hadn't the means to fend him off. So she went with him to Rick's, willing herself to appreciate him as an escort. And indeed, there was a lot to be said in his favour. He was handsome, in what she called a collar-ad sort of way; influential, and had her best interests at heart; and rich, which couldn't do her any harm. He introduced her to golf, and she learned, with some pleasure, to acquit herself on the course. And he owned a yacht, a small 27-footer, but a yacht, and on Sundays he would take her sailing, and even arranged for a publicity shot of Bernice in a bathing suit against the mast, which was used in the *Tribune*; and they would have dinner at the yacht club, by a window overlooking the lake that, to her landlocked, midwestern eyes, was as big as a sea. And she let Francis kiss her at the door of her apartment, the cool, lingering kisses that etiquette not only permitted but prescribed. A kiss, nothing more; though there was a strange, not altogether unwelcome urgency to his embrace. When she went inside she would close her eyes, whispering to herself as the tears rolled down. Then she would shake herself, and, at midnight, or one, two in the morning, she would lift her copper spray-can in a gentle, cradling motion, and start watering her potted plants.

Yet no matter how often she frequented Rick's – and she was a regular customer now – she never saw Danny there. She had thought when she started getting out that that would be her principal torment, and each time she went she would brace herself, rehearsing her responses if he spoke to her or, worse, if he did not. And then, when he didn't show up, she began to wish that he would; if only she could see him again, she was willing to undergo any torture. But weeks went by and he never came and, though at first it hurt to realise that he must have been avoiding her, she began, finally, to feel relieved, grateful even, to be able to relax. So that when he did come she was entirely unprepared.

She was sitting at a table with Francis and a couple of other actors from the network when she saw him enter, his arm around a small, plumpish woman dressed in a neat, beige, scalloped linen dress. In the mysterious fashion in which these things operate, what Bernice remembered best was the woman's bag; which must have been due to the fact that, out of a need to prevent her from taking in much more, she focused on it with such intensity at the time. It was a medium-sized but essentially commodious bag of maroon suede – a useful, all-purpose bag, a bag for the day and for the evening, winter, summer, fall and spring. And the woman who carried it, clutching the tortoiseshell clasp in her capable hand, from what she could see of her through the mist that was coating her eyes, was just such a woman: a useful, comfortable, pleasant, haimisheh woman – a tsaddik if there ever was one – and if it weren't for Francis Lytton at her side, she might have screamed, or fainted, at the sight.

Was it that very evening or the next? To this day Bernice doesn't know. She enjoyed, if enjoyed is the word, the obliteration of feeling the shock of the incident produced. Perhaps there was a week between the time that she saw him and what happened, perhaps even more; she had lost, too, any notion of time. All that is clear is that she was on Lytton's yacht, and whether an excess of liquor or, unaided, her own nihilistic urges brought her there is beside the point. She was there, his reward, as he must have seen it, for many months of patience and finesse. It was a typically hot, suffocatingly sticky Chicago summer night, and she lay on her side on the shiny deck, breathing in the resins of the varnish, observing from what seemed a very great distance the lights on the yacht club and the city's tall towers. Was there music? Probably. Francis would have thought of that, and champagne too; why stint? He lay on the deck beside her, fingering the waves in her strong brown hair, brushing his hand over the small powdered dome of her shoulder and down her arm, slipping it at last into that groove between her waist and her swelling hip that brought in itself such exquisite sensations that the lights on the Sullivan skyscrapers and the marina at the yacht club and their long, wavering reflections on the water began to swirl in her eyes. When he carried her into the tiny cabin and placed her on the bunk, the smell of pine resin seemed to grow stronger as the boat bumped and rocked, and when it was all over he nuzzled her cheek with his lips and murmured, 'You're a virgin'; and she said 'yes' – at least she had been – but she couldn't bring herself to tell him that until that moment minutes before she hadn't really known just what not being a virgin meant; for she saw that he never would have believed her.

It seemed, too, only a matter of days that it hurt for him to embrace her; she couldn't bear him to touch her breasts, they were so sore. She took it for shame, a tenacious disgust that she felt for herself, part of the numbness but more: deeper, irremediable. She began to beg sick when he wanted to see her, and though it was an excuse, she actually did feel sick, and when she wasn't working she would spend all morning in bed. When she was, she could barely make it through her lines. The hair that hung over her forehead would get damp from the effort, and as soon as she could she would step out of the studio and march down the corridor to what she then called, not without irony, the powder room; and once inside she would shove open the door to the first available cubicle and hurl herself against the pocked porcelain of the bowl which, somehow, throughout her spasms, felt cool and comforting, reminding her of her childhood and the coolness of her mother's hand, smoothing the damp hair from her brow.

She told no one – least of all her mother – and after a while was able to bring the whole business under control. She would time each of her speeches and, rehearsing them as she traipsed through the apartment watering her plants, practised keeping the waves of nausea in check; a program that worked so well that a month or so later she hardly felt it at all, and the feverish sensations that went with it were also gone. She was so pleased to be better that she let Lytton take her to Rick's again, where she was careful nonetheless to sit with her back to the door, but she got so sleepy at night that she found herself yawning while Lytton talked and she noticed, as if through a fog, his growing dissatisfaction with her. Her lack of sociability reflected badly on him, she supposed, but she just couldn't rouse herself, and he didn't take her anymore. And because he didn't take her, or because she had lost all interest in going in the first place, she stayed home most evenings reading books and writing circumspect letters to the family in Iowa. If she went to the pictures at all, it was with a couple of other actresses who were her friends, Mary and Louise, their rivalry set aside for the night.

Winter was coming: the leaves fell from the great wide plane trees along Superior, and blew like scraps of paper in the chilling wind that swept in from the lake. All the cocoa Bernice was drinking while she stayed home and read was making her put on weight. She left the buttons on her skirts unfastened and covered her untidiness with coats. She knew; and she didn't know. She walked. She walked all over the city, as if with her footsteps she were gobbling it up, swallowing it with the wind in chunks, and each passing block took her further from what she wouldn't accept. She walked quickly, purposefully, her eyes straight ahead, mindful of what Lytton had advised her that first day, moving so briskly that she would get hot under her coat and would have to loosen the scarf around her head. She marched across the murky river, and along the lake where the icy air flailed her and bit into her cheeks, and she stood at the edge of Grant Park and watched, numb with horror, as the wind whipped the flaps of the tents and blew great hollows in their sides while the panhandlers sang and stood rubbing their hands above the fires. And she felt ashamed about her coat, about being so warm, about wanting to give it to someone and not knowing how, reminding herself that she needed it, to wear inside the lined and heated broadcasting studios where she was lucky to still have work, though not nearly as much as before. And when the snows came, the vision of the tents would haunt her, and the world seemed crueller than she had ever imagined. It was impossible to walk anymore – the wind, so austere and powerful that it made no noise at all, could slam people up against the sides of buildings, and carry them for blocks and across whole streets; an awesome white silence that curled the leaves on the plants in her apartment as she struggled to pay the rent.

But in the spring that brought millions more unemployed the government brought relief and, as the weather broke and Bernice could go walking again, she saw the men working in the streets: broad-shouldered black men in torn knitted caps and overalls at their jackhammers; grizzled miners climbing in and out of manholes, looking oddly mechanical in the strengthening sunshine, like the men in a painting by Léger. Tightly furled leaves perched on the branches of trees, and there was banjo music in the park, a bright, sad sound a little like her laugh, but it gave her a stolid courage. Her perambulations now didn't take her far; she seemed to tire easily; her legs felt swollen, and ached if she stayed on them too long.

One day when she was walking she got a dull stabbing pain in her back and, as though it was a hand guiding her, she found herself at the little semi-circular patch of lawn that lay in front of a hospital on Erie Street. She paused, inhaled, and went inside. The nurse at the admissions desk wrote down her name, and Mary's as next of kin, then took one sharp look at her and called another nurse who bundled her into an elevator. All she could remember after that was the strong, pervading odour of chloroform, different but reminiscent nonetheless, from the smell of varnish on the yacht's wooden deck, and when she awoke she was in a ward but was still so woozy and tired that, despite the glare that was pouring through the windowpanes, she went back to sleep and slept soundly and peacefully until they brought in her baby.

As soon as she was able to focus Bernice began to smile. The baby – a girl, she guessed, from the bow – was the silliest-looking baby she had seen. What a crop of black hair! A head like Topsy's! The nurse who had lifted her from the cart and was handing her over said, 'We've never had anything like her, we couldn't resist,' referring to the ludicrous hank of wispy black curls gathered in the pink satin bow. But the infant's fists were lying so serenely on her chest, and her face was composed with such solemnity, that Bernice felt it would be unkind to laugh. 'You were lucky,' the nurse said, 'with that toxemia.' But Bernice had taken the baby's hand and was watching a finger grip her own.

'What are you going to call her?'

'I can name her? . . . I don't know. I'll have to think.'

The baby began to grizzle. Bernice slipped her expertly on her breast, an act she had seen performed so often in her own childhood by her grandmother and mother and cousins and aunts that she wondered how she had been able to ignore the memory. For a minute it might have been a part she was playing, but she remembered the women, and even the cows in spring, their eyes dopey with love, and then she believed it was real. And after the baby had finished, Bernice slipped off the bed and carried her daughter over to the window, to see the sun rising like a bright ball over the lake; and the water seemed alive with it, flecks of sunlight dancing like millions of incandescent insects skimming the surface, or thousands of flying fish leaping, squirming, struggling to get aloft. She glanced at the baby in her arms, who was screwing up her face with the light, and she saw her years hence, as one of the wise little kids in Danny's story, wiser perhaps than she had ever been, and considered naming her Sylvia, for Sylvia Koppel. But there was too much pain there, so, willing it as a sign that she would have every chance in life, she chose Evelyn – the name of the daughter of the woman from Tennessee and her English lord.

'Evelyn,' Mary said. 'Not bad.' She was sitting on the end of the bed, blowing smoke rings, one high-heeled patent leather pump dangling from her toe, as Louise had the only chair.

Louise was less forthcoming. She was worried that, with the birth over and done with, Bernice would be in circulation again; there were a couple of parts coming up she would have liked for herself. But her good nature got the better of her and, besides, her voice, rather high and nasal, only suited character roles. 'NBC's putting on two more shows in the fall,' she said, 'and I'm thinking of travelling with the WPA Theatre.'

'Sounds interesting,' said Bernice. 'When would you start?'

'Right away, if I can.'

Mary reached down to cup the shoe back over her heel. 'I might go too, Bernice,' she said, straightening up. 'What about you?'

'I don't think so. It wouldn't be any good for the baby.'

'The baby? You're going to keep it?'

'Yes,' she said, 'of course,' as if there had never been any other option.

'You're crazy, Bernice.'

'What are they going to say? You know. Around?'

'I won't hear them.' Bernice sat fully erect on the bed. 'I'll be in New York.'

One more thing. A few years later, Bernice was sitting one night in Sardi's, a classier, Manhattan version of Rick's. She lived in an apartment then without many plants, but an interior decorator had pasted a large paper banana leaf on her dining room ceiling and down one wall. The door to the restaurant opened, and who did she see walk in but Danny Goldring. She waved, he came over to her table, and sat down. He was in town briefly, he told her, working on a revue for the Federal Theatre. Their talk was animated and intense; Sardi's was packed but no one but the two of them might have been there. It started to get late and she had to go home, and he offered to accompany her in the cab. When they were out on the street he put two fingers in his mouth and blew, and a cab came screeching to the curb. Inside, he reached over for her hand, placing it firmly inside his own, and tapped their locked fists two or three times against his knee. The cab took Ninety-Sixth Street through the park and the shadows of the sycamores flickered over his face. 'That night, Bernice, remember? I tried to tell you. You know, the one about the chachem?'

Bernice laughed. 'Oh, no!'

'Really. Listen. The chachem. I had it all memorised. "If I were a chachem, a truly wise man," I tried to say, I would have known how to say the things I wanted to, to the gorgeous dame I loved.'

'I know, Danny, now.'

The cab swung out of the park and onto Fifth Avenue. When it stopped in front of her building she bent across and took his face in her hands, kissed him full on the lips, and jumped out. She found her balance on the curb, then marched across the sidewalk and under the canopy to the glittering glass doors ahead.

Naked

Lena Edelson came with her burden. She was a wide, slightly red-faced, grey-haired woman, her body a monument of generous female flesh. The day was warm; heavy clouds hung in the sky, reluctant to break in a storm. The corn was ripening in the nearby fields. When she reached Miriam Lavan's door she carefully slid her parcels onto the wooden porch and paused for a moment, rubbing the backs of her legs. They were sore, even with the elastic stockings, which made them tacky with sweat. Then she stretched her arms. They were aching, too, from the weight of her packages: the bag of discounted knitting wool and various-sized needles, the envelope of carbon-copied newsletters, the cardboard bakery box filled with her own delicious rugelach and mandelbrot, and the pocketbook full of letters that she'd squeezed between her midriff and upper arm. Before bending down to pick all this up again she brought the heels of her hands to her eyes and pressed them hard against the sockets.

Janet was in the cupboard under the sink, playing radio. Her voice was just the right pitch and she knew all the patter by heart, the station breaks and commercials as well as the different programs. She spoke through the round metal air vent as though it were a proper speaker. For over an hour she had entertained her Aunt Miriam with her broadcasts. She was Stella and her daughter in 'Stella Faces Life'; Mary and Don and Rochester and all the others on the Jack Benny show; she read out the news. She was exceptionally good at the Quiz Kids, even the applause and cheers. 'All right now, who can tell me what the pupa stage of a butterfly is called?' A hush. 'The chrysalis.' 'Hooray!'

When she heard the doorbell, she pushed open the cupboard, unfolded herself and walked down the hall singing 'chrysalis, chrysalis' quietly to herself until she got to the door. 'Hello, Mrs Edelson. Aunt Miriam is in the kitchen.'

'Ah, Lena,' Miriam cried from the hall. 'Come in, come in.'

Janet and Miriam helped Lena with the packages. 'How are you, my dear?' Lena pinched Janet's cheek, squeezed her, and when she let go brushed her hand along Janet's hair. 'Shayn. Such auburn hair! You are getting such a big girl, we will have to beat the boys off with a broom! And how is your mother?'

'We got a letter today,' Miriam said, leading her friend into the kitchen. 'New Orleans! How I do love that place. The most beautiful gardens, with fountains that make their own music. When Morris and I would go . . .'

Lena shook her head. 'What do you think?' she said, winking at Janet. 'Does your mother hear this music?'

Janet blushed. 'Alice thinks it's too hot. I'm not sure about Mommy.'

'She likes the food,' Miriam said. 'And all the time with Herman.' Miriam put the bakery box on the kitchen table and opened the lid. 'Ooh, Lena. You've excelled yourself today!'

After Aunt Miriam had made tea and Mrs Edelson and Janet had eaten some of Lena's rugelach and mandelbrot, Miriam sent Janet to rest on the sofa in the living room. Lying there, she could see the nimbus clouds, and the curved leaves of the fig tree glittering like scimitars in the heat. The blossoms were gone; the last of the purple fruit hung heavy on the branches. There were strands of light coming through the cloud and the tree and the figs made quivering shadows on the carpet. She was still feeling weak, though the swelling had gone, and she was full from gorging, but she wouldn't sleep. She slipped her hand under the cushions and pulled out her mother's letter. *Dearest Janet, We are having a nice time but are missing you, your sister especially, she is finding it much too hot. The houses here are festooned with iron lace and are built right next to each other. Next year you will see for yourself. Daddy likes it so much he would like to come again. I hope you are resting and getting better. What a shame, to miss all of this because of the silly mumps, but wait and see, we are bringing wonderful surprises . . .*

Lena and Miriam were still at the kitchen table, casting stitches on their new steel needles. The rugelach was gone, but two bits of mandelbrot eyed Lena from the plate. She envied her friend's figure, though she didn't envy her diet. Her thick fingers landed on a piece as if of their own accord and brought it dutifully to her mouth; the sweetness spreading over her tongue. She smacked her lips, brushed away a few crumbs and started counting her stitches. She counted once, looked in the pattern book, and it seemed she had got the wrong number. To make sure, she starting counting again.

Miriam began knitting, a scarf of deep navy blue. She always knitted scarves, using a plain stocking stitch; she could read and knit simultaneously. The scarves would grow under her needles without interrupting her thoughts and she could churn out quite a few. This pleased Lena but she often wished she would stop; it was almost as though the clicking of the metal took Miriam inside herself, away from her surroundings and, most disturbingly, away from conversation with her friend. Perhaps it was too much to ask of a heart patient. Studying her, Lena lost track of her stitches again.

'Take your time. They won't be needing any until winter.'

'I like it, Lena. I like to feel I am doing something.'

'You do enough. You knit enough scarves to keep an army warm. And nursing the kid,' Lena said, tipping her head towards the front of the house.

'It's nothing. She's company.'

'You mean she's family.'

Miriam nodded. 'That too.'

No matter how she went about it Lena found it hard to make her talk. Talk in the way they used to, in the old days, when the words rushed out of their mouths and tumbled over themselves and there was never this pressure keeping them in. Of course, it was all in the newsletter; she had typed it herself, rolling the sheets in with the carbon paper and punching the keys, and then repeating the process, so the words that stuck in her throat too, no matter how much she ate to dislodge them, were spread across the pages and then all over the town; but something held her from casting them out in the air, exchanging them face to face. And on that day there was something special, something so urgent, and still she found it impossible to come right out with it and tell her friend.

'Miriam Lavan, I want to say we have known each other many years.'

'I don't like to think how many,' Miriam said.

'Who would have thought then that we'd be old?'

'What are you saying, Lena?'

'Miriam, I want to ask you a favour.'

'You want to take advantage of a poor sick widow?'

'You shouldn't laugh.'

'I know. But it makes it feel better.'

'Shaicovitch, the lawyer.'

Miriam kept knitting, at a furious pace. 'Lena, I've tried. Many times. First of all, he lives in Washington now. Next, he's very busy. He does his best.'

'But Miriam, this one is special. This one we know!'

Janet fought sleep. Sleeping in the middle of the day – that's what babies did. Since she caught the mumps her jaw was so sore that she went to sleep with her thumb pressed against the backs of her upper front teeth, not sucking exactly . . . but she didn't want to do that now. She turned on her side on her aunt's lumpy cushions, and looked out the window at the light threading through the sombre sky and the looping branches of the fig tree. Her mouth held the taste of buttery chocolate, and walnuts, the taste of Mrs Edelson's rugelach, and she found she could keep from sucking by pressing her tongue hard against the roof of her mouth. It was nice for her aunt to have visitors but if Mrs Edelson left she could go to the kitchen and listen to the radio. The serials had started. She couldn't understand why the women were still knitting. The war was over. Aunt Miriam had said something about the camps but she thought that was over too. Miriam explained about helping the people find homes and until they could they had to wait in Europe. Nobody seemed to want them. Aunt Miriam and Mrs Edelson were especially angry with the British. They said they had broken their promise: boatloads of people on their way to Palestine were sent back to Cyprus and had to wait in more camps there. It seemed there were different kinds of camps. She had been to camp and it was fun, although at first she'd been homesick. But this year Daddy was back, and Mommy and Daddy wanted a vacation too, that's what Daddy had said, and Alice and she would go with them to New Orleans.

Only she couldn't go.

She put her hand to her jaw, where only a few days ago the swelling had been awful and even now she could feel a hardness under her ears. Her eyes moistened. So unfair! If only she could fly out of her body and be with them now, walking through the streets of lacy houses, sipping icy fruit drinks through clear glass straws, listening to the tinkling fountains. She could see one, there, in front of her, the water spilling over the top and falling into a kind of pond and each drop making ripples that spread right up to the edge where she'd be standing. She would be wearing the organdy pinafore her mother had bought her instead of these sticky, twisting pyjamas!

She sat up swiftly, seized with the passionate indignation of the young. Never to fly, to be nailed to the ground by a body!

She swung her legs to the floor and pulled herself up on her feet, picking through the dark shadow branches and the shadows of the hanging figs. Then suddenly she lifted one foot high, and brought it down hard on one of the swollen, wavering shadows that looked like a shrinking balloon. It made her feel good to think she had popped it, better still to imagine she had smashed it, just as if it were a giant squishy fig.

Calmed by this, she tiptoed to the hallway that led to the kitchen, and stood in the dark at the end of it, on the edge of the worn red tongue of the carpet.

'No, no, no!' Lena said. She put down her knitting and threw out her massive arms. Her whole bosom shook as she waved them. 'She was married to a Levy, the nephew of my Moishe's brother's wife. Aaron's wife, you remember? The one with the braids. She used to wind them in a crown around her head.'

'No,' said Miriam. 'How would I remember?'

'They were from Budapest, in the chemical business,' Lena said, more quietly. 'Horthy kept them alive, protected them, because he couldn't have run the country without them. Ethel's nephew, he was making ersatz coffee, oleomargarine, soap . . .' She related this with her head down, her fingers playing nervously over the woollen stitches she had dumped on the table. 'I think he wanted to leave but the government wouldn't let him.' She raised her head, to look into Miriam's eyes. 'The Huns went even so far as to disobey the Nazis. They needed their Yidn.'

'This didn't make them love us.'

'No. Towards the end, as soon as it started looking bad, the Germans issued their own decrees For what did *they* need them, when there was nothing to do but surrender?' Lena closed her eyes for a moment before going on. 'I don't know how they rounded them up. Most likely they took Tibor in the factory, when Bella was still at home.'

Miriam's pale face was blotchy, her black eyes dulled, as though a screen had dropped over them, or her mind had gone cloudy inside. She put her knitting down too and rose from the chair, her movements quiet, frail. 'Lena,' she said, 'Why are you telling me this? Isn't it enough that I knit the scarves and do what I can to try to make the immigration people change their ways, even if Congress won't change the laws? Isn't this enough? But though I'm a sick woman, Lena, I gladly do this and more, but please, please don't make me listen. Where does it get us? Where can it possibly get them? I can't stand it, Lena, even if you can.'

'But Miriam, please, this is a miracle!'

Miracle! Aunt Miriam and Mrs Edelson were getting loud. The excitement in their voices stopped Janet from moving closer down the dark hall. There was something frightening about the way they were speaking – she had never heard it before. She realised that it wouldn't be wise to be discovered, that the best thing to do would be to tiptoe back to the living room. If she couldn't sleep she could read.

But books had lost their appeal. Her cheeks were warm, not like when they'd been swollen, but like they were when she was bursting in on a secret, even if she couldn't know what it was.

She could hear her blood move, and suddenly the fear was gone. Instead of tiptoeing back to the sofa she found herself stepping quietly towards the voices.

'Can you believe it, Miriam?' Lena was pacing back and forth through the kitchen. 'Such ingenuity, such courage! You simply have to get in touch with Shaicovitch. He could do it, I'm sure, with her. She's young, with qualifications, and Ephraim Feinstein himself is willing to be her sponsor. But we have to move soon. I can't bear having her wait in a camp another minute!' She stopped at the table just long enough to open the clasp on her pocketbook, rummage among the letters inside and pull out an envelope. Her fingers fumbled opening it. 'Look, I have a picture,' she said, pulling out the photograph, brandishing it in front of Miriam's nose. 'It will be useful,' she whispered. 'Look, how beautiful. Shayn. Like her name.'

Miriam put her hand to her chest and looked at the picture, the portrait of a young woman in a misshapen tweedy overcoat crossed over at the waist and held together by a cracked-looking leather belt, as much an improvisation, Miriam supposed, as the coat. But the woman's hair was stylishly coiffed, teased into a pompadour at the front, and her lips were darkened with rouge; a woman with strength enough, despite everything, Miriam thought, to hang onto some cockeyed sense of dignity.

'Bella,' Lena said. 'Bella Reigel. Born the twelfth of November, 1922. Twenty-four years – a child. But a qualified dental technician. She had time to do that. Although after the marriage, of course, there was no need.'

Miriam gazed intently at the photograph, looking hard at the young woman's hairdo, then at the rounded shape of her chin, then her eyes, vulnerable as a fawn's. She felt part of herself close off, shut down, like a limb going to sleep from too much pressure; and there was nothing left functioning but her head, a brain that worked independently from the sinewy, fleshy organs that were meant to support it.

'The Americans found her,' Lena whispered. 'And this, you know, after they had been expecting the Reds. And the Germans trying to hide it all, burn all the evidence, everything. Everything.'

Lena's voice grew louder, as though defied to increase its volume, to dissipate the horror. 'And they marched the women naked into the forest, Bella in the line to be shot and thrown onto the growing pile of corpses in her turn. But she fooled them, *fooled* them, do you hear? She slipped out of the line, and crept onto the pile, nu?, and lay there listening to the gunshots until it was over, the bodies thrown on top of her all the while. And that's how our own boys found her, our own GIs, flying low in their bomber overhead, and she crawled out of the pile of corpses and they saw her, waving them down.'

Miriam put the photograph down on the table and rested her forehead in her hand, her stare still fixed on the picture, even if she no longer had the strength in her fingers to hold it. Her eye settled on the coat again, how it was drawn across her body, and secured somehow with a cracked pigskin belt.

'A miracle,' Lena whispered.

At last Miriam felt tears on her cheeks: they felt like mere runnels in a desert, rills on a yellowing plain, but she was grateful, even for these. 'You'd better give me the details again,' she said, when she had wiped them away. Then she sighed, and got up from the chair to search for a pencil and paper.

It was then that she saw Janet, white-faced, in the doorway; her deep reddish curls awry.

Later, long after Lena had gone, and the sky was dark and caressing, a deep, dense brown teeming with the secret life of tiny, airborne insects, Miriam sat on the faded porch swing with her niece. She held her arm, old and yet somehow girlish, around Janet's shoulders, which seemed even thinner and more fragile than before, when she had lain sweltering in bed in the grip of her fever. She held the child close against her, as if she could spin from her own feeble body a sturdy, shining cocoon. In the presence of the low tangled branches of the fig tree, a luminously pale shade of green in the night, they shared stories: innocent, innocent stories.

'Did you drink mint juleps, by the fountains?'

'Oh yes,' Miriam said. 'Once or twice.'

'Was it very hot? Like tonight?'

'Very hot. Except the streets were so alive. There were so many people, everywhere. And every one of the houses had a light burning in the open doorway, and your heart would beat to the music, pouring out.'

'What kind of music?'

'Oh, brass. Trombones, trumpets. But also pianos; mostly pianos perhaps. Yes, I do remember pianos, with the water in the fountains. Because they were like echoes, and they set up a kind of music in my brain; a ripple, kindele, over and over – like a lark.'

After putting her to bed and laying a cool sheet over her, Miriam felt behind Janet's ears for the hard knots left over from the swelling, but even they had gone. 'You'll be just fine for school.'

She ran her hand over Janet's forehead, and over the hank of thick hair rising up from her scalp. She took the child's hand and gave it a final stroke. 'Pleasant dreams, kindele,' she whispered. 'Of the beautiful fountains.'

'Good night, Aunt Miriam,' Janet murmured.

She watched the silhouette of her aunt grow smaller against the light coming through the door from the hallway as Miriam stepped out of the room, and tried to imagine her younger, listening to the pianos tinkling through the lighted doorways and mixing with the gurgle of the fountains in the moonlit streets. But when Miriam had gone altogether she saw her father throwing pennies in the water, coins as new and shiny as the buttons on his jacket, though she knew that he wasn't wearing his uniform, wouldn't be anymore, and she made herself see him without it, with Mommy and Alice, and it all seemed safer and nicer.

But she couldn't stop thinking of the uniform; it had made him seem strange, drew him out of himself, so that he seemed part of something sharper, vaster, than the five cosy rooms in their little white house on Eleventh Street. She had always sensed that the house was too small for him. She had seen the soldiers marching and seen pictures of them riding in their jeeps, with their caps just so and their lopsided smiles and the stunning whiteness of their teeth. The whiteness shone hot in the darkness; no, it is the light in the hallway, Aunt Miriam left it on so she could sleep. But she couldn't sleep, it was impossible now, harder, she realised, than when she had been very sick and the fever set her burning. She wanted to get up, run into the hallway and switch off the light but she didn't have the courage, and she sensed that the total darkness would only make the whiteness worse. And then she saw what her own mind and Aunt Miriam had kept her from seeing, and she pulled up the sheet to cover her eyes but she was there anyway just as the whiteness was, the whiteness of her body against the deep green of the forest and how they saw her and she must have seen them seeing her, with no clothes, none of them with clothes, no, none of them, but *she* could see them, must have seen them, how *could* she have seen them, seeing her.

Janet pulled the sheet right over her head and threw herself onto her side. She drew her knees up, pressing them hard into her chest, and brought her hand to her mouth. She felt the tips of her ears burn as she slipped in her thumb and felt the roughish skin slide on her tongue. And she held it there, without sucking, because she knew now it could give her no comfort.

Safar: To Count

Safar, to count, related to our word sapphire and the Kabbalah's sephiroth, also derived from the Hebrew 'sappur', said to be the substance of God's throne. 'Look at Ezekiel,' my grandmother Miriam said. 'Chapter one, verse 26.' Years later I looked it up again, to refresh my memory. This is the chapter about the vision of the angels in the heavenly chariot Merkavah; 'And above the firmament, that was over their heads,' it reads, 'was the likeness of a throne, as the appearance of the sapphire stone.' Seated on this throne was a great personage, described as looking like a man. Another source, which the writer of Ezekiel would surely have condemned as blasphemous, suggests instead that 'sappur' refers to the holy blood of Isis, and that it was her *lap* that was God's throne – a heretical notion if there ever was one. It seems that the Egyptian 'sappur' was related to the Assyrian 'saphuru', a red paste used for ritual purification, and had nothing to do with the transparent blue corundum we know today as sapphire. Isis was what the Egyptians called the Great Goddess, the deity worshipped throughout the ancient world, but by the sixth century AD, when the Hebrews wrote their *Sefer Yetzira*, in which the sefiroth first appear, a sapphire was the brilliant blue stone we can see now in any jewellery shop. And Isis, or Hathor, or Astarte as the Babylonians knew her, or Asherah of the Canaanites, this goddess 'from whom all becoming arose', had become herself a mere sephira – Bina, only third in the hierarchy of ten emanations of Ein Sof, the endless unknowable. But I am jumping way ahead of myself here.

Safar: to count. So there are ten sephiroth in the kabbalistic scheme of things. Ten, to the kabbalists, was the perfect number.

According to an early Mishnah, the world was called forth by ten divine utterances, made out of all the letters of the Hebrew alphabet which, variously combined, make up that holy language, just as the numbers from one to ten provide for all the possible numbers, from nothing to infinity. All this makes a little more sense when one realises that in Hebrew the letters are also numbers, each a veritable powerhouse of symbolism. The sephiroth are not numbers, strictly speaking, but as you have seen, the fact that there are ten of them is significant; 10, the perfect inversion of 01, encloses the entire universe. The sephiroth are manifestations, rhythmic pulsations of the force, the cosmic energy. The twenty-two numbers, especially the first ten, beginning with aleph and ending with yod, are the elements out of which the universe is made.

As well as to count, 'safar' means to write. We too make this connection between letters and numbers, this oneness as the kabbalists saw it; this is what is behind a word like 'account'. An account is a story. And the French word for story is 'conte', a linguistic distortion of the Latin 'computus.' Our own words 'reckon' and 'recount' are also related, as is the American use of 'figure.' I figure this, I figure that, where Australians would say reckon. Then there is the German 'erzahlen', the Dutch 'vertellen,' the English 'decipher'. The ambiguity of these words and their subtle links suggest the very human attempt, I think, to come to grips with the meaning of existence, to measure the measureless, through myths and allegories and stories and numbers, all of which can be seen as merely different ways of reckoning, ultimately one and the same. Perhaps it is not insignificant here that the Egyptians believed the art of writing to be the gift of Isis.

But what on earth, you ask, does all this have to with me, Evelyn Hazelwood, an intermittently employed television comedy writer, eking out a puzzled existence on the eastern edge of a southern continent, once thought necessary for maintaining the balance of the world?

I am thinking back, as it happens, to the time many years ago when I was a pupil at PS Number Six, on the corner of 85th Street and Madison Avenue in Manhattan. I was living there with my mother Bernice – Bernice Lavan, the actress, you may have heard of her. She was working in radio then, and had a nice apartment right on Fifth Avenue, with windows overlooking the sycamores in Central Park. The rear of our apartment building was on Madison. I used to take the elevator down to the mirrored foyer on the first floor (the ground floor as it is called here in Australia), turn to the left into the corridor leading to the service entrance at the back, and race out in all kinds of weather to catch the bus on Madison, which with its bustle and noise and traffic was as different from Fifth as if it belonged to another world.

My teacher that year was Miss Arden, and for the only time in my life I was the teacher's pet. Miss Arden was young and pretty and kind, but basically unhappy in the second grade classroom at PS Number Six, even though the school was reputedly the best, if one of the oldest, in the New York public school system. Miss Arden wanted to be an actress. It might be an exaggeration to say that she had a passion to act, but she did want to act very badly. She had said as much to my mother, or so my mother told me, and though my mother does have a tendency to exaggerate, there was a sad, resigned look about Miss Arden that seems on reflection to bear the story out. In any case, it is highly plausible that leading a gaggle of wide-eyed seven-year-olds into the mysteries of reading, writing and arithmetic was not Miss Arden's idea of perfect fulfilment.

I remember only three of my classmates: a Polish girl named Doris, and two boys - Sammy Goldberg and David Rosenthal. Doris was beautiful, with lustrous brown hair and that translucent skin that reminds one of rose petals. She seemed even then almost archetypically female, and always brought things like fringed shawls and lipstick cases and small embroidered placemats to show the class for news. Sammy Goldberg was short and roly-poly, David Rosenthal thin and wan, with pale green eyes that turned up at the corners like a pixie's.

Sammy Goldberg and David Rosenthal were very good at numbers. I remember Miss Arden with her back to the classroom window, leaning against the steam radiator, and tossing out problems like balls for them to catch. Every once in a while she would turn to look down at the asphalt courtyard below while David or Sammy, or both of them together, they were so fast, shot up their hands and spat out the sums. I was good but nowhere as quick.

It began to dawn on me why. To Sammy and David numbers were numbers, but to me they were like a family. It's all a bit hazy now, but then it was precisely worked out. The odd numbers were men, I think. The higher the numbers the older they became. Nine, I remember, was very much like my Uncle Herman. He had black eyes and straight black hair and wore a dark blue pinstriped suit. He had just got out of the army, and had a job with the family firm. Eleven was a grandfather and could have been Herman's father. I don't know why but the women weren't delineated so clearly, except six, who wore a fitted black dress and looked like my Aunt Zoe.

The point is that all these elaborations were making me far too slow. As soon as Miss Arden mentioned two numbers I had to figure out their relationship to each other and what they were wearing and whether they'd be friendly, when all that she wanted was a sum. I could feel her waiting, her soft blue eyes pleading, I could hear the anxious click of her fingernail against her teeth, but there was nothing whatever I could do about it, the turmoil kept raging in my head, and I never could bring myself to explain to her the reason why the numbers she wanted took so long coming out of my mouth.

She did what she could to help. For all her thespian longings and the dejected look that came over her from time to time, she was a warm, caring teacher. Unlike most teachers those days, she did not use terror to instil a respect for learning in her charges. She was one of a new breed of educators, luckily for us, who took their Dewey seriously. She delighted in the arcana of knowledge and knew how to pass this on. 'Just think,' she said to the class, 'with only these nine figures – 1,2,3,4,5,6,7,8, and 9 – plus the sign of zero, you can make any number you want in the whole wide world.' She had picked me for one who would share her enthusiasm, but the news of the numbers' infinite capacity only inflamed my imagination further, and didn't make the answers come any faster.

She took us on nature study expeditions in the park, and the classroom was festooned with hydroponic potato plants and displays of caterpillars on lettuce leaves and the like; all in sharp contrast to the barren asphalt playground below. To this day when I hear the word 'frog,' I don't think of swamps or streams but of Miss Arden's classroom. The atmosphere was moist and green, and reeked of the mustiness of tadpoles in fish tanks, offset by the fragrances of the flowers that came from her parents' farm in New Jersey. One late spring morning she brought an armful of large, floppy daisies. She arranged them prettily in a tall mayonnaise jar, asked us to gather round, and handed David Rosenthal a magnifying glass.

She pulled up one of the flowers so that it was standing considerably higher than the others. 'Now, David,' she said, 'look carefully at the centre of the flower through the glass, and tell me what you see.'

Even from where I was standing I could see the snow white petals and the yellow centre, so bright it looked like the powdered egg we got on rations. Miss Arden explained how this centre, round and compact and velvety to touch (she passed it around for us to feel), was actually a bunch of tiny flowers packed so closely together that all the pollen collected there so that a bee could easily pick it up. The delicate white surrounding flowers were the ray flowers, and the tiny ones gathered in the centre were the disk flowers, she said, and together they formed the corolla, or crown. She then turned to David, who had begun impatiently to twirl the magnifying glass, flashing beads of silver light onto the worn wooden planks of the floor.

'Now, David, look again at the daisy through the glass.'

On tiptoe, I strained to see what David was seeing. I could only make out a portion of the magnified centre, but could still distinguish the flowers, looking like the separate tufts of pile on a carpet or, as I had first imagined, the fuzzy filaments on a pincushion that Doris once brought to class.

'I see the disk flowers. And how the ray flowers are attached,' David Rosenthal said.

'Good,' said Miss Arden. 'Now count them.'

David held the glass closer to the centre. 'They're too small.'

'The ray flowers, David. Count them.'

David Rosenthal peered again through the glass and, crowding in on him, the rest of us watched him mouth the numbers as he counted, one, two . . . the lashes shading his almond-shaped eyes almost brushing the lens, which shook a bit from the tension in his hand. 'Thirteen,' he announced at the end. 'There are thirteen.'

At this point Miss Arden asked him to pass the glass around so we could see for ourselves, and there were, as he had said, thirteen.

Then she pulled the flower right out of the jar and asked us to examine the stem, emerging a slick dark green. The water dripped onto Miss Arden's skirt as she held the flower up for all of us to see.

Again, she prodded us with questions. Was there anything remarkable about the stem? Its colour? Its hairy texture, so easily detected as it dried? Asking us to touch them, she drew attention to the prickliness of the leaves. And then, in a voice that suggested that this was what she had wanted all the time, she asked us to count them, and to note the way in which they were arranged around the stem. And again, we counted thirteen, which I had heard even then was a lucky number, though some people were afraid of it, so that in an apartment building there would never be an apartment 13. Then Miss Arden held the flower up high and asked us to watch as she rotated the stem slowly in the fingers of one hand, pointing to each of the leaves with the index finger of the other. And we noticed something that we had missed before, that the leaves marched up the stem in a spiral – in fact I think she compared it with a staircase, because most of us had heard of spiral staircases, or had seen them in apartments, even if we wouldn't have known the abstract notion of a spiral – and she showed us how she had to rotate the stem five times before there would be a leaf directly above another one. And she went to the blackboard, still holding the flower by its long leafy stem, and found a piece of chalk, and wrote the number 5 and the number 13, and turned again to face us, with a bold look of challenge in her eyes.

'What can you tell me about these two numbers?' she asked.

Immediately, Sammy Goldberg snapped out his arm. 'Thirteen less five is eight,' he said, barely drawing breath. 'And thirteen plus five is eighteen and thirteen times five . . .'

Miss Arden smiled, her eyes bright, but now more with pleasure than with challenge. 'That's all right, Sammy. You had it the first time.' She stepped over to the board again and wrote 1, then 2, then 3, then 5, then 8, then 13 and, finally, 21. Once more, she turned to face the class. With a smile on her lips she crossed her arms. She asked if we could tell her something about the numbers now, but we all sat silent. Amazingly, neither Sammy Goldberg nor David Rosenthal seemed to have anything to say. She had us stumped. Then she let us in on the secret, drawing the sums very slowly on the board: 'Add 1 to 2 and you get 3; add 3 to 2, and you get 5; add 3 to 5, and you get . . .'

'Eight!' Sammy Goldberg yelled out.

'Five to 8, and you get 13,' Miss Arden said, waving the flower. 'And so it will go, forever, if you like, by adding the two numbers that come before, you get the next one. And there is something very important about these numbers, something almost magic in a way. A long, long time ago, before any of us were born, before our grandparents or great-grandparents or great-great-great-great-grandparents, there lived a man who loved numbers. He was Italian and his name was Leonardo. Leonardo Fibonacci. Leonardo of Pisa, he was called, because that is the town in Italy where he was from. You know about the leaning tower? Well, it was the very same town. And Leonardo wrote a book about numbers, for boys and girls just like you, and in it he set a problem about rabbits. He showed how if you put a pair of rabbits in a rabbit pen, a male rabbit and a female one, soon there would be more rabbits. After a month there would be three rabbits and after another there would be five, then eight, then 13, 21, 34, 55, 89, 144, 233, and finally, after a year, there would be 377 rabbits in the pen. And funnily enough, after Leonardo showed this, people began to see these numbers in all kinds of things – in bees and in plants, like the daisies, and in pine cones and animal horns: the antlers on deer and moose and elk. And though people have known for some time that all of nature is connected, now we can see it in the numbers, exactly as Leonardo did, such a long time ago.'

Suddenly, before I could realise myself what was happening, it was my hand, not Sammy's or even David's, that shot up, straining, in the air. 'Like a family, Miss Arden?'

Miss Arden looked at me hard and, as if it was all her doing, all along, gave me a long, slow smile. 'Why, yes, Evelyn', she said. 'Like a family.'

At the end of the year, when the parents came to see us in some performance or other, I forget what, perhaps it was only our nature display in the room, and Miss Arden told Bernice of my drawbacks and capabilities, probably that I was the most incorrigible of dreamers, knowing somehow that that would sit well with my mother, they made an arrangement to meet during the summer. Usually I went away in the summer, to Connecticut where friends of my mother's had a farm. But that must have been later, in August, because I remember still being in the city when it was so hot the tar stuck to your shoes, and at night people on Lexington sat outside on the steps in front of their apartment buildings, and there were lots of soldiers and sailors and marines standing in line to get into the Stage Door Canteen. Bernice worked there some nights – all the young actresses did, checking hats and doling out cigarettes and coffee and dancing; and she would take me with her, and I would sit on a folding chair near the entrance and watch her wisecracking with the servicemen while she handed out the hat check tickets. She also used to take me to the radio studio, the Trans-Lux on Fifty-fourth and Madison, where I sat terrified through episodes of *Inner Sanctum* and *The Shadow*. One day, to my surprise, Miss Arden showed up there. She looked very nice in a white linen suit and her blonde hair piled up like Betty Grable's, and I felt slightly ashamed that I had almost forgotten her, the way kids do when someone who was once so important fades from their daily routine. And anyway, this was a new Miss Arden, even prettier than before, *glamorous*, without a whiff of the sour, musty smell of tadpoles I associated with her class. I was absorbed as always, and spared to a degree from the terror of the murders and mysteries of the story, by the play of the actors stepping up to their mikes, and the intricate business of the prop man as he created sounds – the slam of a car door with an actual metal door set in a frame; for sinister footsteps, treading up and down a concrete slab – when she squatted down next to me, and I turned and as if by magic she was there, and just by her being there I felt safer, more relaxed. A few minutes later the broadcast was over, and soon after that the three of us were out on the steaming avenue, where Bernice waved for a cab.

I loved the taxis. I climbed in and pulled down the little jump seat that always seemed made just for me and faced the two women fanning themselves with their hands. I saw from the tall facades of the buildings whizzing past that we were headed downtown. Miss Arden seemed very happy, smiling and chatting to Bernice who, I now recall, had a sceptical look on her face.

'But you have security where you are,' she said. 'I wouldn't give up that. At least not until you've had some experience in summer stock. When you've got the summer free. And anyway,' she said, glancing out on the sizzling pavements sweeping past, 'it's no time to be in the city.'

Miss Arden nodded slowly, taking in every word. It was odd for me to see her in this light, as if she were a pupil herself, and it was during the conversation in that taxi that I even learned that she had a first name – Bridget.

We got out in the Village, near the park I now know as Washington Square. My mother had always made much of the Village; she exclaimed over the period grace of the houses which, fenced in with their spiked iron railings, seemed very small and ordinary to me. She often expressed a wish that we could live there, and I was pleased, if bewildered, when she would say that we couldn't afford it. The park as well was too tame and small: not like Central Park with its winding paths, and shaggy sycamore foliage, and granite outcrops that I loved to climb. The driver pushed open the sliding glass window separating the front seat from the back and Bernice handed him some money for the fare, and the two women powdered their noses and tucked in bits of their hair while she waited for the change. It was clear to me now that we were taking Miss Arden to see the actress who had helped Bernice out when she first came to New York. Her name was Adela Mirka, a grand old dame of the stage, and she frightened me more than all the villains ever stalked in the studio by the Shadow.

She met us at the door, her large wrinkled face rucked up in a smile. Her eyes were enormous, but of an indeterminate colour –

hazel or lightish brown – ringed with kohl and watery with age. Bernice had told me that she was once a great beauty, one of the stars of the Yiddish theatre, and despite her appearance I was ready to believe this, because of her one undiminished feature: her rich, clear voice; and the fact besides that anything Yiddish I was bound to think somewhat peculiar. The living room of her apartment, which took up the bottom floor of the narrow brick house, was filled with photographs in old gilt frames, and in some of these I recognised the huge luminous eyes and the hair rolled back from her forehead in a high crown, as she still wore it then.

The light in this room was dim – perhaps she had drawn the curtains to keep out the heat – and while the women talked I wandered about, picking up objects like porcelain roses and small crystal dogs, and pretending I was in a dark cave. The women spoke in their strong, professional voices, but these were like murmurs to me, receding further as my conjurings flickered and flared, and in my imagined hush there was a feeling of otherworldliness about the room, as though this were a place for soft incantations, where secret rites were performed.

Madame Mirka served almond macaroons and tea in glasses. She sat very straight and tall in her chair, even when stretching to let the tea run from the samovar. I remember wondering – worrying, actually – if Miss Arden would find this strange: I knew enough even then to realise that we – Madame Mirka, my mother and I – were different, and Miss Arden belonged to that wider world where tea was made in pots or with bags, but she seemed to like all this strangeness; for her it might have sparkled with glamour, if for me there was always an element of shame. Bernice had called me to join them, and I sat on a little upholstered footstool with a plate of the macaroons in my lap, listening to the talk about theatre and rationing and the war.

'They are such sad, pathetic, *simpering* plays now, darling,' Madame Mirka said. 'And the lines! It's as if they wanted to rob the actors of their power! Have you seen *The Glass Menagerie*, Miss Arden? I have, several times – I am drawn by curiosity, almost against my will. And why? Because of Taylor's performance. How does she do it? How does she make you want to cry out for the character when the poor dear woman is nothing but an overblown

Ophelia? Give me a hot-blooded Gertrude,' she grinned, 'wicked as a pickle, any day.'

'Things have changed,' said my mother.

Was I aware of this? The war in Europe had ended, but there were still soldiers everywhere, and big demobilisation parades, yet all this was on the outside, so to speak; I still inhabited a world where women were in charge, and the three women around the table in the heavy summer shadows of Madame Mirka's sitting room heightened the sense of this, so that in a way they seemed larger than the large things they talked about.

Miss Arden had seen *The Glass Menagerie* and had been to all the revivals as well. 'I would have loved to have seen you as Gertrude,' she said.

The light beamed in Mirka's tremendous eyes; her wrinkled skin seemed as soft as the velvet cloth on Doris's pin-cushion. 'Ah, Gertrude,' she said. 'Sweets to the sweet: farewell! I hop'd thou shouldst have been my Hamlet's wife; I thought thy bride-bed to have deck'd, sweet maid, and not have strew'd thy grave . . .' This said, in her powerful, undiminished voice, Adela Mirka broke into a peal of giggles. 'Oh God, we had fun. Marcel Picon was such a haimish Hamlet, nothing pompous, just a poor tortured boy. And the clowns! One night one of them painted a face on the dummy that was supposed to be the dead Ophelia. Winking, and poking out her tongue – in the *lewdest* way. Everyone who looked in the coffin could scarcely keep from breaking up. "Sweets to the sweet, farewell!" Oh, we did all the classics: Shakespeare, Ibsen, Shaw. At least they made *their* women strong! Something rather more gutsy than a few well-timed murmurs, and for the men some well-chosen grunts!'

My mother and Miss Arden laughed, although I knew Bernice loved the American plays. When she spoke about them at home she said the people in them talked as real people talked, yet the lines captured the poetry of their lives. She didn't care much for Strasberg and the method acting, but she loved Odets and Williams and O'Neill (who were her countrymen and had something personal to say to her) almost as much as she loved Ibsen and Chekhov. She was arranging for Miss Arden to audition at the Equity Library Theatre, but she didn't raise this in front of Madame Mirka.

'It's hard to laugh any more,' said my mother. 'The world is not the same simple place.'

'Oh, my dear, but we must. Especially in the theatre. It will take time, but we must. There must be hope in the world, now more than ever, don't you think so, Miss Arden?'

'Yes,' said Miss Arden. 'I believe there is a good deal of hope. I see it. Every day.'

I put down my plate, which teetered on the fluted edge of Mirka's round rosewood tea table, and stole away into the gloom again. The vacation was beginning to drag. I missed the company of children; my muscles were cramped from sitting and from the small, delicate movements expected of a child in the company of adults. I missed the rocks, and the grassy expanses in Central Park, I missed the bumpy asphalt school playground. The prop man at the studio and the jump seat in the taxi had made the summer tolerable, but only just; and I was saddened further by the knowledge that I was going up a grade and wouldn't have Miss Arden for a teacher; indeed, I think I resented the fact that she didn't want be a teacher at all. I gazed at the photographs on Madame Mirka's wall and Madame Mirka in all her seasons and guises was peering back down at me, as though she shared my sad secret fears and by the tilt of her head and her glittering smile showed that she disapproved of my giving in to them. So I walked away from the wall and began fingering her little crystal dogs again; she had only a few, but I guessed they might be like the animals in that play, and I ran the palm of my hand over a miniature cactus to feel the prickles, and after that I was at a loss for what to do with myself and was just about to sit down on the footstool again when I noticed the tall blue urn filled with sunflowers, in a little alcove next to the shuttered glass doors which led to Madame Mirka's garden.

'The world is too full of judgment,' I heard her say, 'and not enough mercy. Too much reason and not enough heart. Do you know that in the Kabbala it is written that this imbalance is the source of all evil? And could even they have imagined what we are seeing today? Too many men fighting and torturing each other, killing innocent people, and blowing up everything else.'

My mother and Miss Arden were silenced by this, or perhaps

from this distance it seems that they were silent because that is how memory selects and shapes such moments, so that they stand out as clear and shimmering as a star on a frosty night, or a morning after rain. But as I remember it, it was slow, suspended: a soundless replay, the fragment of a dream. I walked over to the urn with the sunflowers, their lolling heads bursts of deep gold sunlight, looking so dry I waited to hear them crackle, but they, too, were silent in the muggy heat; the great blooms poised on the edge of decay, their stems dried to bronze. The dryness had separated each burnished ray of the corolla, making it stand out and easy to discern, but before I started counting I glanced back at Miss Arden, and she nodded wisely, and her smile of sympathy and pride made me think that she had known the flowers would be there; just as she had understood, in the end, about my numerical family.

One afternoon, in what seemed to me an eon after the visit to Madame Mirka's, but may only have been a matter of one or two weeks, my mother and I went to see Miss Arden in a play. As ever, we took an age getting ready. Before showering, Bernice slipped the hangers with her slacks and matching tailored jacket on the hook on the bathroom door (so the steam would ease out any wrinkles – better than using an iron, she would say), and after drying herself and me she let the towel fall to the floor and stepped on the scale. Bernice was always weighing herself and one of my strongest memories is of her standing tiptoe on it peering at the dial, naked except for the shower cap, which she wore after the shower as well as in it – to keep the steam that was pressing her trouser suit from frizzing up her hair. The steam streaked the frosted bathroom window, and the light passing through it coated her faintly freckled skin like a second film of sweat, and she took the towel that she had dropped on the floor between her toes and wiped the bubble over the dial so she could see. And now, in my memory, the image of Bernice poised on the bathroom scale has been spliced, as it were, to a track with Madame Mirka's voice, and the sound coming from the radio in the living room when Bernice opened the door. And Madame Mirka's strong pronouncement – a judgment itself – is louder than anything else, louder than the news that the war had ended, crowned with an apocalyptic explosion: a convulsion of unimaginable fire.

Bernice slipped on the trousers and stood bare to the waist in front of the mirror in her bedroom, slapping a rasberry-coloured astringent onto her face and torso. Her breasts swung with the rapid movement of her arms, and I was conscious of them at the edge of my vision while I prepared myself for the outing by carefully braiding my fly-away hair. When Bernice had applied her makeup, she wriggled into her bra and thrust her arms into the sleeves of her shirt.

Was it really that day that we heard about Hiroshima? It seems too contrived that the day that I saw Miss Arden on the stage would be the day that Enola Gay dropped a bomb of such fantastic destructive force that the fragility of the physical world could never again be in doubt. Yet this is the way that it has lodged somehow in my brain. Stranger still to me now is the realisation that at the time I was filled with no particular horror. And surely my mother must have stopped her skin-toning to register the news, if only to cry for joy that the war was over. But in my memory this is not so. There I find a woman before a mirror, young, but appearing very old and strange to her daughter (those bobbing breasts at eye level), and a skinny, dark-skinned child with reddish lips, trying to tame her refractory hair. Two very feminine creatures in their steamy boudoir, a subject for a painting perhaps: Bonnard, Degas. And in the background, wafting on the thick and humid city summer air, from the blond-wood Magnavox in the living room, a disembodied voice, a voice with no more resonance of dread than the Shadow's or the gravelly penetration of the man who every Saturday evening introduced us to *In-n-n-er Sanctum*, but a flat voice, a matter-of-fact voice, a *reasonable* voice, above all an *authoritative* voice, telling us that we had split the atom – and changed the world forever with its bomb. What could this matter? My fears had already found their expression, were subsumed, I suppose, in the messages of those chilling mysteries, pinning me as millions of others to a terror I could never escape from, though it came from afar.

Bridget Arden's theatrical debut took place in an upstairs room in the New York Public Library. It wasn't actually a play but a series of readings. Bernice had a collection of blue-covered books full of scenes from modern plays that she had used in auditions before she restricted herself to working in daytime radio so that she could look after me; it must have been in one of these that Miss Arden had found the monologue from O'Neill's *Anna Christie* that she was to perform. She was very nervous. She was wearing a sort of sleeveless turtlenecked jumper and a beret. Bernice offered her a cigarette to calm her nerves, but she wouldn't take it, she said she was nauseous she was so nervous, it would only make her stomach worse.

'That's the way it should be,' my mother said. 'If you don't have butterflies, you won't be any good. You'll be wooden, flat.'

'You're just saying that to make me feel good.'

'Honey, *nothing* I say is going to make you feel good right now . . . Except . . .'

'Except?'

My mother smiled. 'That you look terrific in that beret!'

There were plenty of people in the audience, in uniform and out. It is hard to imagine them absorbed in such sober entertainment on VJ Day, but maybe it was so. Only in the newsreels perhaps do you find that programmatic representation of history, with celebration following immediately on victory. Maybe in real life people took time to let the impact sink in, embraced and made themselves cups of tea. Or maybe the ritual of performance, however small, *was* a celebration, a pause, a solemnisation before the eruption of bacchanalia in Times Square, with its jubilant coils of tickertape and night-long jitterbugging.

Miss Arden, being unknown, must have been the first to go on, because I don't remember being bored waiting as I usually was on such occasions; there is no image of me playing on the great wooden stairs, or catching jacks with a sweep of my hand on the broad marble floor. What I remember is that room, with the soldiers and the WACs and students and widows sitting solemnly on their folding chairs, almost as quiet and respectful as they would have been in a church, and far more so than I have ever seen in a synagogue. I helped Bernice and her friends from Equity hand out the roneoed programs; Madame Mirka arrived, tall as a queen, and my mother gave me her pile to hold while she led Madame Mirka to her seat.

Miss Arden delivered her monologues with all the emotional power we could have hoped for, my mother and I. Taking a speech from each of the acts, she wove the character of Anna with depth and warmth, transforming herself from the cynical, weary prostitute of the first act to the girl in love in the second, then the woman betrayed in the third; and, finally, the woman whose tragic fate is only underscored by the hope awakened in her heart. Did I see this then? Did I know what a prostitute was, precocious creature that I was? Hardly. But I was swept up in the wizardry of her transformations, the changes in her expression, the removal and repositioning of the beret, an inexplicable increase in the strength of the light radiating from her eyes at certain moments when her voice went very low. Oh, I had seen my mother in real theatres, where the footlights and the spruikers and the tattiness of the costumes and the harsh grease of the makeup made everything seem exciting and frightening, wonderfully *extra* real; and the actors in the radio studios had impressed me with their syncopated movements to and from the mikes, although theirs was a far more workaday charm. But Miss Arden was doing something marvellous with her voice; she had an accent – *yust* for just – and a fractured, slightly halting syntax. Was this my teacher? This utter change in her was different from the grandiose posturings of Madame Mirka: it was the power of one human being – a grown-up, no less – with the barest suggestion of costume and no more than a prop (Anna Christie puffed on the cigarette that Bridget Arden had refused), to become someone else entirely, to make you believe this so completely, that anything was possible, anything at all.

When the piece was over there was much applause and Madame Mirka rushed up and clasped Miss Arden to her breast, and Bernice went up and placed an affirming hand on her shoulder. But it took some moments for her to float down, and it took me time too to snap myself out of the spell, so that even in the taxi taking us home I was unusually quiet. 'Didn't you like it, Evelyn?' she asked, and all I could do was nod like a good child in reply. My mother kept chattering about everyone needing a 'first big break' and planning future moves for her, but Miss Arden was mostly silent too and, as if somehow to distance herself from mundane, professional considerations and shore up the mood she had attained through her performance, she responded as little as possible to Bernice, continuing instead to pay close attention to me. At last she turned to my mother. 'I feel awful,' she said. 'I of all persons should have realised. That was too old, far too sophisticated, for her.'

'No!' I cried out, surprising myself, but not wanting Miss Arden to be blamed in any way. In any case Bernice soon said, 'Don't worry. This one's old before her time.'

'You're too good,' I blurted out. 'You won't be a teacher now!'

My mother laughed and Miss Arden, in spite of her concern, looked pleased. 'There's no reason to take it that way. You'll be up a grade. You're going to have a new teacher anyway.'

I smiled weakly at this and, gulping back confused tears, adjusted myself on the jump seat, thinking hard about what had been said. I knew that I had lied – not that I hadn't been disturbed about the loss of Miss Arden to the school, but it wasn't that which was making me feel such a stranger to myself; it was the occasion, and the astounding transformations it had wrought in her. Then, in a way that only reinforced the feeling that there were parts to me, too, tamped down, kept secret, but with the energy to change me in an instant, I quietly asked: 'What made you say them? What made you say . . . those words?'

Miss Arden looked at Bernice, and Bernice looked at me, and the two of them laughed.

'Why honey,' Bernice said. 'They're written – on the page.'

'But who put them there?'

'A man did,' Miss Arden said.

'You know, Eugene O'Neill.'

O'Neill. How many times had I heard Bernice invoke that name? I knew that there were words on the page, in those blue-covered books that Bernice held in her hand while declaiming in front of the mirror, and on the roneoed scripts that the radio actors scanned before taking their turns at the mikes. But because I had been so immersed in it perhaps, never before had I realised the power of it, the joyful, soaring, dizzying *power* of it until that day. It was a revelation – of religious intensity – and the joy of it was on a par with winning the war. No, it seemed to my childish self more important than even that, and my wonder made me exclaim, 'He *made* them, he made them come out of your mouth!'

Miss Arden came to the apartment that night, and she and my mother put me to bed before leaving me with a babysitter to go out. It was a hot, sticky, noisy night and words danced feverishly in my brain: bright words, broken words, the words O'Neill used in his play. The sheet twisted round my waist as I turned them like counters in my head. I jumped out of bed and leaned on the window, looking up at a placid moon and a fog of neon floating from Times Square in the dense deep blue of the sky. The sky, sky, sky, sky, sky, sky; over and over, whispering the sound, so that in the end it was merely a sound, echoing, a sound without ballast, like a kite let free. And I stepped back from the window and went back to bed, to fall into a fitful sleep.

In the morning I found Miss Arden on the sofa in the living room. She was wearing the clothes she had worn the day before: the sleeveless shirt had worked loose from the waistband on her skirt, which had ridden high up on her leg; there was an afghan folded at her feet, but it had been to hot for it, and the morning sun streamed over her naked arm. Though I made myself quiet she must have sensed I was there and, rolling over, opened her eyes. Then she pulled herself up to a sitting position, holding her head the way Bernice did when she had a hangover. She didn't acknowledge my presence, but did what I had also seen Bernice do sometimes in the morning: move very quickly but gingerly to the bathroom. It seemed a sad way to end a triumph, but was all of piece, I supposed, with her becoming an actress. The door banged shut but I could still hear her awful retching inside.

At breakfast she had nothing but a piece of dry toast and Bernice's strong black coffee. My mother gave her some clothes to wear home; she showered and dressed, and when she was ready to go, gave me a kiss on the top of my head. Standing at the door she studied me for what seemed a very long time before waving to us again and moving off towards the elevator. I cleared the breakfast dishes while Bernice listened to the news again on the radio, and then I went back to my room; and, resting my chin in my hands and my elbows on the windowsill, I looked out again on the patch of sky that was visible from my window.

My bedroom was on the side of the building away from the park, and faced a small courtyard similar to our playground at school, only this one was almost empty except for the tall garbage cans and one of the janitor's large grizzled brooms. Looking down there through the summer haze after flinching from the bright heat of the sky made me feel sombre; depressed. The more I gazed the more I thought of school, a school without Miss Arden, where I would be lonely and unloved again, and soon the courtyard below was swarming with noisy children playing hopscotch and stickball and bursting out, here and there, in schoolyard scraps – an amorphous, swirling mass that slowly coalesced when the shrill attendance bell rang and then streamed out once more into a pattern of parallel lines. And with barely an alteration in the focus I could move the scene back again, and move in closer, as if I were a camera, to the spot where David Rosenthal and Sammy Goldberg would be playing, each of them down on a knee spinning marbles towards the circle chalked on the seething asphalt. And I could put words in their mouths, words about the war and the cloud that rose like a huge black hat over Japan, and words about numbers as they counted their marbles: one, two, three, five, eight, like the petals on the daisy or the drooping sunflower in the alcove in Madame Mirka's parlour; and as I gazed I was struck by the connectedness of things, how it *was* all related, like a family: I saw Doris with a patent leather bag swinging out from her shoulder as she rushed to get into line, and I followed her into the classroom and made her open it in front of us and show us the secret compartments: And these are the secret compartments, she said, for powder and lipstick and perfume and pills. And suddenly the words didn't sound silly at all, though on the surface they were; and I could see myself, watching her, chewing the end of my braid.

It was then, in a kind of trance, that I wandered into the kitchen again and, taking a pencil and a handful of scraps of paper from a drawer, sat down at the table and scratched out the words: Act One.

Gambling

'I don't care, Sid. It's a vice. Like booze, or stuffing your kisser or beating your kids. It's not relaxation, it's not entertainment, how can you call it a game with those stakes?'

Bernice had planted herself in the curved adobe archway that divided the living room from the den in the small apartment on Roxbury. Her hands were on her hips, her tongue moved as if it had a demon of its own, her green eyes were flashing fire. No mistaking it, Bernice was furious. Why? Because Sid was setting up the card table for the Wednesday night poker game. The men took turns having it: Toots Bauer, Freddie DeCastro, Maxie Kearns, Hank Devine. Tonight it was Sid's. And if she could only just tolerate him gambling in other houses, she found it unbearable in her own. She had not always been so opposed. Once she had found Sid's connections and preoccupations fascinating, they were so refreshingly different, she had thought, from her own. But now that difference was hurting.

'It's crazy, Sid. A long drawn-out convoluted form of larceny. They'd throw every one of you in jail if you robbed each other in the street!'

Sid had unfolded the card table and was snapping out the legs. With a final flourish he turned it upright and checked to see if it was stable. Then he dragged it directly under the shade of a lamp that hung from the ceiling. He adjusted the height of the lamp by pulling on its cord.

'At least in jail there's no rent!'

After checking again that the table was steady Sid brushed down the baize with several short swipes of his hand and then, bending closer, blew away any fluff with his breath. The light from the lamp with its wide, conical shade, softened his features, flattening them somewhat, so that his thin, pointed face seemed more rounded, more innocent and benign. Whereas Bernice, in shadow, was as dark as her mood.

'We can't go on living on credit. What are we supposed to do when it runs out? Move to Boyle Heights? Your buddies would really love that! And you know what? It would serve them right. We'd have just enough room to hold the games in the bathroom. You hear me Sid? It's meshugga, absolutely, totally, to even *contemplate* the risk.'

She knew as the words spurted out that she was taking risks of her own, but the demon had hold of her and she couldn't stop. Though on the surface Sid was a mild, good-humoured man, it was dangerous to push too hard. There was a point at which he could change, quite suddenly, and plunge into a recklessness that would beggar anything that had gone before. But her demon possessed a logic that was too compelling, too irrefutable. She tried a new tack.

'You're not sleeping, Sid – soon you'll be giving it up altogether.'

On a small rectangular server on wheels, to the side of the green baize card table, Sid had piled plates with sandwiches (corned beef and dill pickle, pastrami and dill pickle), a bowl of chopped chicken liver with a small tray of melba toast, and some glasses and an ice bucket and a packet of paper napkins. He moved this closer to where he'd be sitting and began setting out the chairs.

This absorption of his was infuriating. Her voice was rising again, shrill, infused with all the power of her profession: 'So what if you lose this time? What are we going to pay for it with? We can hardly afford the cold cuts. I'm getting embarrassed to walk into Nate n' Al's in case they ask about the account.'

Out of his trousers pocket Sid pulled the brand new deck, still in its glossy wrapper; he patted it and put it on the table, near the edge. 'Don't go to Nate n' Al's. Go to the guy at the market.' He started whistling as he began setting out the chips.

How could he be so maddeningly cheerful? She hadn't paid the bill, and neither had he, and they weren't making any money, either one of them, that she could see.

He lifted the bottle out of a bag and set it on the server beside the ice bucket. 'You can't be serious. Sid! Johnny Walker Black!'

'The guys don't drink that much, Bernice. Freddie's got an ulcer, Toots has to watch his heart . . .'

With a mob like Toots Bauer, Hank Devine, Maxie Kearns and Freddie DeCastro on the premises, who would have thought Paul Hazelwood, a young rugby five-eight from Queenscliff, was the wild card? He looked mild enough for a gathering force that could blow events either way. He looked puzzled, even a bit cowed. He stood on the steps leading to the Cowans' front door, one foot on one step, the other on the step lower down, his shiny new chinos straining on his muscular thighs, and ran a hand over the short stiff curls on his head. Across the lintel hung a band of crepe paper, one blue streamer twisted around a white streamer, dangling from which was a cardboard H-A-P-P-Y-H-A-N-U-K-K-A-H in gold. And just below, on the door itself, pinned underneath the knocker, was a large Star of David, again in blue and white: the top, inverted triangle in blue, the bottom, intersecting it, in white. There was a yellow harvest moon ballooning over the roofs of the Spanish Mission apartment blocks, though it was late December, and the sky to go with it was a gaudy blue, a backdrop blue, flat and electric as if it might have been painted. All this seemed strange yet not entirely strange to Hazelwood – it was as warm here as it was in Australia at Christmas – but the not-quite-real-sky and the decorations especially bewildered him. He heard the rumble of male voices inside and who knows? perhaps this is all that he needed to restore his mettle, although he hesitated again before lifting the brass knocker and letting it drop with a thud against the Star.

'Evelyn! Your date!'

'She's always late,' Bernice said with a grimace to Paul. 'Come sit down.'

He followed her to the den where the television set emitted a cool blue light not unlike the glow from an ice cube. When he sat down she turned the set off, and he watched the cube melt to a drop then disappear. He heard the men's voices more distinctly then.

'Would you like a drink? May as well.'

Bernice went to a cabinet and opened the door. A light came on and Paul realised it was a fridge. He looked around at the rest of the room, at the pictures of circles and triangles and little stick figures on the walls, and at the lamps recessed into boxes cantilevered just below the ceiling, noting that they were made from the same sort of mellow wood as the cabinet with the fridge. Evelyn's mother poured Budweiser from a can into a glass. She was small like Evelyn, and there was a youthfulness about her – not what Paul would have expected from a girl's mother – but there were also lines around her mouth, deep ones that ran from her nose to the corners of her lips in a kind of disappointed pout. She wore a pair of old slacks with paint or something on them, a green jumper unravelling at the waistband and cuffs, and her hair was matted down under a scarf.

As she was handing him his glass one of the men came in from the other room, started for the fridge, but stopped on seeing Bernice. 'Hiya, Bernie,' he said with a sheepish smile. 'Got any sarse?' He was a short, rather delicate man, with regular features and acne-scarred skin and a spotted bow tie. 'The quack says I should go easy on the booze.'

Evelyn's mother went back to the fridge and peered inside. 'We've got root beer. Will that do?'

'Sarse, root beer. Same diff. Either one's gonna pickle my insides quicker than any booze would, but doc's rules.'

'Freddie, this is Paul. Paul . . .'

'Hazlewood.'

'From Sydney.'

Freddie took Paul's hand and gave it a light shake. 'Freddie DeCastro.'

'Sydney, Australia,' Bernice said.

'Wooo. That's a long way. What are you here for kid?'

'I'll go see what's holding Evelyn up,' said Bernice.

A guy in the fraternity house where Paul had been staying had lent Paul his Chevrolet, a convertible; they had the top down. A breeze blew off the ocean, stirring up the slipstream from the car. Paul had taken Evelyn to a bowling alley downtown, and her ears were still ringing from the crack of the balls against the pins. In the short time he'd been in Los Angeles Paul had become a regular; he got on better with the patrons of the bowling alley than with the guys at the fraternity, a group of them even let him play occasionally in their band, and he liked the cheap beer. Because he had drunk so much of it Evelyn was driving, and she was driving without purpose, or rather, with the purpose of staying in Paul's company as long as she could. As they rode down Olympic towards Santa Monica, right past the grassy park opposite the apartment on Roxbury, she told him (only because he asked) the story of Hanukkah, of how Judah the Maccabee led his band of Jewish guerillas against the Seleucid tyrant Antiochus, who had desecrated the temple in Jerusalem by staging orgies there in honour of Zeus. She made it sound like five hundred skinny Mort Sahls brandishing sticks, holding off the mighty Seleucids against all odds. 'When they got to the temple they found it burned and sacked but Judah rededicated it, lighting the lamps of the great menorah – you know those candlesticks?. Only then they used oil. Anyway, there was only enough oil to last one night, but God kept the lamps alight for eight. It's what we have instead of Christmas.'

'I'm not religious myself.'

Evelyn's hair flapped round her face and now and then into her mouth. She had to brush it aside. 'Things have been going badly for Mom and Sid. I think she's got it in her head that she's done the wrong thing or something. That maybe she's being punished. We've never gone in for much of that palaver before. But there's a game you play, with a draydel – a kind of top. We used to play for pennies, my cousins and I, when we were kids. It's symbolic I guess.'

Paul recalled the tattered green jumper and the paint-spattered slacks. 'What happened?'

'Happened? Oh, I don't know. They got crushed.'

'With your mother . . . and Sid.'

'With them?' Evelyn sighed. 'Nothing. That's just the point.' Evelyn raised her eyebrows, in the knowing way people do when speaking about their parents. 'It's been going on for a while. Sid can't get work, but he doesn't want Mom to. Mom thinks it's her fault, so she goes ahead and tries to get jobs anyway, but she hasn't been able to land anything either. Well, maybe the odd commercial.'

'Why can't they work?'

'Ever heard of McCarthy?'

'You mean the jockey?'

'The *jockey*?'

'Darby McCarthy. Okay, he's only an apprentice. But he's run some bloody good races.'

Evelyn laughed. How good it was to be with someone who didn't even *know*. 'There's a senator here.' She took a small swallow before going on. 'You see, back in the thirties, forties – whenever – Mom was a communist.'

Paul blinked at the picture in his mind of the lady in the scarf and slacks. 'For long?'

'She says like twenty minutes. But it was long enough.'

It was Maxie's deal. Maxie was a burly man, with big beefy hands and a round red face and a round fleshy nose. In other places and other times he might have been a butcher, a ritual slaughterer, but in the Los Angeles of 1957 he made a living in public relations.

The cards flipped out of Maxie's sweating hands. So far Sid had a pair of sixes and the jack of spades in the hole. When the jack of hearts came flopping towards him he saw he had a chance for a full house – three juicy jacks and a pair – but glancing around the table told him that the chance was slim. Maxie had a jack face up, so did Toots. So that meant one left in the deck, if it wasn't somebody's hole card. Sid thought maybe he should fold. If he had any sense he'd get out, cut his losses then and there. But he still might do well with a pair, or three of a kind, if he got dealt another six . . .

'I'm raising,' said Toots, in a haze of cigar smoke. They'd set a limit but Sid hadn't wanted it low and now Toots was raising again. Toots was back at Universal and could afford to. He was so small he had to jump out of his chair to push in his chips but two months on a salary and he was throwing his weight around. Did something for a guy, getting a job back after all that time. Things were loosening up a bit at the studios. Some they take back, some still forced to diversify. With the small fry, who's to know? And now Hank was following. Was he kidding?

Sid felt almost dizzy watching the piles of chips slide across the baize, charging towards the pot in the centre of the table like battleships, destroyers, funnels glittering in the glare, or slipping off in the moonlight out of some distant island harbour. There was that story about the Pacific theatre I'd always wanted to do. Great material. Pity Stanley Roberts and everybody's uncle beat me to it.

He was conscious of the others waiting; a restlessness crackled around the table.

His chance was slim but the pot was looking good.

'You hear Fox's taken up the option on that Roth book, what is it? Call it, something or other. You ought to look into it, Sid.'

'Don't bamboozle me, Hank.'

'*Call it Sleep*? They'll never make a picture out of that. Just look at the title. It doesn't move. Fox has had the option for years.'

'So what does Sid care? They'll be more likely to take a script of his if they think it won't hit the screen. Then they won't have to worry about the credits.'

Sid took another moment to study the table then looked up at Hank. As a player, Hank was so-so. Cunning but less than cool. The very fact that he was introducing the subject of work meant he had a lousy hand. Anyone else it could be bluffing but not with Hank. There he was, a tall gangling schlemiel with hollow cheeks and a bony nose and an adam's apple that couldn't stop bobbing, and he didn't have the savvy to wipe that smirk off his face.

Sid pushed his chips into the pot. He was staying in.

There were two favourite spots for lovers in Los Angeles: Mulholland Drive at the crest of the Santa Monicas with a view of the sparkle in the brown velvet night below, or the ocean. There was a joke about submarine races, to be spied from the top of Mulholland, but the ocean didn't seem to need an excuse, ironic or otherwise. The ocean was a rich lode for lovers, a vast swelling volume of possibilities, with auras and fragrances redolent of other possibilities, echoing patterns devised a long time ago. Pelicans with wobbly beaks plucked anchovies from the brine, anemones opened and closed to its sluicing, shrimp floated down through its shadows, tuna and bass and barracuda flashed beneath the glassy rhythms of its waves. Evelyn, out of some instinct perhaps, was heading seaward. In spring, she remembered, the grunion flared like torches on the sand. The long supple drive along Sunset and down the canyon, with the smells of cypress and fresh, sea-salt air, was intoxicating enough in itself; and when they reached the highway and the concrete parking lot facing the breakers, joining the line of other cars poised as if waiting for the movie to come on at a drive-in, they might have switched off the engine and stayed in their car like the other couples did and necked.

But Paul, a foreigner to this custom, opened the door on the passenger side and jumped out. He clasped his arms behind his head and inhaled. The night was balmy in spite of the breeze, the moonlight on the tumbling water enticing. Yet something checked him, primed with beer and the ozone as he was, from doing what he would have done without thinking at Curl Curl or Bilgola. So instead of stripping down to his briefs and racing headlong into the surf, he walked with Evelyn along the littered beach, the soft wind tingling round his jaw, his shoes filling up with gum wrappers and sand, until they both got tired or thought it might be nicer just to sit and watch the splash and foam and spray. They sat with their arms around their knees, in full view of the couples petting in their cars, if any of them had been interested enough to see what might be going on ahead.

But Paul and Evelyn sat chastely, absurd perhaps for both of them, certainly for this spot, and why? Maybe it was because of that ocean shivering and swelling before them, such a huge, prodigious expanse. So they talked; talked about things they thought they understood, grabbing them like rafts to carry them through the waves. They talked about jazz, and about America, about their courses at the university where they had, most improbably, met.

'Primitive Lit. What the hell? I reckoned it would be nursery rhymes, that sort of thing. An easy cop.'

'Beowulf? Gilgamesh? They're adventures, quests.'

'You know them?'

'A little.'

'Then you could help.'

'Like I did with Ancient History? No thanks.'

'But I passed!'

Evelyn scooped up a handful of sand, waited a moment, and tossed it.

Ducking, Paul laughed. 'But you're such an excellent teacher,' he grinned.

'Don't you think it's horrible that you can pick my brains an hour before the final and walk in and take it without ever once looking at the text? What do you learn by that?'

'Look,' he said, tapping her on the knee. 'I'm having a bloody good time. That's what I'm here for. To play football and have a good time.'

'It's horrible.'

'Why is it horrible? What are you going to do with Gilga – whatever it is. You'll get married, have kids . . .'

'You make it sound like a sentence.'

'It's the way it is.'

'Don't you have any dreams? Something you want to do with your life? Besides knocking around bowling alleys and bars?'

'Sure. I'd like to play for Australia. Get the goal-kicking record and play for Australia.'

'That's all?'

'That's all? It's not that easy.'

'Yeah, but what are you going to do then? You can't play rugby union forever. Besides, it doesn't pay.'

'You play for the love of it. It's an art. Money doesn't come into it.'

'Money comes into all art, unfortunately.'

'It shouldn't.'

'But it does. Money, and politics. I'd always wanted to be a writer until I saw what happened to Sid.'

'A rough patch. He'll come good.'

Evelyn shook her head. 'I don't think so. I think it's knocked it all out of him. I've seen him, sitting in front of a typewriter day after day, with nothing to show at the end of it but a blank piece of paper in the carriage. The thing is, it's so unfair. It wasn't even him who was the communist.'

Bernice mixed her colours on the breadboard on the kitchen table. The problem was keeping them from getting muddy. A picture was taking shape on the easel but of what? It was green, it was brown. She forced herself to imagine a tree in a leafy wood, a man with an indistinct face. But no. What she admired was the whimsy of the Klees in the den: his arrows and wheels and delicate little machine birds suspended in colour-washed clouds. And what did she get? This soup.

Hobbies. They were something that actors accumulated, time-killers, and, if they were good enough, second strings to their bows. The trouble was, she simply wasn't good enough. Bernice, you're an amateur, the paint on your canvas is too hopelessly, *hopelessly* mired.

Her nose twitched from the reek of the paint, the turps, the rag soaked in linseed oil. She bit her lip. She took the palette knife, mixed a bit more prussian blue with the green, and slapped a gob of this onto the canvas. Then she spread it, as she would butter, down the right side, taking care to keep her hand steady and the paint thick and ridged. But the new paint was sucked up in the old, and the whole thing was so dispiriting that she felt like flinging the breadboard at the canvas. And the house was so deathly quiet, which wasn't good; the game must be getting serious. She sighed, and wiped the knife clean on her rag, and peeked out the door.

The men formed a grotesque tableau under the dusty cone of light, the coarseness of their features accentuated by the strength of the colour all around them: the green of the baize, the red and the black on the clean white shine of the cards, the red, white and blue of the chips. And there was Sid sitting like some mesmerised chimp as if nothing at all were happening and those other ghouls weren't about to gobble him up for another snack. Two writers there'd been in her life, and she had to end up with the one who had no sense. She couldn't stand it; seeing him sitting there actually hurt her eyes. She squinted, and the whole scene changed. Tattered clouds drifted across the face of a bright moon, and moonlight cascaded onto the dark green bay. Tall ships were floating into port, their masts and sails smudges against the silvery pastels of the sky. But she opened her eyes again and all she could see was the spittle on Toots's cigar.

She let the door swing close again and stared disconsolately at the canvas. Then, after a moment or so, in a sudden fizzy spurt of inspiration, she turned around quickly and squirted a gob of titanium white onto the lump of green on the breadboard.

Evelyn got a shock to see all the lights still on. 'What time is it?' she whispered. Paul checked his watch. 'After three.' They stood there looking at each other. A kiss seemed, well, inadequate. They had told each other too much. She is too like a sister – a mate – thought Paul. He will never know me, thought Evelyn. How long did they stand there, pondering the next move? Did they hear the noises of the poker party breaking up? The door with its Hanukkah regalia opened, apparently without their noticing, and there was Hank Devine with his jacket collar turned up and a white silk cravat at his neck. His foot was poised to step out but his head was turned inside. 'Wait till next week, Sid you bastard. And you better get on to Fox about that script. You're not on this run for long.'

'I'll call Ed Gottleib in the morning,' Sid's voice rang out from the foyer.

'That a promise? Gotta go for it while you're hot.'

With Paul on one side and Evelyn on the other, Hank Devine passed through the door. And Maxie Kearns and Freddie DeCastro and itsy bitsy Toots Bauer. It was Toots who first noticed Evelyn in the semi-dark. He reached across and tweaked her on the cheek. 'Waddya getting up to, Evie? Somebody spike your Shirley Temple?' He gave out a squeaky laugh and snapped down the brim of his hat.

When they all had ambled down the path to their cars there was only Sid at the door. A splendid grin lit up his face, as if in an access of grace. The big moon shone on his receding forehead.

'Evie,' he said when he saw her. 'It's late.'

'Sid, this is Paul. Paul, this is my stepfather, Sid.'

'Well, what are you standing out here for? Come inside.'

Evelyn gave a silent groan when they entered the living room, the scene of a deserted battle. The ashtrays were full and still smoking, there were plates with the chewed crusts of sandwiches at the feet of the chairs, the cards were strewn like bodies over the baize, and the great piles of chips in front of Sid's place were wobbly, uneven, as if dented with shells. A bottle of scotch stood on the table but Sid had gathered up the glasses on a tray.

'Cup of coffee?'

'Thanks, that'd be great.'

'How about it Evie? Bernice's gone to bed.'

Was Evelyn conscious of her grimace, or that it was so like her mother's? In any case, as she picked up the tray with the glasses and slipped through the swinging door to the kitchen, Sid threw himself down on a couch and spread his arms wide. 'Been a big night, sonny. A big night.'

'I take it you did well,' Paul said.

'Cleaned them up.' He lifted his arm and tapped the side of his head with his forefinger. 'Brains, sonny. Genuine bona fide grey matter. Sachel. That's what it takes.'

'What about luck?'

'Yeah, you've got to have some of that. But luck on its own will get you nowhere. Hey, do I detect an accent there? You from England?'

'No, Australia.'

'Australia? Go on. Evie didn't tell us. What brings you here?'

Reddening slightly, Paul told Sid about the rugby scholarship, about the rivalry between UCLA and Cal, and how the coach at UCLA set up this scheme to import players from Australia, to show the Yanks how rugby should be played.

'I've seen a couple of those games – no pads, no helmets. They're rough. Crazy to me.'

'Well, it's passing and kicking, not tackling. More of an art, I think, than gridiron. I can't work out how anyone can move around a field with all that ironware. It seems to be more about contact than the ball.'

'Nope. You've got it wrong, football's a science. It's all in the formations. Though since they've changed the old single-wing for the T the game's lost a bit in my opinion.'

'Sid used to be a sportswriter for the New York *Evening Post* before he went into movies. He covered the Giants,' Evelyn explained, returning with the tray that held the glasses and now rattled with coffee cups, the percolator, a bowl of sugar and a small jug of cream.

'The Giants. They're from San Francisco.'

Sid shook his head. 'Started in New York. After the war some of the teams moved out west. Baseball too. The Dodgers? They were from Brooklyn. You been to a game?'

'That's Sid's real love – baseball.'

'I wouldn't say that, exactly. Football, baseball, the races. I like them all. Australia – now there's a racing country.'

'Everyone loves the ponies at home. It's the betting. We'd bet on two flies crawling up a wall. There's this game – two-up. Blokes bet on the flip of a coin. It's illegal but no one can stop it.'

'Excellent odds.'

'That's what they say. It's never worked for me but, or my old man.'

'So what's the problem? You've got to have a fifty per cent chance in any throw . . .'

'But there's the averages.'

'Forget the average – it's a myth.'

'Sid's a real gambler,' Evelyn said.

'Sure. And why not? Now Evelyn's mother, she's a different story.'

At the open door again, next to the Hanukkah decorations, Paul took courage and kissed Evelyn goodnight. A warmth spread through her that she had never experienced before. Oh, she had kissed other boys – and more. She was what in those pre-pill times was called a demi-vierge, had indulged in practices touted as safe sex today. But this was different. Delicious but hard – as hard as the muscles in his athlete's body. It felt as though she was on the brink of a journey, at the start of her own private quest. Perhaps she had never savoured male beauty before, or recognised it as beauty, so much of being female as she had understood it was feeling herself desired. She liked the spring of his gold-flecked hair, the outward curve of his nose, and the inward curve of his cheek below the bone, So what did this mean? How far might she go? There would come a time, she supposed, when she would never see him again, so would this make her bold? When the kiss ended he touched her gently on the tip of her nose. She nodded and closed the door.

The light in the tiny parqueted foyer seemed to shine with a special intensity. The living room, though, was a pool of darkness – she was glad to see that Sid had gone to bed. She tiptoed down the passage so as not to wake him or Bernice, to keep the night to herself. But as she neared the bathroom she saw the thin strip of light under the door and heard the watery gulp of the toilet and before she could get any further her stepfather had emerged. He was wearing his grey towelling dressing-gown and with the greying stubble on his chin and the dust of silver in his hair he looked ethereal, insubstantial, a little like a ghost. A happy ghost, with a kind of cockeyed beneficent luminosity. 'Night, Sid,' she whispered, and he responded with a vague, misty smile. She was on her way to her room again, her breath still exquisitely shallow, when he called her back. 'I like your young man,' he said. 'Better than those other pishers.' And maybe she gazed back at him with an expression on her face that he recognised because he said, 'Do you want to talk? I think I'm going to have a hard time getting to sleep.'

'You lose this time, Sid?'

'No, not at all. But I'm feeling wound up, too excited.'

He flicked the master switch in the living room and the lights came on again, one after another, like a medley. The lamp over the card table threw a spire of light over the stacks of chips and the dusty baize and the tawny bottle of scotch. Sid lifted it off the table and held it closer to the light so that it shone like a hunk of topaz. 'Your mother was in a state when I bought it and look at it, hardly touched.' He put it back down on the table. 'So who was going to drink it? Hank Devine. The rest? They couldn't be bothered. The Irish drink, but gambling is the Jewish vice. Except, of course, for your mother.'

Evelyn stared at the man in the lamplight as she thought of her mother. No, she wasn't at all sure.

'What do you say, Evie? This time it's love?'

'*Sid.*'

'This is such a crazy question?'

Evelyn's blush deepened and she waved her hands in helpless denial in front of her chest.

'As I said, he's a helluva lot better than those other pishers.'

'But he's . . . Australian.'

'So, is this the moon? I knew some guys who went there, during the war. According to them, it wasn't such a bad place. I'm sorry I missed out. Great jocks. The islands . . . *Bali Hai will call you* . . . Me, I never got further than boot camp. Dreaming up quiz shows and crime shows for *other* troops.'

'It was safe.'

'Safe? What's safe? Security is an illusion, Evie girl. Life is a precarious business, don't you know? For us maybe more than most. And in my book the best approach is to learn to like it that way.'

Noon light the following day: bouncing in hard clear shafts on the kitchen tiles. It was a late lazy stretch of time for Evelyn. She walked in her nightdress into a dreamy silence. Bernice must have gone out shopping; it seemed she had the apartment to herself. Then she thought she heard the tip-tip-tip of Sid's typewriter faintly through the walls, and she stopped to listen, but as soon as her attention focused it was gone. She opened the refrigerator and the interior light beating against the white metal was even more blinding than the sun had been, belting through the western window. Blueberry muffins, waffle mix, orange juice: none appealed. She grabbed the carton of cream for her coffee and closed the door. There was coffee in the percolator to heat up on the stove.

She sat at the table with her hands around the cup and the smells of Bernice's paints wafting about her head. Oily, pungent, dark, not unpleasant; they drifted through her thoughts. There was a musty astringency to them that she might have felt had accompanied her all through her years had she been sufficiently aware of them. Yet Bernice had only taken up painting recently, after the trouble began. Then, as the steam rising from her coffee cup prompted her to sip, she grew conscious of the swirls and dabs of colour on the breadboard, the streaks of green on the palette knife, and her eye lifted, with the fumes or the steam it's hard to tell, to Bernice's canvas propped up on the easel, and the limp smelly rag on the ledge below. She smiled; well, it was more a wince than a smile, for what daughter is in a position to assess her mother's accomplishments? She sighed. At least this looked more like a picture than the ones that had gone before. Abstract, but a picture. She could make out a greenish-blue, rather luminous background and, in the centre, a white triangular shape, slightly skewed, a kind of cone, like the lopsided bottom of the Star on the front door, or one of the dotty geometrical shapes that cropped up here and there in the prints Bernice had hanging in the den. Evelyn bent her head to the side, to level in her line of vision whatever it was that this white thing was meant to be. Then she brought her head up, yawned, stretched her arms, drained her cup, and, after scraping her chair back, walked over to the sink to rinse it.

The next time Paul and Evelyn went to the ocean they took Bernice's car – an ancient Studebaker whose paint had become frosted from the salt in the air – and they slipped out and walked over to the galvanised iron railing that marked off the parking lot from the sand. They rested their elbows against the cold metal and were lulled by the long twinkling rolls of brine as if they were already at sea. They stayed there a while before climbing down the worn granite steps towards the beach. Flecks of quartz twinkled in the granite like the glances of sunlight on the surf. They had reached a stage where silence was as appropriate as words, and Evelyn was certain that her thoughts were flowing with his, and she felt exhilarated and brave. The air was sharp with the smell of kelp. She watched the wide foamy tongues of the ocean roll out and remembered the grunion, those long silver fish the tide brought every spring – hundreds of them, like silvery comets streaking through the waves, then wriggling across and burrowing into the moonlit sand – and then she thought of more ancient amphibious creatures. A teacher had told her about them once, when she and Bernice were living in New York and Bernice had plenty of work. Bernice, and her sad green paint. But she swam around that black rock in her mind, swam strong and fanciful and free. Those brave fish, her teacher had said, and strange, she could smell even then, as though it had never left her, the moss-green moistness of that classroom. They were her ancestors, she had said, and the ancestors of all the creatures of the land: the reptiles, the mammals, the birds. What a wonderful thing was the sea, Evelyn thought, inhaling it deep into her lungs, and doing this she could imagine that first fish, the very first one, and what it felt as it dragged its body over the cold wet sand, and how it breathed, and what it ate, and where it lay its eggs, and what were the odds.

Parramatta Road

The trouble with Ida was that she saved seats. Not just a few but a whole solid row of them at the front of the lecture theatre. This wasn't the worst of her failings but it was the one that most offended Evelyn before she got to know her better, although the last thing Evelyn could have imagined was that one day she would. Evelyn, habitually on the late side, would rush down the aisle, to encounter Ida standing in the middle of the row, her arms outstretched as if she were herding a group of children. She would shake her head importantly and announce in a low, heavily accented, rather gravelly voice that the entire centre row was taken. Taken? Evelyn would give an embarrassed smile, turn, and eventually spot a less conspicuous seat up at the back and to the side, where she shored up her dignity and had difficulty hearing the lecturer.

Perhaps it made Ida feel important, more secure. It certainly attracted attention, but she didn't seem to notice, or care, how irritating it was. After a while Evelyn saw that even the people Ida saved the seats for weren't all that grateful for the trouble she'd taken on their behalf. From her seat high up in the lecture theatre she could observe them straggling into class, still chattering among themselves, or shouting cryptic remarks to someone a few steps behind – the fag end of a session in the buttery or the union bar – to settle into the seats Ida kept for them, with all the nonchalance of lords straddling their mounts, or nabobs taking their rightful place at table. And this only seconds before the arrival of the lecturer, in his absurdly draped, chalk-dusted gown.

Anthropology was a relatively new subject then, a bold innovation for the university that stuck nervously to the old traditions and still called its terms Trinity, Michaelmas and Lent. Someone must have decided that anthropology was a fitting discipline for a university in the antipodes. After all, chairs had been established at Cambridge, if not at Oxford, and both Malinowski and Radcliffe-Brown had spent time in Australia. But in fact it took the war to push things along – governments needed to know about the strange customs and mysterious ways of all those backward peoples whose lands the Europeans were fighting in. And ever since the first war Australians had been responsible for New Guinea. But Evelyn was only dimly aware, if at all, of any of this. She hadn't really wanted to take anthropology. She had wanted to enrol in French but that began too early in the morning. This was the year she was taking off work so she could go to classes in the daytime, come home at a decent hour and get to bed before midnight, but she knew it would turn out differently with Paul for a husband. Because she was no longer supporting him she would be a proper wife again and the flat would be awash with people and booze and there'd be piles of dirty dishes in the morning, and even the walls and floors would seem to undulate like liquid in the bright morning glare. There would be nothing solid or stable in her freedom.

So she decided on a ten o'clock class. To give her time to nurse him through his hangover and get the flat in order before running up Walker Street to the station. Sometimes she even had time to stop at the cafe on Mount Street and sit at one of the laminex tables and watch the women push their foldup prams in the rain.

By the end of lent term she had long ceased bothering about the front seats and seething over Ida. Evelyn had grown fond of the steepness at the back. She liked looking down at the lecturer, it made him look small and powerless, and she developed a cold, detached interest in the spectacle of Ida and the coterie of smartarses she was trying to ingratiate herself with.

Every Monday, Wednesday and Thursday the drama would repeat itself: Ida with her arms spread wide or lowering them to brush her fingers possessively along the seats and then the parade of them: boys in grey raincoats with sleek brown hair flopping down on their foreheads, the prim-looking girls in suits and gloves whose appearance hadn't caught up with the recklessness of their language. Though she would arrange it so that she was sitting in the middle of them, smack in the middle of that centre row, Ida was as out of place in their company as a duck in a wedge of swans.

Evelyn took pains to examine herself, to make sure that it wasn't the rebuff that made her see Ida in such an unattractive light. But the truth was that Ida *was* unattractive, not because nature had made her so but because she seemed to have gone to a great deal of trouble to make herself grotesque. Her hair was defiantly frizzy at a time when the slightest curl was a transgression, and Evelyn suspected she dyed it, because her eyebrows were brown and the hair on her head was a vivid strawberry colour. Her face was a perfect triangle, not perfect in the sense of those faces that taper gently from a broad spread of cheekbone to a sharp, dimpled chin, but a triangle like you see in a geometry text or in those felt play sets for children. And because of this stark regularity, her face seemed quite flatly two-dimensional. Over it she slapped a thick coat of whitish powder and ringed her large exopthalmic eyes in black. She dressed dramatically too – a chartreuse jumper with a chunky brass medallion was a favourite – in a style that just missed being bohemian because it was far too conscious of its effect.

They were learning about the difference between cultural and social anthropology. Cultural anthropology emanated from America, its pioneers people like Frank Boaz, Ruth Benedict and Margaret Mead. Social anthropology was basically British, its contemporary practitioners in a direct line of descent from the great nineteenth-century eminences, Edward Tylor and Sir Henry Maine. Cultural anthropology was suspect, lightweight; it concerned itself with customs and mores, so many Indian potlatches and pow-wows, and made no attempt to analyse the organisation of the societies in which these curious practices took place, or how they might fit into the overall evolutionary pattern. There was an even subtler difference, a difference of far wider importance, but Evelyn wasn't to see this before a decade had passed and she was no longer a student and was thinking more or less for herself. She learned then that Boaz and Benedict had deliberately avoided placing the societies they studied into any evolutionary hierarchy, that their approach was a reaction against the pernicious social Darwinism that underpinned the class system and still informed the kind of anthropology that was being practised among the British and in their colonies. By the time Evelyn became aware of this the American approach had become a denial of class politics altogether and she found problems with that, but back then in the winter of 1962, all she could detect was the air of superiority over Americans that she could only acquiesce in, because her marks depended on it, and because she had made a choice, and was looking for any justification she could find.

The winter was colder than any she could remember. Now that she wasn't typing all day in an office and rushing after that to a class, or searching desperately for books in the old panelled library in the quadrangle and running for the bus and then the train late at night, reading what she could as it rattled over the bridge and through the darkened tunnel, she had time to notice the weather. She was in and out of buildings more, buildings that on the whole were underheated and draughty, including her flat. It was hard to imagine that she had been a child in Chicago and New York – the years spent in semi-tropical climates had thinned her blood. She shivered under her umbrella, hunching her shoulders like a refugee as she scurried down the hill to Parramatta Road to catch a bus to Wynyard. She shivered at the kitchen table reading Dryden and Pope. She shivered drinking espresso, watching the women in the rain. She could never get used to the rain.

The rain was bad for business, too, which meant that Paul was often home during the day and would drive her mad with his records and the mess he made in the kitchen while she was trying to study. She kept a corner of the table for her books and spiral notebooks and a box with the index cards she filled with quotations for essays. Before she set to work she would clear away the dishes and the crumbs and the newspapers and get a clean ashtray, but when Paul was home he would make devon and chutney sandwiches and sit down beside her and ask for her opinions about his lists. He made lists of things he had to get for the business – cash and receipt books and cardboard ledgers, materials for tenders. He made lists of indoor plants he was going to buy for the flat and seemed mildly hurt that she didn't take more interest. He wore his overalls and boots and drummed his fingers to the music and made more sandwiches waiting for the rain to stop, and didn't leave until it was time for training. He would train in the pouring rain. And when he got back she would stack up her books and papers and the card file and soak his muddy football shorts in the bathtub while they ate dinner.

After too many days of this she would leave herself when he was there, even when the rain was at its heaviest, pounding against the windowpanes and bouncing in thick needles against her umbrella as she ran towards the station. She would flop into her seat in the train and worry about the relationship. The rain made her worry about money and loaded her with guilt for not working. But she was determined. A degree? A piece of paper, it meant nothing. But she had the feeling that if she got one her world would set itself right. Her idea of it was almost talismanic. It would be a ticket, somehow, to the kind of life she had left behind. So she stuck it out: the rain and the football shorts and the late night booze-ups and the seat at the top of the lecture hall and the frequent references to the shallowness of American scholarship and the loneliness that would overwhelm her at odd, unexpected moments such as catching the eye of a stranger across the table in the library, or looking through the window of the espresso lounge at the women hurrying in the street with their groceries piled high on the hoods of the foldup prams.

The year was harder than she had thought or hoped it would be. Because she had time, more than she'd had in previous years, she had more time to brood, and the brooding made it harder. She expected more of herself, because there was time. And yet the time, which seemed to move so slowly that she felt as if she were treading the swells of an ocean, in fact moved all too swiftly, and before she knew it had tossed her up on a breaker and now she was facing exams.

It was the day of the anthropology final. She got off at the bus stop just outside the union building on Parramatta Road and climbed the steps to the little bistro next to the theatre. The sun was out and made the quartz flecks in the granite shine. She bought herself a cup of coffee and lit a cigarette while she glanced through her notes. She was not at all confident. As usual she had tried to digest too much, wolfing down great gulps of knowledge instead of selecting carefully from the menu. And now she was forgetting it all. Radcliffe-Brown and the Tiki, or was it Raymond Firth? There had been a segment, too, on ethnic tensions between the Chinese and Malays on the Malaysian peninsula but the lecturer for this part of the course had been a young guy with very pale skin who wore a grey gabardine suit without a gown and raced through his lectures in a Midlands accent that Evelyn, high up in her eyrie, found impossible to understand. She regretted this because he had seemed to know what he was talking about. She hadn't got the knack yet of second guessing what the questions would be and was wondering if there would be something on this since Malaya and Singapore were on the brink of becoming a nation, when she heard a familiar voice asking if she could sit down.

Evelyn resisted saying that the seat was taken.

'Thanks. I'll just go and get myself a coffee.'

It was only when she came back and introduced herself that Evelyn learned that the woman's name was Ida.

Ida poured sugar from the dispenser into her cup, stirred for a moment, staring at Evelyn with those huge black-ringed eyes. 'I was wondering, dear, if I might have a cigarette.'

Something curious was happening. It was as though all her efforts, against Paul and his dirt and his noise and the cold and the rain, had been futile, and there was no use struggling anymore. Evelyn opened her bag and handed over the packet.

Ida struck the match, held it to the cigarette dangling on the skin of her lip, and threw her head back to drag in the smoke, releasing it in a cloud as she came forward. She glanced at Evelyn's open spiral notebook. 'I see that you are prepared.'

Evelyn smiled meekly. 'Not half as much as I'd like.'

'Do you usually come this early?'

'No.'

Ida gave a hoarse laugh. 'Neither do I,' she sighed. 'But last night I didn't sleep. Not at all. All night.' Her look was heavy with meaning.

Evelyn laughed herself, out of impatience perhaps, or a keen sense of the irony of her situation. 'I haven't slept much myself,' she said. 'But it mightn't be all that bad.'

'Feh,' said Ida, with a wave of her hand. 'I don't care about the exam.'

Evelyn stubbed out her cigarette, closed her notebook and brought it to her chest. Maybe she could look at those Malayan notes in the library. But she felt the power of this strange woman's gaze again and the notebook slid back onto the little round table as if of its own accord.

'I don't care about anything, you see.' The large green eyes were filled with moisture. She lowered them to the smoke rising from her fingers. 'My husband has left me,' she said, directing her gaze upward again towards Evelyn.

'But . . . when?' Evelyn asked. It was hard to take in somehow that Ida too could have a husband.

'Two weeks today.'

'That's too bad.'

'I feel terrible,' Ida said.

'You would.' And Evelyn began to feel quite guilty for disliking her, not the least because she couldn't imagine what it would be like, to be left on her own, without Paul, even though he drove her crazy.

'I'll tell you, darling. I haven't slept for three months. Because I knew, I did know all along, what he'd been up to. Long before he packed up his bags and left.'

'It must have been awful.'

'Every night he said he was working late. But then he wouldn't bother to ring at all. I would think he was in an accident.' Her eyes brimmed with tears again.

'But how did you find out?'

'I saw them together, darling. That is, we were often together – her husband and my husband and she and I. We were friends. Old friends. Every week we would go out, the four of us, to dinner. To a show or a film. And I saw how they looked at each other. It was the way they looked at each other. They couldn't disguise it.'

'You would think they would stop. Going out with you, I mean.'

'How could they?' Ida's husky voice was getting louder. 'They would have looked suspicious. It was a regular thing. Ever since we came here. We all came out together, you know.'

Evelyn opened her bag and took out her packet of Marlboros, offered one to Ida although she had only just crushed one out, and lit one for herself. And she asked Ida where they had come from, she and her friend and these two husbands of theirs.

'Hungary, darling. We came after 56. We had to come. We were students, you see.'

Evelyn smiled. 'And you are still students now.'

'Only me. My husband has already graduated. I worked so that he could finish.'

'And now it's your turn,' Evelyn said.

Ida started crying then. She propped her elbow on the table and rested her wide forehead on her fist; the tears spilled over the eyeliner, onto her cheeks and her blouse. Evelyn, too, was assaulted by emotion. To avoid staring she looked down at her notebook and then began to feel desperate about the exam, but despite this found herself reaching across and touching Ida on the arm. Closer, she was even more conscious of Ida's heartache. She could feel the depth of her sobs, smell the staleness of her sweat. 'We really should talk about the exam, don't you think?' She spoke softly, adding, 'We only have a few minutes.'

Reluctantly, Ida glanced at her watch. 'A half an hour.'

'Not very long.'

Ida's cigarette was damp from the tears. She left it smouldering in the ashtray. 'I think I'll go home.'

'No!' Evelyn protested. 'I can help you. Except for that stuff from Dr Enfield. I couldn't follow him very well . . .'

But Ida was still weeping and wanted to go home.

'Well, maybe you should straighten yourself up then. Come, we'll powder your nose.'

But even after Evelyn had gone with her to the ladies' room and stood by her while she splashed water on her face and dried it and re-drew those eyelines with a shaking hand, Evelyn couldn't get Ida to come with her. As it was she only just made it to the Great Hall herself before they closed the big doors behind her.

Fortunately the exam was so structured that she didn't have to answer the question that Dr Enright had set on the Chinese in Malaya.

Evelyn was pleased that it was summer. Exams were over and, for the first summer since Paul had brought her to Australia, she wasn't working. She took her time over things, singing as she vacuumed and washed up, all the Sinatra songs that were Paul's favourites and that, in spite of herself, she too had come to love. It didn't take her long at all to clean the flat, no matter how much Paul and his mates and their loud-voiced women had messed it up the night before. It was hot and she would walk to St Leonards Park and catch the 144 to Manly, prop herself against the stone wall on the esplanade and read the books she had picked up from the library, a wild, eclectic assortment consisting of Neville Shute adventures and the novels of Miguel Asturias. In the back of her mind she knew she ought to look for a job to help them over the summer, though the business wasn't going so badly now that there were stretches of fine weather. But she loved the feel of the hot sand through her towel, the way it moulded to her shape as she imagined it might around the roots of a plant, a sensation of sinking that had become the most calming she knew. It made her feel she could be part of the place, as much a part as the towering pines along the esplanade and the long rickety pier being licked by the swells in the bay.

There was such peace and delight in that week of freedom that she forgot she had given Ida her number. So when Ida did ring at first she didn't know who it was. But gradually that morning came back to her and she caught the pain again in Ida's voice. And with the same mix of irritation, pity and resignation she'd felt before, Evelyn was agreeing, no, suggesting, that they should meet for lunch.

Ida lived in Bondi, in a flat on the ground floor of a liver-brick building on the hill. Sitting in the lounge waiting for her to get ready Evelyn could see the dense cobalt tones of the ocean over the roofs of the houses. There was a fresh smell from the sea. The flat was filled with the kind of furniture Evelyn longed for. A dark mahogany table with carving on the edges stood near the window where the gauze curtains billowed in the breeze. She realised that she had been waiting rather longer than she'd expected to when she caught herself watching the sunlight dapple the floating gauze.

'Evelyn,' she heard Ida call. 'Evelyn. Please, can you come?'

Evelyn shook herself, rose, and followed Ida's voice down a corridor. She caught sight of Ida when she came to the threshold to the bedroom, and it took her perhaps a fraction of a second to realise that what she was seeing was Ida's reflection. It startled her, and it startled her more to see her own reflection above it, the two of them held in the architrave. Ida, in a mauve satin negligee, was seated at a dressing table, powdering her face, dredging it with such thick applications from a large cotton puff that it looked even whiter and flatter than usual. When she saw Evelyn she gestured towards an armchair near the bed. 'Darling, I need to talk.'

'Well, yes,' Evelyn said. 'Over lunch.'

'I don't feel very hungry,' Ida said. She leaned closer to the mirror, holding her cheeks as though forcing them into place; and she registered a look of such self-loathing that it frightened Evelyn, even as Ida twisted round so they were sitting face to face. 'You don't mind?' Then, turning to the mirror again, she gave herself a grimace, pitched herself forward and broke out in a series of morbid, wrenching sobs.

'You were a singer?'

'Oh, yes. I sang in a little cafe not far from the university. I was a student also, you know, but the truth is I much preferred to sing.'

'What kind of songs?'

Ida smiled. Her red frizz stood out against the peach-coloured pillow, ash from her cigarette fell in flakes on the sheet. Her makeup was smudged from the tears and the face-cloth Evelyn had used to calm her down. 'At first, romantic songs. Torch songs. You know we knew a lot of jazz. We studied it very thoroughly. It was serious, like rock and roll today. There were records, too, from before the war. Billy Holliday, Ellington. I knew them all. I learned to sing blue notes. Do you know about blue notes?'

'Well, yes. My husband used to play in a band.'

'Really?'

'Just for fun.'

'Blue. Neither sharp nor flat. Somewhere in between.'

'Do you ever sing now?'

'No, darling. I am too sad to sing. Even blues. The bird inside has flown.'

She stubbed out her cigarette and gazed for a moment at its remains in the ashtray. 'Besides, I'd already given up jazz. We were singing protest songs. I would lead the crowds in the cafe and, then, before we knew it we were out in the street . . .'

'You were brave.'

'Feh, brave. Darling, by then we had nothing to lose. And let me tell you, it was exciting. You know,' she choked, 'I was very much in love.'

Ida began to weep.

'You know, darling, the worst thing is that's she's such a Magyar. A shiksa. Blonde, blonde, blonde, with cold, narrow blue eyes. She's even anti-Semitic. I can't imagine how he stands it.' Ida rubbed the large white bones on her wrist. 'Maybe he doesn't remember her snide remarks about Jews or even hear them now that he's so ga-ga.' Her laugh was bitter but almost, momentarily, zestful. 'Probably she's learned to hold her tongue. She's clever, I'll give her that. I suppose when she thinks about his nice, established practice it doesn't matter at all that he's a Jew.'

'You're Jewish,' Evelyn said with surprise.

'Of course, darling,' Ida smiled.

'So am I.'

'I thought so. I think one can always tell.'

Evelyn nodded, slowly, less in agreement than grappling with the implications.

'So you see, that is what makes it so awful, so unbearable. After everything we've been through.'

Evelyn didn't even try to stop her weeping again.

Seeing Ida became a habit. Business was going well for Paul and there seemed no reason for Evelyn to get a job for the four-month student vacation. In any case, Paul never worried about money, the worry had always been hers. She remembered when he had put their last seventeen dollars on an Irish filly at Santa Anita and Evelyn couldn't even watch her win. She sat in the bleachers with her palms pressed over her eyes and missed the thrill of the finish. So Ida's need served a purpose. Listening to her, helping her were acts of atonement, keeping that vague, generalised guilt that continually threatened to engulf her at bay. That Ida was outrageous made it all the better.

Two, sometimes three times a week, Evelyn would take the train to town and catch the bus to Bondi, revelling in the smells of tar and petrol and the salted sea air. And when she got to the flat it was always the same. Ida would be in the mauve satin dressing-gown, which was beginning to smell itself from the weeks of constant wear, smoking and ringing her large, crusted eyes with the thick black liner. Evelyn would bring rye-bread sandwiches that Ida would lunge at, then refuse, and then it would be time for Evelyn to listen again to the awful story of the besotted husband, the conniving Magyar and the sacrificing, sacrificed wife. Once she brought a record from Paul's collection in the hope that she might get Ida to sing but Sinatra only made Ida sadder. And once she ran a bath for Ida and shampooed her hair, hoping that she would get to like the feel of being clean, but that failed miserably too. She never told Paul of these visits, or anything at all about Ida. But for some reason she hadn't quite come to grips with, she made a special effort with his dinner each night when she came back from Bondi.

One morning towards the end of summer, when the days were still as hot as she liked them and Paul had gone off to the site and Evelyn had planned to go to the beach, the phone rang. She took her time answering it; she expected it was Ida and the morning was too beautiful for Ida. The bag with her books and the towel and a sandwich dangled from her shoulder, bumping her hip as she sauntered to the phone. But it wasn't Ida, it was an altogether strange voice which chilled her for an instant, until she was made to understand what the call was about, and then the chill went deeper and spread. It was a neighbour of Ida's, a woman who lived in the adjacent flat and ran errands for her and brought her meals from time to time. She was agitated, distressed. 'Come quickly,' she said, in an accent almost as thick as Ida's. Ida had slashed her wrists. They had rushed her to the hospital in the night but she had been released. Evelyn rushed over in a taxi.

When she got there Ida was in bed. The neighbour had tucked the bedclothes in firmly and Ida sat serenely propped up on the pillows, her bandaged wrists laid gingerly on the counterpane. All colour was gone from her face, so that only a light dusting of powder was needed to achieve her characteristic pallor. But she looked comfortable, quiet, and in fact was smiling, though the smile was sheepish and wistful. 'Thank you for coming, darling,' she whispered. 'I knew you would come, but I would have been so unhappy if you hadn't.'

Evelyn took her seat by the bed, reached across and touched one of the bandages. She raised her head then and looked quizzically at Ida.

'Forlorn,' Ida said. 'I was too forlorn.'

'You might have succeeded.'

'I wanted to. I wish I had.'

'Don't be ridiculous!' Evelyn huffed. 'You wouldn't want to give him the satisfaction.'

'Darling, he wouldn't care.' The tears rolled quietly down Ida's cheeks, streaking the light film of powder.

'Doesn't he know?'

'Who would tell him? As a matter of fact, it's seeing him that sets me off. If I never saw him at all it might be better.'

'You see him?'

'Too bloody often, my dear.'

'But when?'

'He comes here. Because he still wants all this.' She winced as she lifted her arm and spread it wide. 'He wants a divorce. And wants me to move out. So he can move in and she can sleep in my bed, eat at my table, seat his guests on my lounge suite—'

'But that's unbelievable!'

'And I said no. I told him I could never consent to it.'

'So what will he do?'

'Give her up. Or wait five years.'

'Ida, if he wants her –'

'But don't you see? He doesn't. He can't have anything with her as he's had with me.'

Evelyn feared that the force of Ida's words would make her break down again but Ida remained calm. There was such conviction in what she said that Evelyn found herself believing her. She imagined Ida arm-in-arm with her student husband – he would be dark, dashing, tall. They walked over the cobblestones in a street in Budapest. All she could imagine was the slick wet cobblestones and a painted wooden sign swinging over the door of a cafe and the crimson scarf that flowed from the young man's neck. But the images stopped just there, she had nothing more to sustain them. Budapest. Hungary. Was it defensiveness that made all of Europe a blank?

'And he comes *here*?' she asked, to firm things up in her mind.

'Here, or sometimes we arrange that I meet him at his office.'

'Where's that?'

'In Randwick. On Alison Road. Not far.'

The neighbour, Mrs Cernak, came in solemnly with a tray and just as solemnly withdrew. Evelyn and Ida lunched on tomato, cream cheese and olive sandwiches. They were delicious and Evelyn forgot all about the one in her bag. She noticed that Ida, too, ate with a hearty appetite, and when they had finished she asked Evelyn for a cigarette.

That evening Evelyn, silent, reflective, watched her husband Paul. All evidence in her own life to the contrary, she believed marriage an immutable state. Where had she ingested this notion? From her grandparents, from the movies, the songs? How had it stayed with her? Paul was in the lounge room, what she would have once called the *living* room, and he was listening to his records. He had got home before she had, having knocked off work at half past four, and was sitting there when she walked in the door, her beach bag filled with provisions. After dinner he went back to the music. For some reason she hadn't wholly explored, his continued passivity irritated her. Even though she knew he was resting after a hard day's physical work in the sun, it was irritating. She wanted to see him moving, as though it was his mobility, the powerful grace of his body and limbs in motion that made her own shifting nature bearable, and to see him stationary, supine, left her alone with her discontent. He was lying in his shorts on the divan, his hands tucked under his head, his muscular legs bare and sprawling. She wanted to kick, or at least rearrange him, but knew that if she did make him move he might only do something more irritating, like decide to cook something, or repot the plants, or sit in the kitchen and compose another of his lists.

She sat down and lit a cigarette instead, imagining she was somewhere else altogether, in that cafe, for instance. She imagined Ida singing in the smoky room, easy to do with Sinatra on the phonograph, Ida's voice so strangely low, and there it was, the whole scene, the one she had tried to conjure up in the afternoon but wasn't in her, or so she had thought. The students in their drab shirts and trousers, smoking and whispering, Ida in a tight skirt and beret, her broad hands pressed on her narrow hips, and the tall dark man, a boy really, with his deep red scarf and shining eyes, the only bright objects in the room, getting up from the table, pushing it forward with a scrape, coming towards her with those dark shining eyes.

The record stopped. Paul was asleep. Seeing him, his stiff sun-brightened curls nearly covering his eyes, Evelyn felt suddenly desolate, as if she were losing all contact with him, forever, and there was nothing between them but a chasm of howling silence. She whispered, the strange, irrational fear lodged in her throat, 'Paul?' She slipped her hands through her hair and over her ears, until the silence came into proportion again. Then she went over to him and, kneeling, ran her finger around the sun-roughened shell of his ear and lowering her lips to it blew softly until he woke. They made love then, on the divan and on the floor, and when she was at peace again she told him about Ida. 'It isn't fair,' she said. 'That he should take *everything* from her. You would think since, after all, he's the guilty party, he'd be more reasonable.'

'Maybe he doesn't know how much he's hurting her,' Paul said.

There was an orderliness to Evelyn's personality; with the summer coming to an end she had begun to think how nice it would be if Ida could be free of her sorrows before term began. She saw that her desire for Ida's happiness was partly a hope for herself, though it was too arduous and ultimately pointless to work out who might benefit the most. She rang Ida the following morning, concerned about how she had got through the night.

'You're better. That's good,' said Evelyn on the phone.

But Ida was still feeling shaky, so Evelyn made the trip once more to Bondi. Ida was dressed this time, her face powdered thickly again, the bulging eyes ringed. She was wearing a cerise cotton sack dress and her arms looked very white and thin. They sat at the carved mahogany dining table. Ida would oscillate from heavy bravado ('You wait and see, Evelyn dear, I shall make him pay!') to abject self-abasement ('Look at me, how thin and scraggy I've become. How could he love me this way?'). Evelyn could see how much Ida depended on her for the merest shred of confidence. She made the tea, poured it out in the green and white gold-rimmed Noritake set that she knew by now exactly where to find in the sideboard, made toast and jam because there wasn't much else in the flat, and suggested they go out shopping.

'No need,' Ida said, with the wistful smile of the invalid. 'Mrs Cernak will bring in some things this afternoon.'

'You should go out, Ida. At least once a day. That's what a friend of mine told me. Rain or shine. Even if it's to the corner shop to get the afternoon paper.'

'Tell me, darling. When do you read the afternoon paper?'

Evelyn laughed. 'I don't. But Paul brings it home for the form guide.'

A mistake, to have mentioned him. Ida looked alarmingly glum. 'We could go for a walk along the beach. If I'd thought I would have brought my bathing suit,' Evelyn said. And wondered why she had never considered it before, swimming while she was at Bondi.

'I would look simply awful in a bathing suit.'.

'Come on, what do you care? What do any of us care?' Evelyn, laughing, lied.

'Seriously, I don't want to go out.'

'But why?'

'He might be coming,' Ida said abjectly. 'I don't want to miss him.'

Evelyn threw her arms down on her lap, rose from her chair and went to the window. She lifted the gauze, and the white light poured like wax over the sill and the table and onto the floor. She blinked and, looking across to the water, said, 'It's crazy that you're even seeing him.' Turning to Ida, Evelyn moved her head slowly from side to side. 'He can't understand how he must be hurting you.'

'I only wish someone would tell him.'

Evelyn dropped the curtain and watched Ida for a moment. Ida, her eyes protruding more than usual, returned the stare. Evelyn stood motionless by the window, experiencing a keen excitement, only too conscious that this transfixed look of hers was the gaze of a doomed animal, a rabbit or a hare. Later, a day, a week perhaps, or even after many months, if she were honest with herself and not so quick as she normally was to parcel blame, she would have been hard put to say whether it had been her impulsive suggestion or Ida's, born of desperation, or something that Ida had long since nursed in her mind.

'I think that someone should tell him,' Evelyn heard herself say.

She said nothing to Paul. He wasn't likely to remember discussing Ida; it was the sort of thing he would encourage as a routine marital courtesy and immediately forget. Yet that made what she was intending even more of a trangression, stepping into waters unforbidden only because they were unknown. She could expect neither help nor sympathy nor, ultimately, rescue. If he was, as she knew, for all his superficial quirkiness, a basically sensible, kind but conservative man, he would respond from a deeper self-interest, which bonded him not to her, but to the stranger, the man in the flowing red scarf.

She found his name easily enough in the phone book, his office on Alison Road, Randwick, as Ida had said. Reaching for the receiver she felt a pang of fear but went through with the dialling nonetheless. She was jolted by the man's voice on the end of the line, she had assumed he would have a secretary. Although she hadn't meant to, she led him to believe that she was a prospective client. 'I need to see you,' she said. 'About some trouble I'm in,' she said, and made an appointment.

For the two days she had to wait she was in a state of high perturbation. Contradictory feelings of pride (for going out of her way to help a friend), shame (she recognised that curiosity was an equal, if not more powerful motive) and, though she could scarcely acknowledge let alone articulate it, a burgeoning sexual frisson assailed her. She channelled much of this nervousness into an uncharacteristic concern over what she would wear. In a kind of parody of the stories she had read in the women's magazines she used to pick up to read on the train home from work, nothing in her wardrobe seemed suitable. She spent hours before the mirror holding dresses, tops and skirts against herself, shifting the combinations with such pertinacious intensity that the tiny bedroom was swirling with colour and her arms ached at the end of it. She settled finally on an olive-green linen dress that she considered a little too dressy but went well with her tan and dark hair. On the morning of the appointment she drew it back into a neat french roll and was as ready as she ever could be for her adventure.

The day was hot, a blowzy, languorous day in February. The streets smelled of tar and dead jacaranda leaves. The Randwick bus was crowded with mid-week punters, round little men with wrinkled gabardine suits and grey fedoras pushed back on their toupees, and chainsmoking gaunt ones reading their folded form guides. They tumbled off at the entrance to the racecourse. She rode for a few more stops, her senses tingling with the smells of rank decay, sharpened by the tang of the approaching sea.

His office was on the first floor of a two-storey red brick building with an estate agency and a sandwich bar on the street. She walked up the stairs and opened the door to the waiting-room. To her surprise now there was a secretary; perhaps when she had rung that afternoon the woman had already gone home. Evelyn could take in the fact of her, the woman's clothes, features, hairstyle, but little else; everything in the room was a bold if blurred abstraction, accelerating in a sequence of colour and shape. She stammered out her name and the secretary – blonde, thin, red – led her to the inner door.

'And you say that you are wholly dependent on your husband.'

'Now, yes. But you know what the building game is like, he could go broke any time.'

'It is a wonder you haven't formed a company before.'

'There were so many other things to think of,' Evelyn said.

'A businessman thinks first of reducing his liability. Always.'

He was not as she had imagined. Medium height and build, clothed in a dark blue, three-piece worsted suit. His hair, too, was a middling shade of brown, cut close to his head but long enough to show its wave. There was a very slight plumpness about him, no more than a suggestion that he was fond of good food, and dined out frequently. She was conscious of cologne and a guarded, worldly, appraising look in his eye. When he spoke he often brought his hand up to rub the back of his neck, a gesture which seemed to say that, though he was accustomed to encountering the failings of his fellow humans, they never ceased to astonish him. He spoke in a modulated, barely accented English, with none of the impassioned cadence of a dissident. In fact, the only part of him remotely similar to her previous image of him was his tie, which was red but much darker than the flowing scarf.

'How long does it take, then, to register a company?'

'Longer than it should. The registrar's office operates like any other band of commissars. You can get them to move sometimes if your client's a big-time developer setting up a holding company . . .'

'I'm afraid my husband isn't in that league.'

'May I ask what his assets are?'

She shrugged. 'A utility, a mattock, a spade. He contracts out,' she explained.

'And you have no regular solicitor?'

'I told you, no.' She held her breath, and let it out as slowly as she could. 'To tell you the truth I wouldn't know one solicitor from another but at least I'd heard about you.'

A light leaped, heedless, into his guarded eyes.

'From someone at the university,' she said.

He nodded, rubbing the back of his neck. Then he smiled. 'There's a very nice cafe not far from here. Would you care to join me for lunch?'

Had she expected this? She looked at her watch, as much to steady herself as to determine the time. It was not quite twelve.

'It's yes, then. Come,' he said, taking her by the elbow. 'I'm hungry.'

He led her out onto the street. The bright noon light hurt her eyes. The heat had intensified since her bus ride; she felt it in the sudden moisture under her arms. He slipped off his jacket and slung it over his shoulder. Walking, they talked in a quick, bantering way, on all manner of subjects, distant from them both – the coming federation of Singapore and Malaysia, confrontation with Indonesia, Cuba after the Soviet backdown. She gave vent to her exasperation with Australia, it was easy in his company; their common foreignness allowed just this sort of release. (Such an insignificant, self-important place, the people with so little savoir-faire.) These unexpected turns in the encounter were so encouraging that she lost her anxiety over how to broach the subject of Ida; Ida was fading rapidly from her mind. This niggled, and the niggling annoyed her. She brushed it away as she would a fly at a picnic.

For now, they were walking through an alleyway surrounded by paling fences and the aroma of frying chops, the tar soft under their feet. They came out of the alley onto Glebe Road. The cafe was one of those restaurants with dark tinted windows and cool, dusky interiors, the carpet as yielding as the pavement had been in the alley. A woman, the hostess – blonde, svelte, dressed in black – took them to a table at the side. His table, she grasped. She looked at the menu, thinking in a flash of the sandwich that she usually packed for lunch and the ones she made for Paul. 'We shall have some wine. A Penfold's Chardonnay, Bin 35,' he told the hostess. The food was rich, middle European; she ordered fish, the lightest meal offering. To her surprise he ordered pork, though all her life she herself had eaten it. Why had she supposed Europeans would be less assimilated? While they waited for their food he made polite inquiries about her life, where she had been born, why she and her husband had come to Australia.

'Paul is Australian,' she said.

'I assumed he was also an American.'

'We met over there. He went to teach us rugby. A date took me to a game, the Wallabies against UCLA, and there was this party afterwards.'

'There is always a party,' he smiled.

A waiter brought their food. They busied themselves laying out the starched white napkins in their laps.

'So this husband of yours, he played for Australia.'

Evelyn blushed slightly. 'He still plays. But he hasn't gone overseas in a while.'

He raised an eyebrow, then picked up a fork and nodded her

way. 'We'd better eat before it gets cold.'

They were silent for several moments, attending to the meal. She was aware of the tinkling of cutlery and her chewing. The food had little taste. It was as if she were watching this scene of two strangers in a restaurant and couldn't convince herself that she was actually part of it. Perhaps it was that guilt again. It wasn't right that she was enjoying herself, therefore it couldn't be. She made herself think of Ida, Ida propped against the pillows, clutching the counterpane.

'Your husband is very fortunate,' he suddenly said. 'To have you as a partner.' He fingered the stem of his wine glass and spun it slowly. 'Do you handle all these matters, looking after the books and so forth?'

'Yes,' she said. 'Though not entirely.' She could feel the heat rise at the back of her neck. She searched her mind for holes in her story, something contradictory she had said: a danger, because she hadn't in fact involved herself much with Paul's affairs. She knew when they were in the red and in the black and that was it. At least she hoped she knew.

'It's said to be good for a marriage. Husband and wife working as a team.'

Evelyn took a slow sip of her wine. She was feeling very shallow and silly. The whole occasion, the restaurant, the linen, the wine, this stranger. Something dreamt up by a randy schoolgirl. Was she dreaming? What she was doing was unconscionable; moreover, risky. She felt an urge to make a clean breast of it, as if by that very act her waking, conscious, sane world could be restored. But she didn't quite trust him; she even sensed that he might be egging her on.

She laughed. 'That's the sort of thing you read in the *Women's Weekly*. You know, next to the astrology column.'

'You read the *Women's Weekly*?'

'Not regularly. But I get a kick out of the astrology column.'

'Don't tell me you believe in astrology,' he smiled.

This forced her to admit that she did. A little.

'That reminds me of a woman I once knew. A full-blown certifiable. Her speciality was hypochondria. Always something wrong with her. She loved going to doctors. And one day I discovered that what she liked almost as much as buying the attention of the various physicians she visited was sitting in their waiting rooms reading the magazines. She also believed in astrology. A little.'

'You seem to have known this woman well.'

'Well enough,' he said.

She glanced at her empty plate and pushed her knife and fork together, with scarcely a memory of having eaten.

'Did they have astrology columns in Hungary?'

'I honestly can't remember. I suppose they did. But it would have been counter to party ideology.'

'And you were opposed to that.'

'It was very hard not to be.'

'But hard to express it.'

'Do you know about Hungary?' He didn't wait for her reply, perhaps he was used to negative ones. 'On the surface it was looking pretty good, after the war. Popular front, then a people's republic. The AVO, the State Security Department, got rid of any opposition. But then Nagy came, a Muscovite, but a Hungarian. His sympathies were with the people. He made promises – no more forced collectivisation, he would release the prisoners, close the internment camps. Moscow, of course, wouldn't have it. Nagy was dismissed, expelled from the party. But we were emboldened, you understand, by Khruschev's speech at the twentieth congress and by the Polish challenge that summer. By autumn we were marching and no sooner were we doing that than the police were shooting at us and we were in total revolt. Nagy came back and things were looking good again, with him at the head of a coalition. Social Democrats, peasants, Catholics. The popular front again, only without the Reds. But Nagy got cocky, announced our withdrawal from the Warsaw Pact, and that was the end of it. And now I am here.'

'I suppose it was even harder for Jews,' she said.

'Those of us who were left tended not to make much of our Jewishness. We were socialists, the new Hungarians. As a matter of fact, I was brought up a Catholic.' He gave a quiet chuckle, crossing himself.

'We think of nations as people almost, as unified entities,' she said. 'And yet they are always divided, if not by religion, then by race, or ideology. Look at Malaysia. My anthropology lecturer doesn't hold much hope for it, what with the racial tensions, but when I think about it, a nation is a pretty artificial thing in the first place, nearly always a compromise between primary allegiances. A coalescence at best, but hardly ever that.'

'You're a student,' he said, and she couldn't tell if he was surprised or if the discovery confirmed what he'd already suspected.

'Why, yes. In fact that's how I heard about you,' she added, quite casually, in no way revealing that here was her opportunity, at last. 'I met a woman in my class. Well, actually, it was your wife, Ida.'

'Ida,' he said quietly, nodding as if in appreciation. He smiled, rather guiltily, she thought. 'And what did Ida tell you about me?'

'That you were a solicitor and your office was in Randwick.'

'That was all?'

'No, not all. She did give me the impression you were making her rather unhappy.'

He rubbed the back of his neck then, slowly, tenderly, not merely in urbane astonishment this time but as if he had received an actual blow. Then he looked up at her, his eyes defensive and reappraising. 'She put you up to this.'

'No,' she could truthfully say.

'You mean you really do need a solicitor.'

'Maybe not as badly as I made out.'

He threw his serviette down on the table. 'Mrs Hazelwood – if that indeed is your name. Perhaps you have all the time in the world for games, but I have more pressing things to do.'

'I'm sorry,' she said. 'Genuinely sorry. I suspected it was crazy all along, but—'

'It was.'

'I felt I had to do something! She tried to take her life!'

'On *numerous* occasions.'

Evelyn covered her mouth with her hand. Only after some moments could she remove it. 'But doesn't that make you think about how you've been treating her?'

'What *has* Ida told you, Mrs Hazelwood?

'She's heartbroken that you've left her, that's all.'

He sighed.

'And she's very hurt about your wanting the flat.'

This time there was genuine anguish on his face. 'The flat?' He was silent for a few seconds. 'Listen, are you mad? To look at you, you seem a perfectly pleasant woman. Young, intelligent. And yet underneath you must be as cuckoo as she is. Whatever did you expect to achieve on a mission like this?'

'I don't know,' she confessed. 'I really don't. Perhaps I was curious.'

He eyed her carefully. 'Now that makes more sense.'

'It seems I was being far less noble than I cared to admit.'

'You are remarkable, nonetheless. And a much better friend than Ida deserves.'

'I'm not feeling like that just now.'

'What has she done to you?'

'Done?'

'Look. I don't wish to appear unkind. But since I'm already the villain of the piece I suppose it really doesn't matter. You must know what I'm talking about. You have eyes in your head. Do you honestly believe that I could have stayed with Ida? That any man could have stayed with Ida? You have to admit she's incredibly ugly!'

Evelyn gulped. 'Then why did you marry her?'

'Things were different then. It was an act of generosity.'

'That's pretty arrogant.'

'Yes. But it's the truth. And there was no reason in the world I could think of for being miserable the rest of my life because of it.'

'But she supported you while you were studying and now you even want the flat.'

'She told you that? Oh please, Mrs Hazelwood. Evelyn. The flat was hers with the divorce.'

'She said she won't give you a divorce.'

'She wouldn't, at first. But the law, harsh as it is, will grant one in respect of a separation that has lasted five years.'

That long?

Evelyn leaned back in her chair and let her arms hang loose beside her.

Over the next couple of weeks she rang him a few times. She had felt the need to make it up to him, considering how gracious he had been. She racked her brains trying to think of some kind of work she could bring him, and finally came up with a contract to be drawn up for Paul's bricklayer. It was a piddling job and she felt a bit ashamed that she couldn't present him with anything bigger, but he could tell from the extent of it how small a builder Paul was, and was as gracious as he had been over their first transaction. Between the phone calls about the bricklayer she wondered if he usually invited clients to lunch or if he had sized her up the moment she stepped through the door. But from what he had said it seemed unlikely that he had had any previous delegations from people in sympathy with Ida. She supposed from what he revealed that he had been a philanderer, and it was not especially vain of her to imagine he'd been moving in on her. But that didn't square with Gryzyncka, to whom he seemed happily married, and on at least one occasion he suggested that Evelyn might like to meet her. Sensibly, Evelyn declined. But she found it harder to quell her curiosity. 'Tell me,' she said, as they were making arrangements for the brickie's contract to be signed. 'That day when I came to see you. Did you suspect?'

He laughed gently over the line. 'I wish I had! No,' he said, his tone betraying more regret than perhaps he wished. 'It never occurred to me that someone would feel so strongly about Ida. But I was curious. It's not often that clients come in off the street, from the blue, so to speak. They usually drop a name or two. I wanted to know your connections.'

When the university year began – the start of Lent term, as Evelyn herself had begun to call it – she enrolled in the honours course. This included a class in prehistory, held in a room with long form tables and the hazy sunlight of early autumn pouring through the venetians. The lecture room was, of course, much smaller than the vast theatre where students the previous year had learned of the superiority of British anthropology and the troubles facing Malaysia.

She began to get friendly with other serious students. The cliquey sophisticates of the year before faded from her consciousness. It was clear that too many sessions in the buttery had had an effect on their marks, and they had a hang-dog, vanquished look, perhaps all the more so because they had to find seats for themselves. Although Evelyn never rang or went to see Ida again she was counting on seeing her at the university. Naturally, Ida had failed the exam so she knew that she wouldn't be in this class, but she had thought that she might run into her on the quadrangle, or along the stairs, or in the library with its cushioned linoleum and polished oak shelves. And after a while she seemed to be halting for moments in these places, long enough to be almost waiting, even at the bistro outside the theatre on Parramatta Road.

Misty Harbour

Marseilles or Cordova tile, the hipped roof, the boxed eave, the fretted bargeboard, the ubiquitous triple-fronted bungalow. Evelyn was attentive to these details because Paul, her husband for a time, was a builder and, without really knowing it, she would observe them – randomly, lovingly – and so the sense of them, their essence perhaps, crept through her skin and latched onto her organs, her soft body tissues. For the truth was that she, who had no house, and on the surface regarded houses with the sort of mild disdain reserved for life's inconsequentials, loved houses, all houses, even those distinguished by their apparent lack of distinction. She was familiar with the shades and shapes and textures of their bricks; their windowed expressions, astonished, complacent or sad. Her gaze would savour the angle of a roofline the way one might respond to the rakish tilt of a hat. She was, unconsciously, beckoned. Walking the streets, or riding the trains, she would be charmed by the sight of them as if by a mirage; gardens and gates and facades in one sense so inviting (and arranged, as it happened, to evoke just that illusion of welcome and cheer), and in another, utterly, absolutely, outside her reach. Like other people's marriages, she would muse, when consciousness of these feelings drifted up in odd snatches, as the train sped her past the yards and skillions and spider-web laundry hoists circling slowly in a morning's breeze. Or at night, their glazed eyes flickering under the moon.

In dreams she had special houses, houses whose beauties only she could fathom; she was always pointing out their hidden features, explaining their possibilities to friends and strangers, persons fleeting and shadowy in a way that her visions were not.

And why do I speak of her now as though she herself were another person, fleeting, insubstantial, this shade of a young woman who is as difficult to catch hold of as the faceless visitors to her dreams? Well, the simple answer is that she is another person, and so I must continue to speak of her, this tender, ignorant, innocent who was me.

It's interesting that in none of these dreams did she actually build a house; odd, when she understood the process so well, the step-by-step construction from its foundations, and through her daily proximity to Paul knew precisely how long it took, weather permitting, from the time the concrete was poured to the lock-up stage, when the slow, fiddly business of 'finishing' was begun. But in her dreams the houses were always found, fully-formed, signs of a wondrous serendipity, unimaginable, if it weren't for the very fact that they had been imagined, and were there. And that was it: they were there. And often it was not simply the case of Evelyn having found them, but *discovering* that these wonderful edifices had been in her possession all the time. One in particular I remember. It stood on a stubby projection of shale, in the shape of a thumb poking pugnaciously into the water, with the foaming waves slopping over the land and dovetailing under a high, bright, but snug and glassed-in verandah. Evelyn would lead her guests up a steep set of stairs into her look-out and her heart would swell with wellbeing and the muscles in her face would spread in a deeply satisfied smile as the glaucous waves met and curled and subsided, entwined and murmuring under her house. Water. The key, I see now, was the water. The joy of being safe and snug and anchored to the land, yet all the while surrounded, licked and soothed, by the tamed, endlessly encroaching water.

This was how it was in her dreams; what it all meant wiser folk than she could say. In real life she knew that water was trouble. Always, Paul would take elaborate precautions against it. Where other builders might lay strips of bituminous felt two courses above the ground, Paul would lay his at five, and in high foundations would lay an additional one, as well as flashing all the bearers and floor plates. He laid felt under windowsills, too, and below all slabs, and above any openings, or next to abutments, cut and wedged into wall joints, folded, and tamped into the roof.

He distrusted flat roofs, but if for some reason one was specified, he argued for a pitch of at least two inches for every ten feet of battening, by raking the rafters towards the guttering, and if he failed in the end to persuade a recalcitrant architect or client, he made sure to install the best metal sarking. His conscientiousness prevented him from ever accumulating much in the way of profit or even, let it be said, a reasonable working capital, but it did gain him a reputation, and he came to be sought by the better architects and the more discerning home-owners. And this, more or less, was how he got to know the Barretts.

It all began when their roof caved in, a roof that Paul hadn't built, and never would have had anyone asked him in the first place, but they brought him in to repair it. It was an unusual roof in an equally heterodox house, looking circular but actually structured as an octagon. The roof was made of concrete tiles, graded upwards and outwards to eight points from the centre, where a wrought-iron down-pipe was set, to carry rain water through and then under the house. From these eight points, which occurred at three-quarters of the extension of each of the sides, the roof dropped again in a series of hip formations ending neatly at the gutters. From there the walls hung in sheets of shimmering plate glass. The effect was of a highly stylised rose, a kind of origami flower, set in an angular glass bowl. The architect – a Brazilian – was far away, having gone off to help Oscar Niemeyer with extensions to their capital, and the Barretts were left stranded, so to speak. For one stormy night the rain and the wind proved too much for the one black wrought-iron pipe, which served far better as a decorative feature than as a drain. Flying debris got caught in it, the driving rain collected in the hollow of the rooftop, water began seeping in through the tiles, and in a matter of hours the entire sunken centre collapsed, and the Barretts were awash.

'Any mug could have told them that would happen,' Paul said to Evelyn as he peeled off his sodden workclothes, after a day of digging out waterlogged twigs and bark jammed in the downpipe with one hand, while clinging to the single remaining rafter with the other. His face, dark with a reddish-brownish silt, was dusted as well with plaster, and lumps of it were scattered through his hair, and when he was finished and wearing nothing but his underpants, he fell onto a chair, too exhausted to drum up the energy to make it to the shower. His elbows dropped to his knees and he held his head in his hands. But then he raised himself. He thrust out his legs and flopped against the back of the chair. 'But, oh my God, Evie, what a house! What a dream of a house. A fucking pain in the arse, but a beauty. You should see it, Evie.' He turned his head slowly from side to side. 'What a man would do to have a house like that.'

The day that he drove Evelyn to see it was a fine bright one in early spring. The roof, repaired and newly reinforced, showed promise of bearing up under any future quirk in the weather, and the Barretts, in gratitude, had invited the young builder and his wife to a Sunday barbecue. The sky, I remember, was that peculiarly rich, dense shade of blue that carries scudding white clouds as the deep voluminous sea carries ships. And as the road wound down towards the peninsula that leads to Misty Harbour, everything had a quality of sharpness and brightness, was illuminated as in the borders of those finely figured medieval manuscripts and books of hours. There was a creaminess to the light, yet the colours of the birds, the parrots, rosellas and lorikeets, had the incandescence that you sometimes see when the sun is much lower in the sky. Every leaf, every spotted or corrugated tree trunk, every twig and curl of bark, every wallaby or hare scampering through the brackened bush, had a reality intensified by the fine, sparkling detail which gave it life. What houses there were had been set well back from the road, and were almost hidden by the gums and tangles of creepers, so there was as well a sense of stillness, a quietening of human desire. The light passed through the windscreen of Paul's utility and this patch of glass, separating Evelyn and him from their surroundings, only strengthened her feeling that this was a scene she was observing, a tableau, recorded by some monkish anonymity whose hand had been moved by a simple, pious trust. And she wondered about the Barretts again and their extraordinary house. Responding to the invitation she had spoken to Mrs Barrett – Marcia – on the phone, and the voice seemed confident and authoritative, the voice of a woman who often entertained, the kind who wore leather trousers and chunky gold jewellery with egg-shell white shirts when she opened the door to her guests. But she had formed no picture of the husband at all, Phillip she reminded herself, and because of the scene and the associations it evoked in her she began to imagine him as that monk, someone reserved, gentle, artistic and reflective, altogether different from his stylish, convivial wife. And then it occurred to her that this was because he was a scholar, a mathematician, Paul had said he lectured at the university, and she could see how the pieces were fitting, that she had always associated scholars with this kind of temperament, her own great-grandfather had been one, and despite an exterior roughness, she remembered him as such – a deliberate man, gentle and responsive to beauty, an echo of a past that she could barely lay claim to as her own.

Suddenly, with another turn in the road, the brightness, that quiet, vivid sharpness disappeared. A cloak of fog fell over everything, the bitumen, the verge, the trees, the ferns. Misty Harbour – obviously this was how the place had got its name. Evelyn twisted herself around to see if it was clearer behind, but the heavy mist was everywhere. Facing ahead again she began to feel nervous, not knowing whether to be soothed or not by Paul's easing his foot on the accelerator.

'Can you see?'

'Not well, but I'm used to it by now.'

'Is it often like this?' Paul had turned on the lights and was peering over the top of the steering wheel.

'Most days. It's the lie of the land.'

She was getting a fit of the nervous giggles. 'What's that supposed to mean?'

'The lie of the land,' he persisted.

'It sounds funny. Quaint.' She began to mimic him. '*The lie of the land*. You sound like . . .' she wasn't sure. But in her mind she saw a man in worn denim overalls, on a wagon, with a lantern. A farmer perhaps, but someone who knew which way the hills ran, the valleys and streams, a man who chewed a stick of straw. But how would she say this in Australian? She shrugged self-consciously. 'Some . . . old okie or something, a hick.'

'You want to know about this or don't you?' Paul had rolled

down his window and was shouting at her with his head outside the cabin. He drew it back in with an exasperated sigh, whether for her or the fog she couldn't tell. 'It's an inversion. The cold air from the water passes over the land and gets trapped.'

Evelyn nodded, uncomprehending. Paul was still intent on the driving and wouldn't have seen, though it would have been fine if he had. Both of them had come to expect that she would fail to understand those solid, homely facts that he was bound, by some code, to provide.

'The air that's been in contact with the water's got a different temperature. It's colder than the air above, so it's stuck there.'

'You said it was the land,' she teased.

But looking around she saw only the thick, white, rolling air. Even in the cabin of the utility now, with the window wide open, she could feel the slow tumbling chill of it, the prickling of the droplets on her fingertips.

'Sure. The way it sticks out flat into the water but then it rises just as you're getting to the tip. You can feel the grade of it driving, through the fog. But some days you see really well, a bloody fantastic view of the harbour from the rise. But you don't usually clap eyes on the water till you're there – right on bloody top of it . . .'

There was a bump, a little thud that sent a shudder through the metal.

'Shit.'

Paul flicked on the indicator light, stopped the car and got out. The rust-eaten door gave out its squeaks and knocks, all the more deafening it seemed in the uncanny silence of the fog. Evelyn rolled down her window – where was the side of the road? Instinctively, she twisted in the seat again to see if anything was coming. She had a terror of things creeping up on her, grabbing her, slamming her from behind. She opened the door and climbed out, feeling with her foot for what she recalled would be the loose dirt of the verge. She called to Paul over the top of the bonnet, 'What is it? What's happened?'

'Buggered if I know.'

'Do we have to stop here, right in the middle of the road?'

She saw him in the beam of the headlights, squat-legged on the bitumen. With his hands open and splayed he was patting the ground in small, swinging arcs, turning on his soles when one small area was covered, and repeating this maddeningly patient groping over an adjoining patch. Evelyn, too, kept turning as she watched him, swivelling her head towards the tray of the utility and the lone winking indicator light and glancing back. She marvelled that he was so thorough, so patient, so trusting. One winking indicator light. Was there so little traffic here, even on a Sunday?

'Jesus, here it is.'

He was out of the direct beam of the headlights now and it took her a moment or so to find him, on his knees, huddled over the ground, a strange wheezing whimper of a sound seeming to come from his chest. When he pulled himself up and started heading towards the utility she saw the limp, twitching bundle he had been leaning over, and the small irregular puddle of blood, bright on the gravelled bitumen. Evelyn's face screwed up and a churning began in the pit of her stomach. The dense air pressed hard on her brain and lungs. She could hear Paul rummaging through things, the clunk of his tools, though the noise of this and his footsteps only just filtered through the circle of pity and horror and helplessness that held her to the spot, and she felt his presence beside her again long before she was able to tell herself that he was there, or notice the hammer shaking in his hand, or ask him with a wild, pleading look in her eyes what he was planning to do. The rabbit then gave its own violent flinch, a movement that spread like quicksilver though the blackness of its one visible eye and a dull gleam flashed on the edge of Evelyn's sight as the hammer came down with a crack on the animal's skull. Evelyn didn't move. She watched the blood seep further across the stony bitumen; she watched Paul kneel and pick up the animal and lay it in some nearby scrub. She followed him back to the utility, and crawled in when he opened the door. He got in himself and started the engine and for the three or four more miles it took to reach Misty Harbour neither of them spoke a word.

Marcia Barrett was nothing at all like the brisk, efficient hostess Evelyn had imagined her to be. She was a large-boned blonde woman with something reckless, something Wagnerian, something of the Valkyrie about her. She wore a loose blouse and a full, gathered skirt and leather sandals, and her hair, which was tied back loosely in a knot, was fine, wispy, alive with electricity. She met them at the door with glasses of flagon wine, and Evelyn accepted hers gratefully, if only for something else to do with her hands. She'd been smoking continuously since they'd resumed their drive through the fog, and the first thing Marcia Barrett did after saying hello and giving her the wine was to take Evelyn's wrist and light a cigarette from the tip of Evelyn's own. 'Dear God, you look totally fagged out,' she said. Come, come and meet the gorgeous Phillip.'

Evelyn glanced at Paul. Somehow, for they did not often get these things right, so vastly different were their notions and experiences, a difference that could startle, confound or enrage them at any other time, it was understood that nothing would be said about the rabbit. She saw that Paul was quieter than usual, uncharacteristically subdued, and his awkwardness, a barely perceptible abstractedness, strengthened her interest in him, reminded her of the admiration she had felt all through the rest of the drive, a deep, pure admiration that she knew he would not have her express. But there was effort for her in this, it was foreign to her, as either keening or exclaiming was to him, and as far as she was able she pondered this, giving in to it all the same.

Marcia crooked Evelyn's arm in hers and led her over a breadth of worn, water-stained carpet and through a galley kitchen to a patio, not far from which smoke was pouring from a rudely-made stone barbecue with the deceptively jumbled look of a dolmen, or a cairn. The smoke wove through the slats of a wooden pergola and an arabesque of overhanging vines, and Evelyn was dimly aware of the same sharpness of greens and greys and browns she had witnessed earlier on the road, and she could only just smell the smoke, with its strange astringent sweetness of eucalypt. And the fact that the man she saw tending the barbecue with such seriousness was so like her imagined version of him would have been astounding, if she hadn't lost for the time being her capacity for strong reactions of any kind. He was tall, balding, and somewhat stooped, with slender, knobbly wrists and fingers, though she wouldn't have imagined the tinted clip-on lenses that hung on the frame of the glasses that sat on his nose. 'Phillip, this is Paul's wife, Evelyn,' Marcia said, and Phillip put his long-handled fork to one side and offered his hand, welcoming her in a voice as gentle and deliberate as his wife's had been confident, reckless and loud. He told her how grateful they were, what a fine, honest tradesman Paul was, and she agreed, and he smiled, and the water she had waited all morning to see lay only a few hundred feet or so to the left: a vast ridged expanse of it, blue as she could have wished, with slivers of golden sunlight capping the stiff, scallop-shaped waves. And when she turned back to him she could see it all reflected in his shades. The cries of children rang through the air, and she had the sense of a great number of them running over the lawn and in and out of the house, but could seize on nothing particular, no one pair of limbs or shock of hair. 'I'm a student,' she told him. 'Well, that is, on and off. It's embarrassing – I've been one so long.'

'In mathematics you come to expect that. You're always a student.'

She thought that was gracious, considering.

One of the children came up then, a boy of about twelve, catching his breath in gulps from the running. 'Freddie wants to know if we can go in. Mum says there's time before lunch.'

'No. It's far too cold.'

'The sun's been out for *days*.'

'Tell him it's far too cold.' Phillip took the fork and turned a sausage, raising it first to check that it was cooking evenly. 'Besides, these'll be ready soon.'

'What about the pool then?'

'The pool needs cleaning. It hasn't been used since May.'

The boy's eyes brightened. 'We can clean it. And fill it with warm water. Some from the hose, some from the jug!'

Evelyn excused herself to get another cigarette. She pushed open the sliding door to the kitchen where Marcia was making salads and Paul was helping, slicing radish. Marcia took a drink from her glass and went to the fridge. Evelyn was conscious of the clutter and jumble in the kitchen, and the haphazard furnishings as she moved into the large open lounge room. But the lines, the boldness, the intricacy of the house's design, its marvellous outlook on the wide, secluded bay where white-sailed boats scampered with the breeze over the water's crisp waves, were lost on her, and it was only much later that she realised what she had seen. For now, she fished through her bag for the cigarettes, found them, and sat on her haunches to light one.

They lingered at the table on the patio under the grape-vines, the sun making dancing patterns on the weathered wood. They picked at the remains of the meal – bread and olives and cheese. The children had been fed earlier and had raced off to continue scrubbing the pool. For their parents it was a coup, occupying several hours. Each time one of them came to announce that the job was done Phillip would rise, nudging his metal-rimmed glasses with the clip-on shades up the bridge of his nose, and march off to inspect. And come back grinning to say, 'I found another filthy, dirty, dangerously unsanitary spot.' The four adults had gone through two flagons, and Paul had long since relaxed. Music came from a stereo somewhere inside the house, through a special set of speakers Paul had hung for Phillip just under the slope of the roof in the kitchen. The two men tapped their feet and drummed their fingers to the rhythms. An early release Brubeck was playing – one of Paul's favourites – that he had brought especially for Phillip to hear.

'Listen to him, will you? Listen to the fluid purity of that sound. Desmond's the greatest.'

'You haven't heard enough Hawkins.'

'Okay, no one's better than Hawkins. But Desmond's beautiful, really beautiful. Hawkins has the vibrato, but I love a melody. I love his easiness with a melody.'

'Too popular, too tame.'

Evelyn poked a finger into her cigarette packet. There were only two left, and she felt a stab of panic – from the sound of things they were in for a long night. The sun was low over the hills behind them, the outlines of which had blurred somewhat with the descending mist, and the breeze from the water had cooled.

'Tame? Hell no,' Paul said.

Phillip began to pull himself up from the bench. 'The more I hear of this the more insipid it sounds. I'm going to get the Hawkins.'

'You're fucking wrong, totally fucking wrong.'

Marcia laughed. 'There aren't many who'd challenge the man about his music,' she said, cocking her head towards Phillip.

'Trouble is, everybody here's a purist. Years of listening to Eric Child and it's like they *own* jazz. People are a lot more . . . tolerant in the States, aren't they Evie? It's because there's so much of it. They like Teagarden, Shearing, Armstrong, Norvo, Coltrane. Black, white or brindle. No one gives a stuff.'

Paul glanced at Evelyn and winked, as he sometimes had in those bars, the dim smoky ones anywhere from Central Street to Long Beach, in what seemed a century ago.

'You've no idea what a favour he's doing for you, even listening to it.'

'Whaddaya mean?'

'Phillip has his opinions.'

'I like Desmond,' Phillip conceded.

'What about "Time Out", "Blue Rondo a la Turk"? "Time Further Out"?'

'For God's sake, Paul. You don't believe Brubeck was the only one ever to experiment with tempo?'

'Don't care. He certainly made it sound good. And how about Coleman with harmony?'

Phillip was standing now but his hands with their long bumpy fingers were still on the table, carrying the weight of his body. Evelyn couldn't tell if he was doing this to steady himself or if it was a gesture of belligerence. She hadn't suspected this in him. He staggered slightly, then lifted his leg over the bench. 'I'm going to get something.' She watched him as he moved inside, grabbing hold of the architrave for a second or so.

She looked over towards Paul then; he was rocking in time to the music. He held his head back and his eyes were closed; a fine film of sweat shone on the skin of his cheeks. He was drunk, very drunk. She reached into the packet and pulled out a cigarette for herself and handed the last one to Marcia. The two women smoked without speaking, listening to the the piano tinkling and pounding, the brush of the drums, the thrum of the bass, the glides and ascents of Desmond's alto sax. And the sound of it to Evelyn evoked its lack: the roughened line of a melody like the song of a human voice, a voice that dipped and wavered and held, the voice of Billie Holiday, which she loved, the voice of June Christie, *the misty Miss Christie*, a voice, any voice, the voice of the cantor even, singing what was it? the Kaddish, no, the Kol Nidre, in her great-grandfather's schul. It seemed to fit her mood. All the rest – the clash and jangle of the instruments – she could have done without.

'You know, music's like sex,' Marcia said at last, in something like a murmur. 'Good music, that is. I've always thought so.'

'I'd like to hear a voice sometime. Words.'

'The orgasmic moan.'

'I'm sure that at first people sang. Someone listened to a bird's song and copied it, made it his own. No. It must have been a woman.'

'A keening, a lullaby. Yes.'

The light on the water was dimming, a pale, delicate light: everything – water, sky, hills – a very pale shade of lilac, not pallid but porous, the fading sunlight no more than a skin of pale lemon coating the surface of the waves. In the gathering dusk Marcia herself seemed softer – there was a vulnerability that hadn't been evident while she was organising the children and the kitchen and the dining under the midday sun. Close to her Evelyn could see even in the fading light the delicate network of veins that scrolled across her face, and there were tiny grains on her lids where the short, straw-coloured lashes failed to shield them from the sun. The children had finally tired of their chore – it was much cooler than it was when they thought a swim would be a good idea – and they were out on the lawn again. The older boy, Alec, the one who had come up to Phillip earlier, had organised a game, and inside the house the lights had come on one by one.

'Let's go inside,' Marcia whispered.

Evelyn crushed out her butt on a plate and started filling her arms with dirty dishes.

'Leave those,' Marcia said.

'What about the kids?'

'They'll be all right.'

Marcia stood up, holding her glass to her chest, delicately, as if it were a bouquet of the most fragile of flowers. She stepped to the door and swayed, stopping to balance herself in the shaft of electric light.

'Paul, Paul. We're going inside.' Evelyn held him by the shoulders, nudging him, trying to whisper it into his face, but his head had dropped forward, floppy as a doll's. From the lawn came the excited voices of the children who she now realised were playing hide and seek, a game she had loved once herself, and she was at that moment overcome by such a fierce nostalgia that she could almost taste it in the cool sea air floating off the bay. The mist that wound around the trees and the rocks and the fleeting children and the masts of the yachts at anchor seemed to mirror a tenacious, eradicable sadness in her heart. And suddenly it seemed that the image of the dying rabbit – the bright red of its blood on the dark, rough road – had settled itself firmly on her vision all the while, so that she had seen little else or, rather, everything she did see she saw through it, like an image superimposed on the subsequent frames of a film, or a reflection on the surface of still water. Her grief mixed in with a grief for melodies receding, the knowledge of them receding, tangled in the music pouring through the speakers, a single piano whose notes seemed to mingle with the shouts of discovery in the game: the solitary voice of a straggler. She shook Paul again, violently this time, because she needed him, and she hated it when the booze took him away from her, left him oblivious to her need. 'Paul, Paul!' She took a handful of the hair at the back of his head and pulled, so that his face came level with hers. 'Wake up.' And when he did wake soon after, with his forehead in his hand, and moving his head from side to side in feints of disbelief, she realised it was because of the change in the music rather than anything she had done or said. But she put her arm around his waist and he threw an arm around her shoulder and together they pretended that she was dragging him off the wooden bench and onto his feet and was carrying his full weight as they made their way across the patio and into the house.

She held his hand as they went through the kitchen, its clutter of ashtrays, smeared glasses and teetering piles of dishes on the periphery of her vision. When they got to the lounge room Marcia was sitting cross-legged on the floor, her back against the wrought-iron drain pipe and her glass on the triangular patch of carpet formed by her folded legs. Another flagon of red was by her side. Phillip was in a chair, upholstered in a nubbly tweed fabric and with polished wooden arms, and, as it happened, the only chair in the room. There was a large matching sofa nearby that Paul and Evelyn managed to fall into, and the upholstery felt lumpy in spots, she supposed the foam had been damaged in the downpour, and in places the tweed was snagged and torn. Phillip had three neat piles of long-playing records at his feet. His glasses, minus the shades, were dangling by an ear-rest from the fingers of one hand, his hands resting on the polished chair arms, the gaze of his unshielded grey eyes fixed on some point at the far end of the room, which Evelyn now saw was not really a room but a space within a larger area comprising the kitchen and another space for eating. It wasn't clear if this area was marked off from the rest of the house or if it were merely an illusion of separation produced by the angles of the outer walls, and this spaciousness, the absence of boundaries, she found strangely troubling, though there was a partition of some kind on the other side of the kitchen. On this side the whole of the area was wrapped by a view of the mist on the bay, which would come and go according to some rhythm that Paul perhaps could have explained; but no one was speaking because Phillip was listening and something about the authority with which he did so compelled them, even Marcia, to join him. More than listening herself, Evelyn wondered how much Paul was hearing. She held his hand, occasionally sneaking a glance at him; he was wakening but nowhere near sober. What she heard to begin with was a shapeless progression of dissonant chords, slower but not dissimilar to the jazz the men had been arguing about outside. But then the music quietened again, the piano became softer, and the notes grew apart and that wave of exquisite sadness came over her again, as though a nerve like a string inside her was being wound and jerked and stretched. And when the music finally stopped, with the most inaudible of sounds, Phillip rose from the chair and started it again, but lowered the volume this time, and Marcia looked up at him and twisted her neck to look at Paul and gave a quiet smile.

'Debussy,' Phillip announced. He was still by the stereo, itself an elaborate array of chrome, black enamel and burning red lights, with another set of speakers, Evelyn saw, set up at different points along the gigantic pane of sheet glass. It was clearly the most lavish, most cared-for item of furniture she had seen so far in the house, and Evelyn guessed it must have been new, purchased after the storm. 'Images. *Reflets dans l'eau.*' He enunciated the French with care, out of reverence it seemed and especially because his speech was now rather slurred. 'There it is,' he said, flinging his arm towards the glass. But it was quite dark now and all they could see was their own reflections, and those of the stereogram and its spinning record and its little red lights, and the massive ceiling that Paul had restored, with its beams and rafters of ash. And, after glancing again at Phillip, Marcia brought herself up, teetering for a second on her knees, and headed towards the kitchen.

'Impressions,' Phillip continued. 'Imagine, the moon reflected on the water, the stars, the clouds passing, the inversions of the sails and masts, the bands of mist . . . Vague, impressionistic! That's what they said! But he was nothing of the sort.' Phillip came away from the turntable and shuffled across the carpet towards Paul. 'He was a genius, a *modern* genius. Everything he did was mathematically precise. He overturned the laws of harmony that had been dominating western music for four hundred years. A stone is thrown in a pond, and the ripples flow . . .

'An octave, with twenty-four semitones, but for the sake of a keyboard reduced to twelve. Arbitrary! So why stick to one basic C major scale? It can be enriched, varied, subverted, built upon, using enharmonic modulations and incomplete chords, sliding without effort from key to key. Proust's immeasurable keyboard is what it is, long before Proust nutted it out in his cork-lined room.' Phillip was away now, declaiming, his voice still gentle and measured, more so perhaps after the wine, but impassioned nonetheless. And Paul responded with a look of consternation and Evelyn with fascination, though she guessed she was finding it even harder to follow than Paul was.

'The sounds of the piano keyboard *are* immeasurable. The possibilities limitless. All the keys, black and white, arranged on the Fibonacci sequence. Thirteen white keys, eight black. You hear that climax?' He wandered back to the stereogram, stopped the machine and raised the perspex cover. He lifted the needle and let it down again, turned the machine on, stood back, and when the sound that he wanted entered the room he closed his eyes and brought his hand, with the glasses, down like a baton. And Evelyn imagined the leaves from overhanging trees swaying over water, and a stone tossed in, the ripples spreading, getting wider, a wind ruffling the lambent, silken surface. All dense arpeggios, circling glissandos, sharp harmonic progressions tapering off to a quiet rippling, quiet harmonies; she could see the moon over the water like a drifting balloon through the swatches of cloud and heard in the midst of it a voice perhaps, quiet but clear for a second or so until it was lost in the sudden gusts of wind and the pattern of concentric rings breaking the reflection of the clouds.

'That climax is built on the golden section, the ratio of one Fibonacci number to its succeeding one – 0.618 – each change in character corresponding exactly to the sequence: listen: 1,2,3,5,8,13 . . . da, da, dum, da, da, da, dum, da . . .'

'I know that,' Evelyn surprised herself by saying. 'I had a teacher once who told us about that. In New York.'

'We built this house on the proportions of the golden section. The distance from the centre of the roof to the highest point of each of its sides and then to the ground centre works out almost exactly to 0.618 . . . '

Paul was impressed. He straightened himself up on the sofa and brushed his hand over his forehead and the fuzzy curls on his head. 'That's pretty fucking amazing, cobber.'

'Miss Arden,' said Evelyn, gazing up at the immense, raftered ceiling.

'Goodnight Dad.'

'Goodnight Dad.'

'Goodnight Dad.'

One, two, three – in a row on the edge of the carpet, just in front of the hanging cupboards and benchtop that divided off the galley kitchen from the living area stood three rather scruffy-looking boys. Marcia hovered behind them, her hands on the two outermost shoulders, looking as though she were leading a pack of friendly puppies. They had the tired, happy expression of children who had played themselves out, and they brought in a fresh smell of the night with them, the smell of salt water and moist grass. Now that they had been separated off from the gang of children their identities crystallised; there was Alec, the oldest, with his lanky, bony, developing body and wiser-than-his-twelve-years eyes; Nicholas, a bit younger, perhaps ten; and Charles, whom Evelyn guessed was about six. They all had their father's nondescript, sandy-coloured hair, and his slenderness, without his slight paunch, only Charles, being little, was chunkier. Marcia prompted them to say goodnight to Evelyn and Paul, which they did, in the bored, embarrassed, self-conscious way that children farewell visitors, except for Alec, who for some reason looked Evelyn straight in the eye, and let his gaze settle there for a moment. It was as if he were appealing to her for something, but she couldn't imagine what. The little one barely noticed her. Marcia shepherded them through the living area and then around the curves of the wall until they were out of sight. She still had her glass when she lowered herself to the floor again. She jiggled her buttocks and thighs, working them into position, brushed the stray wisps of her hair back and hooked them behind her ears. She sighed, and filled the glass, raised it, and smiled at its ruby gloss before taking a sip.

This was Phillip's cue to resume. 'We were given the land for a wedding gift by Marcia's father. But it was such a remote spot we didn't think of settling here. We used to come on weekends and camp. There weren't many houses at all. A few beach shacks.'

'And a boathouse, and a jetty,' Marcia added. 'Phillip used to fish and work on his thesis. We'd get here late on a Friday afternoon . . .'

'Pitch a tent and light a fire.'

'*I'd* pitch the tent and light the fire.'

'Well, yes.'

'And Phillip would take long walks along the beach.'

'It wasn't much of a beach then. A few feet of sand. Rocks. Saltweed. But plenty of fish. Still is.'

'Then the boys came and we found we weren't getting down so much. We missed it – thought about it a lot. So, we decided to build.'

'By that time a few proper houses were going up.'

'As was the value of the land.'

Evelyn, losing concentration, forced herself to speak: 'You don't find getting from here to the university . . . a chore?'

'Not really,' said Phillip. 'I don't go in every day. Don't need to go in at all during the term breaks.'

Marcia took a deep draught of her wine and polished it off, levered herself off the floor, and began filling everyone's glass again. 'One thing, it's been wonderful with the boys. I hardly see them from morning to night.'

'Lots of kids.'

Evelyn laughed. 'I've noticed! How do you keep track ot them all, tell yours from the others?

'Most days we don't.'

But the house – Paul wanted to know more about the house. 'How did you get the plans through the fucking council?'

Phillip was back in his chair. 'Beach shack territory. They weren't much concerned.'

'Oh, come off it, Phillip. There weren't many fibro shacks then! The *council* was added to the cost,' Marcia said to Paul.

Evelyn curled down, dropped her head on Paul's lap, her legs dangling over the arm of the sofa. She was giddy and sleepy. She had drunk too much claret because she'd run out of cigarettes. God. She stared at the huge ash ceiling, the rafters reaching across and up to the centre like the inverted ribs of a fan or the beams of a ship, the cavernous skeletons of dinosaurs in the museum of her childhood, the museum that Miss Arden took them to. And she smiled to herself in a dopey, drunken, tearful kind of way about the smell of moss and tadpoles and damp gritty seashells wafting from the nature table in that classroom, and she counted the petals on the daisy Miss Arden had held in her hand, seeing the drops of water slide like so many tiny pearls down its leafy stem – 1,2,3,5,8 – trying to impose the pattern of the rays, yes, she remembered, the ray of the crown, it was the crown, on the music as Phillip had done, da, dee, dum, but she couldn't because the music was different, had changed, and maybe it wasn't true, maybe it was just the sort of thing a mathematician would say. Miss Arden. Paul's thigh was hard and warm and muscular; comforting under her head.

'He doesn't. Not even remotely. Phillip knows nothing about these things,' she heard Marcia say, and something about the confidence with which Marcia said it jolted her, but made her uneasy enough to pretend she was still asleep, if she had been asleep. Something ominous, as if that splendid confidence were about to turn and crack – had she foreseen it, earlier, in the dying light? 'Not a thing,' Marcia continued. 'There's not a practical bone in his body.'

'Marcia,' she heard Phillip murmur. 'Don't. Please don't.'

'The trouble is, he always had too much. Never had to think about it. Turn on the tap,' she said with a limp twist of her wrist, 'and it was there. What do you think, Paul, is there such a thing – too much? Can anyone ever have too much? And now it's not there. All gone.'

Her voice had diminished to a rough whisper but retained an astringency that made Evelyn wince. She blinked hard, so that if she opened her eyes the awful sourness might go. But when she did open them, rolling her head to the side on Paul's thigh, Marcia was crying, the wayward tendrils of her hair plastered to her cheeks, her mouth distorted by a fury long-suppressed, the fury of a caged Brunhilde. 'You see Paul, there you are, working every day; your head and your hands. Together, earning your bread. And my prince earns nothing. Never has. Hasn't worked for years, never worked really. Makes a good pretence of it though. Setting off to the university with his briefcase, as if I would never suspect. And all the nice theorems, the treatise on Cantor, the earthshattering expositions of Pythagoras's laws. Never finished. Not one. Were they phantoms? Is my prince a phantom? But what did it matter, when Daddy's money was always there—'

'Marcia, please. We've been through this before.'

'Oh, you should have seen him then. A golden boy, Paul. Straight out of Kings School to Cambridge. And the pride of the dons he was there. The brightest, deepest, most visionary student they had. Can you imagine my golden boy rowing on the Cam? I fell in love with that. I did . . .'

Her mouth quivered. She began to blubber; fat tears fell from her face and soaked her blouse. Then she stopped, and wiped her eyes and her nose with the back of her hand.

Phillip got out of the chair and crouched beside his wife. He lay his arm across her back. 'She's upset,' he said. 'She's upset about the insurance.' He reached into his trouser pocket, pulled out a crumpled handkerchief and placed it in her hand, so she could blow her nose.

'The insurance?'

'Well, yes. We're living off it now. What we didn't use for the roof.' He took hold of Marcia's hand and looped her arm over his shoulder. 'Come on now,' he whispered. 'We'd better get you to bed.'

Evelyn lifted her head, and Paul pulled himself to his feet. 'Evie, you coming?' But just as she stood he wavered slightly and slumped back down on the couch.

'Don't worry,' Phillip said. 'It's too late to drive back. We can make up the bed.'

Evelyn woke with a monster of a headache and a screaming thirst. Her back was sore from the bed Phillip had made by extending the lumpy sofa, the mattress of which had caved in where the water had collected and dried, leaving patches of hard, crumbling foam with no give. Paul was asleep and snoring. She swung her leg over the side and pulled on the stretch pants she had pulled off just before blacking out herself. How long had she slept? The sunlight burned through the salted sheet glass. She rubbed the grit from her eyes and made her way to the kitchen. Once there she went through the cupboards, found a mug and a jar of Nescafe, and stacked a few of the straggling plates to make room next to the jug. She hadn't learned yet, as she would years later, to fight her dehydration with copious draughts of water, and she made the coffee good and strong. She was also tempted to light one of the butts that lay about in acrid, larval piles, and went so far as to choose one from an ashtray and straighten it, smoothing the crumpled paper with her fingers. But the smell was too vile, and she ended up dropping it through the lip of one of the empty flagons, waiting with a kind of anguished expectation for the sound of it plopping on the bottom. She took her coffee outside to the table under the grape-vines and sat there a while warming her hands on the cup. But it got too cold sitting there (even though the sun was shining and she could hear the sounds of morning – the calls of birds, the gargle of an engine on the water), and the dew on the bench was seeping into her pants. She got up, brushed them off and headed in the direction of the bay, where the boat was ablaze with sunlight and its wake spread in long, smooth, platinum arcs that reminded her of loose folds of satin. There was no sign of the mist, and the thoughts in her aching head drifted back to the mist on the rise, the mysterious ways in which it came and went. She tried not to dwell on the rabbit, that splinter of pain still lodged in her gut, or the rings of melancholy radiating from it, but there was no way to express this, even to herself, and besides, her head was throbbing too, and that was the pain of the moment. Her feet in their black, flimsy, pointed leather shoes sank in the wet spongy grass and its smell tingled in her nostrils. Her throat and chest were tight, sore, yet it seemed, through the lunatic reasoning of the addict, that only another cigarette would soothe them, and her fingers twitched.

When she had walked a few yards she turned on her heel to look back towards the house. The glare of the sunlight beating on the glass was harsher on her eyes than the stream of it had been inside, but by squinting and forming a shield with her hand she had a sense of the shining clarity she had experienced on the road. And the brightness of the light, the sharp clean angles of concrete and glass rising from the frizzy bushes and the grass brought her closer to comprehending Paul's admiration for the house, its order, its grandeur, its power, and in spite of what she had seen the previous night, she could even share in the admiration of the man who had created it or, if he hadn't actually designed it, whose passion had brought it into being. She stood there, with the sun warming her back and drying the sodden seat of her pants, taking in its reflection in the thick salt-dusted glass, and her own, which was dark, and dark too were those of the few trees behind her, their smooth trunks and patchy barks, the strands of bark hanging from their upturned branches, and in the distance the pearly, silky glimmer of the bay and the solitary yellow dazzle of the aluminum, *aluminium* boat, aluminium, aluminium she repeated to herself, illumine, luminous, alight, and even the clutter she could see inside, superimposed on those other, more ethereal sights, the dining table with the papers and books on its cloth of faded batik, the water-marked chairs and the magisterial drain-pipe, the gleaming stereo, the albums on the carpet, not far from the one remaining, half-empty flagon of claret, the tangle of blanket and sheet that wound around Paul's legs but failed to cover his feet, drew her eye as through a tunnel on a passage towards some new understanding. She studied this, the layers of images deepening the perspective on the glass. Then she heard it, she heard the cry.

A girl was running towards her, all bones it seemed, jerking like pistons through the thin clinging cloth of her dress. But before she could take proper stock of her, recognise her as one of the clump of children that had moved through the previous day in a writhing, erupting mass, or diffused in the twilight, running to separate hiding spots and coalescing again on the silvery grass, the girl had grabbed hold of her, was clutching the sleeve of her shirt. 'Quick, quick! It's Adam!' Evelyn struggled with this. Adam? She remembered a Freddie. Adam? She followed the girl, still tugging at her sleeve, her excruciating head pounding to the rhythm of their steps. She was running now, but stumbling on the rocks and twigs and hardened curls of bark strewn every which way on the ground, and though the girl's stride was rapid and sure, even she was breathless. 'He went missing after breakfast,' she called out, panting hard.

They had rounded another corner of the house and Evelyn saw ahead, on a level patch of grass, a long, old-fashioned clothesline, the kind that worked like a see-saw, and nearby, propped on a wooden platform, was the pool. A round one, with sides of aluminum – aluminium like the boat she had just seen chugging through the still opalescence of the bay. There was a ladder to climb into it, and a hose, curving like a green snake on the platform. As she came closer she saw that the wood was wet, dark with water trickling from the hose. A plastic bucket was over-turned on the grass, and Evelyn, catching her breath, got a whiff of the sharp, strong, stinging odour of scouring powder. It burned through her chest and nose. The girl was crying, her mouth contorted as she tugged and gasped, and Evelyn stumbled one last time as she was pulled up onto the platform. And there, like a stone in the murky, soap-scummed water, was a very small child, and his face was dark, dark blue.

Evelyn scrambled up the ladder and threw herself face-first into the pool. She grabbed the child by the arms and pulled. The force of her effort threw her on her feet but the weight of the boy dragged her down. She gathered him in her arms and pushed herself up through the water, bitter in her mouth and burning with traces of the cleanser. She waded with huge sloshing sounds to the ladder and with the boy a sagging weight on her shoulder climbed out.

'Get your mother,' she cried hoarsely to the girl, and she lay the child on the grass and kneeled over him, a leg on either side of him. He had a round face, round like the pool, or the moon. Like a little moon. Blue. Blue moon. In the sun not so dark, but blue.

Evelyn lowered her face to the cold blue face of this tiny stranger, his body in its striped cotton teeshirt and faded cotton shorts gripped by her knees. His eyes were wide open, but were they pleading? She stopped in mid-air, frozen, unable to do it, unable to press her mouth on his, and the blood roiled in her head. She rolled to one side and pushed herself up, at the same time, in the same motion as she grabbed him by the feet. Why hadn't she thought of this before? Dear God, why not before? She hit him, hard on the back, and again, but his body was stiff, unyielding, unresponding, so she lowered him to the ground again. She was conscious of the mother's arrival, her screams, and the gulping sobs of the girl. She bent down again, her throat and bronchial tubes raw from the compulsive smoking she'd indulged in the day before, and the sour taste of claret invaded her mouth, but she leaned towards him, but was stopped yet again by the blueness around his lips, around his eyes, under the folds of his chin and down his neck. She is frozen, she cannot move, it is as if a barrier, impenetrable, invisible, has slid between their faces: hers red from her posture and the rush of blood it drags to her cheeks, his a strangulated blue. It is too late to consider that she doesn't know how to do this. She tries to bend closer, keeps trying, but for all the effort her head has not moved. She looks up wildly at the mother and springs to her feet. Does she tell her to try? The mother, hobbled with fear, confesses that she, too, does not know how. Maybe she tells her she will get someone, maybe this is not what she's thinking but she runs, runs so the crystalline angles of the house race as film past her eyes, thinking kiss, kiss, God, kiss of life, and when she gets to the door to the kitchen Alec is standing there making toast. She calls out to him what has happened. 'Where's the phone?' He points to the benchtop and she nods and says, 'You go,' and she dials for the ambulance and realises then that she doesn't know the address. 'Wait,' she says. 'No, go!' and runs to Paul, shaking him, 'Where are we? Where are we?', and when he sits up and rubs the top of his head and looks at her she says, 'The address, I need the *address*,' and befuddled as he is and as angry as he can be in his state of sleepy befuddlement he tells her and she runs back to the phone.

Sooner than she would have expected he was standing behind her while she shouted the address and the directions. 'What's *wrong*?' Perhaps she didn't speak, this is a part she couldn't recollect very well, perhaps it was just the wild panic in her eyes that made him see it was serious. He jumped into his pants and followed her over the grass, catching up to her where it gave way to the rougher ground and they heard the sobs and the cries and once again Evelyn was suddenly struck by the shimmering clarity of the day, that dense blue of the sky, the white white clouds, the sparkle and warmth of the light, as if its beauty had been devised all along to mock and torment her. What did this sky have to do with the horror ahead? And she felt herself longing for the mist to come, to mute it, disguise it, blot it out.

Alec was giving mouth-to-mouth resuscitation while the mother and the sister of Adam paced the ground, the mother grinding her fist against her teeth. He was working hard, pushing the last of his breath into the boy's mouth and pushing down with his hands on the chest to force the air out while replenishing his own shrinking lungs. In, out, in, out, in, out, with a harsh, choking sound from his throat, never tiring, in out in out in out, but crying, Alec was crying. Paul put a hand on his shoulder and might have taken over but Alec was giving every inch of himself and couldn't stop. Evelyn went to the mother, a young, dark-haired woman like herself, and whispered, in between the cruel hoarse expulsions of Alec's breath, that the ambulance was coming.

Finally, they heard the shrill wail of its siren and saw the wink of its spinning roof-light through the trees. It seemed to have taken an age to get there; several times Paul was on the verge of driving the child to the hospital himself, but it would only have added to the confusion. By then a small crowd had gathered, other parents, the children, Marcia and Phillip. They would have cheered when the creamy white of the ambulance emerged through the fog thickening on the rise and swirling in thin strands through the trees, had they been that sort of crowd. Instead there was a hush. The driver got out, ran over to the spot where Alec was still pumping his breath into the child, then ran back to the ambulance for his oxygen. He was a man of about forty, with brilliantined hair combed flat to his skull, which with the shorts and long socks and his neatly pressed shirt invested him with a macabre if potent authority. When he came back with a stretcher and the canister of oxygen, Alec released his grip, reluctantly, for the synchronisation of his breath with the pressure of his arms on Adam's chest had become automatic now, part, as it were, of his own central nervous system, and when the pattern of it broke, he struggled for air and fell back in his father's arms and sobbed. And Phillip Barrett stroked the hair on his eldest child's head and, like the others, looked desperately on.

The ambulance driver said nothing. His face held no expression. He bent down and attached the canister of oxygen with a tube to Adam's mouth, slipped him onto the stretcher which he covered with a plastic sheet that glittered strangely, with the aqueous solidity of a jellyfish in the sun; and Paul came forward and helped him carry the stretcher with the body to the waiting doors of the ambulance. For it was a body, that much was now clear. But at what point had this been so? What moment? Did the ambulance driver look at her with a solemn shake of his head, or did Evelyn imagine this? She glanced over at Alec weeping in his father's arms and wondered with horror if all the boy's efforts had been futile, if it had been her own paralysis that had done it; and she could feel her heart turn to stone.

She had been standing with the mother, holding her, squeezing her hand whenever she felt the fear pass through her. But now the woman and her daughter were to follow the driver to the ambulance and the woman began to disengage herself and said, still holding Evelyn's hand and looking deep into Evelyn's eyes, 'How can I thank you? You are an angel. You are an angel,' she said.

It was the beginning of the unravelling. There was, perhaps, only one thing that could have saved them, but as so often happens, it was that one thing that couldn't come. Evelyn and Paul went back to Misty Harbour a few times, then their visits tapered off. It is hard to say whether or not they were relieved, or even if Evelyn was; perhaps she had forced herself to endure the returns and found a salvation of sorts from that. It became hard to know whether Misty Harbour was a dream – the house, the water, the conversation, the music, the trees. As the years passed it grew sharper, clearer – not, as you might expect, hazier as it receded into time. There was a sense of unreality about it, the hyperreality that belongs to a dream. But if it was a dream, it was Paul's dream, not Evelyn's. She remembered their driving home that day, over the road where Paul had spared the rabbit from its pain. She thought she knew the very spot; she felt the thud of the animal's body against the tyre, and it was in that very moment that she would have cried out, would have told him of her shame. But in the face of his honour all she could do was repeat in a careful monotone what had happened: the girl's cry and her stumbling over the rocks and the trickling hose and the burn of the cleansing powder in the pool. And Paul drove on while she went over the whole of it again, the body, the blueness, all of it up to the moment of her paralysis, when she would go back: the scum on the water, the dark blue child near the bottom amid the folds of bright blue plastic; all the elements twining in a cruel unremitting arabesque. 'For God's sake, Evie, will you stop? You're torturing yourself. He's dead! There's nothing we can do.' He took his hand off the wheel for a second and patted her, and the words wound back, to do their damage inside.

The Googol and the Tripwire

Alice opened the door for the paper and her nipples went stiff with the cold. She clasped her breasts with her arms, bunching herself as far as she could into a warm, propelling ball and, shivering, reached down and snatched up the paper. She had heard once that breast milk could instantly freeze from sudden exposure to these temperatures, not that this was much of a danger for her now. The snow was swirling, a thick white mist gyrating in sudden puffs across her line of vision, brushing her cheeks like the touch of cold fingers. The tightness grew in her chest and she ran back inside.

Leaning across the fiery geraniums on her windowsill, Alice watched the snow. Now the flakes blew in a sheet of white, so dense that the bushes lining the path had no more definition than the faint smudge of fingerprints on a plate. All those tiny snowflakes, each one different, millions and millions of them, not one of them the same. She dropped her heels on the solid floor of her kitchen, and stepped over softly to the toaster. She waited as the little red bars of heat extinguished themselves and four gritty slices of bread, warm and dark brown, rose slowly in unison.

'It's rye, Dad,' she told her father, handing him a plate. She walked over to the window again, thinking of the story her aunt had told of the beautiful young widow who died of hunger in a blizzard. But she, Alice, had a freezer full of food, enough pizzas to keep Mitch quiet all winter; briskets and tenderloin and chickens and bags full of succotash, tucked safe behind the left-hand door of the huge Amana she had bought after eight months at the packaging plant and kept as white as the flakes that were flurrying outside.

'We might not get out,' she said.

Herman sat poised over the toast, his grizzled hair a surprise of wayward spikes. She had given him Randall's bathrobe, and it hung over his shrivelled frame in ridiculously abundant folds, like a flag drooping on its pole. He took a moment to reconnoitre the table – the unfamiliar cutlery set out on the unnervingly cheery placemats; the two white plates, each with its offering of toast; the marmalade jar glowing a rich liquid orange; the squat mug of coffee steaming to the north of his bread knife; the still-folded morning edition of the *Standard* to the east of that.

'Mitch!' Alice called. 'You're going to be late!'

'What's the hurry?' said her father. 'The guy on the weather said it was settling in.'

The week before, when she had picked up Herman from the penitentiary, the sun was bright in a blue sky and the snow was crunchy on the ground. She had stepped inside the grey stone walls and onto the brown linoleum of the foyer. Because he was leaving she did not have to wait in line as she normally did, in the bank of mothers handing bottles of fruit juice to their toddlers and the sullen chainsmokers in their wet-look boots. She strode ahead, with not even so much as a glance at the signs warning against the smuggling in of contraband or the use of gang insignia that once, in the very brutality of their language, had transfixed her with horror. She went right up to the guard and, almost laughing, handed over her driver's licence, took the pass permitting her to enter another hall where on any other day she would have filled out a form which was yet another step that would get her to the visiting room. There she would be locked behind iron bars, as if her stubborn association with the criminal somehow made her one, too; and there she would stand, waiting in a stew on the cold concrete floor, until they brought him in and let her speak to him over a telephone, he sitting handcuffed on the other side of a thick grimy pane of bulletproof glass. Throughout the two years she had been the helpless witness to his accelerated ageing, exacerbated by the fact that it seemed to be a wholly random matter whether or not he would be allowed to shave, or the prison barber had been by to give the men haircuts. She had seen men in striped suits in the movies of her childhood, but that had been no preparation for his grey infirmary pyjamas with the starched blue cotton tunic that went over them, or the stoop that he developed, weekly, before her eyes.

But that day she had found him waiting in a kind of foyer that she had never noticed before, off the hall where they filled in the forms; and she felt somewhat disoriented by not having passed through enough stages, by not having to work hard enough to get to him. He was smiling, rather sheepishly, she thought. They had given him back his clothes, but they had that look of mothball storage about them and no longer fitted him, and she had had to bring Randall's old overcoat for the cold.

She felt that it was bad for him to come out in winter, when the long flat land was dead, and shrouded in snow. She couldn't help thinking it a bad sign. If it were summer she could set him to work in the garden or get him to paint the house, or he could take Mitch to the baseball or fishing. She tried to imagine him doing these things: stretching up on a ladder to reach the eaves, clipping the privet, his elbows bent and flapping – all the things that Randall might have done, if he had been anything like a husband or a father. She felt herself getting cold with anger again. She set the tray with the Diet Coke and the pretzel sticks on the coffee table, walked over to the television and turned down the sound.

'A Canadian show. *Seeing Things*,' Herman said. 'It's good.'

'I thought you were doing your homework.'

'We are,' Mitch said. 'But Grandpa likes this show.'

'Mitch, you're up far too late.'

'What does he have to get up for in the morning?'

'It's AO, isn't it?'

'You haven't seen it, Alice?'

'I'm usually in bed by now.'

Herman laughed. 'Oh really?'

'What's so funny about that?'

'You never used to be. I used to stay up waiting for you, remember that? Sit down,' he said, patting the cushion on the modular sofa. 'You'll like it. I watched it every week inside.'

Mitch added, 'It's about a reporter, he solves these crimes with ESP.'

'I don't know how either one of you can distinguish one program from another. It's been on non-stop since this morning.'

'We've had our eye on the news, Alice. Wouldn't you like to know when this storm is going to end?'

Alice had a job at the container conglomerate that had swallowed up the wholesale glass company her grandfather started and had been kept going by the men in the family ever since. Kozminsky and Sons was now just a division of Krista and her cousin Abe was the only one left in it except herself. She was secretary to the new head of the accounts section, a man from Lincoln who had been friends in his youth with Starkweather, the boy who dressed like Jimmy Dean and shot dead nine people in the town. Mr Earnshaw. A wiry man only a few years older than she was, with a conspicuous nut of an Adam's apple and face turned a mottled red from lunchtime exercise. He would often talk about the massacre. There were hard times then just as there were now, people with nothing to do but cause trouble, but some rose above it, he would say. It crossed her mind that Earnshaw was hinting at something here though she could have been reading too much into what he said. But his quiet ruthlessness made her uneasy: she sensed he enjoyed his brush with savagery, was secretly proud that whatever had turned his friend into a monster had also made him what he was.

She had been desperate when she went to her cousin to see if there was an opening for her. Operations in the packaging plant were being rationalised – that is what they called it – but what it meant was they had installed computers in the office and two-thirds of the bookkeeping staff lost their jobs. She had a good typing speed and shorthand as well but with the new machines these skills were no longer at a premium, so she took her redundancy pay and went back to business school to learn how to operate the Wangs. The redundancy package wasn't much and Randall was always hopeless with the alimony. Whenever she saw him he said that he had left her the house and everything in it and wasn't that enough? Her mother had always said that she would realise one day how important family was – she said it first, now that she recalled, when she had married Randall. The crunch came when her father was convicted. She swallowed her pride and went to see Abe at Krista. She knew he would help although his own position there was none too secure. But Krista was a growing company, a medium-sized multinational with branches opening in Canada and Mexico. They had room for good stenographers and the pay was even better than she'd hoped.

But thinking about it, in the warmth of her house, with her father and her son by her side, she discovered a twinge of hope inside her that the snow would keep falling and that she might never go back. Maybe this, too, was a bad sign. She took her tumbler of Coke from the tray, sat back on the modular sofa and tried to find her way in the story about the clairvoyant reporter finding his way around the back streets of Toronto.

'Don't ask me,' Alice said early the next day. 'I never understood it. I went to a liberal arts college and learned about history and literature, not that it did me much good. Your grandfather's the one to help you.'

'If I ask any more he'll think I'm dumb,' Mitch whispered.

'He likes it, Mitch. He really does. He wants to feel useful.'

She leaned against the architrave in the hall and watched her son hesitate, then stride into the living room, an exaggerated bounce in his step. Her father was lying on the sofa with the newspaper over his face but when Mitch called he sat up. A lurid glow from the television danced in the lenses of Herman's cock-eyed reading glasses, and cast yellowish shadows on the window. Behind, the snow kept whirling, drifting, tumbling, descending.

'Five hundred and ninety-five, say, by seven hundred and thirty-six . . . How much have you got?'

'It doesn't fit on the calculator.'

'Let me see.'

Herman took the calculator and started punching out the figures. 'What was it, five hundred and ninety five . . .'

'By seven hundred and thirty-six.'

Herman put the calculator aside. 'Your mother should get you a better one. Tell you what, I'll get you one myself – for Christmas. A Casio, the best. But for now, let's see you do it in your head. You know, your great-grandfather could do it in his – he counted those bottles, one, two, three, up into the hundreds, as they came off the truck. He didn't need a calculator. Come to think of it, I'm surprised they let you use these things in school.'

'They say we should concentrate on the principles.'

Herman laughed and ruffled Mitch's hair. 'You got me there. But let's see you do it anyway. I bet you can't.'

Mitch scrunched up his brow and concentrated.

'Five hundred ninety-five by . . .'

'Shush, Grandpa.'

Herman nodded, and to quiet himself looked up at the soundless television, and saw a woman acting in a daytime soap. Her facial expression was anxious, her hands were pushed on her hips. It was an inept parody of emotion, but caught by it unawares, its crude stylisation made him wistful and Herman tried to calculate how long it had been since a woman had looked at him like that.

'I don't know. Four hundred thirty seven thousand something. Four-hundred-thirty-seven-nine-hundred-twenty . . . I forgot the last number.'

'That should be the easiest. Six times five, it's got to be a zero.'

Mitch was annoyed with himself and slapped his forehead. 'Okay, what did I say, four-hundred-thirty . . .'

'Seven, nine hundred twenty.'

'Twenty!'

'Four hundred thirty seven nine hundred and twenty. Good. Now multiply that by three thousand seven hundred and sixty.'

Mitch squealed and threw himself back on the sofa. 'Go suck yourself, Grandpa! In my head?'

Herman stared at his grandson, feeling the blood tingle in his cheeks, as if he were a sixteen-year-old virgin. As if there were such a thing as a sixteen-year-old virgin anymore. 'You know, Mitch,' he said, conscious of a deepening roughness in his voice, 'no one ever spoke to me that way, not even in prison.'

'I'm sorry, Grandpa.'

'Did you learn that in school? Along with those principles?'

'I'm sorry, Grandpa.'

'All right, son.' Herman lifted a bit of fluff off the sleeve of

Randall's sweater. 'It slipped out, we'll say. What we need is a calculator, a pocket one I mean, that'll go as high as a googol, ten to the hundredth power, or a googol*plex* – you know what that is?'

Mitch shook his head.

'A one, followed by a googol!'

'Almost infinity!'

'Why almost?' Herman grinned. 'A calculator for infinity. Why not?'

Mitch looked up at his grandfather. They both fell back laughing and Herman gave Mitch a gentle punch on the arm.

For dinner on the second day of the storm Alice served individual frozen chicken pies and succotash.

'Can't we have pizza?'

'We've had too much pizza,' Alice said. 'It's not good for you. Or me. Or Grandpa.'

'You could have thawed out some pizza when you thawed the pies. I really *hate* succotash.'

Alice pressed her brow against the heel of her hand. 'Please, Mitch. Just eat your pie.'

She sighed, and glanced at her father.

Herman gave Mitch a sly grin. 'I'm not too crazy about corn and beans myself. But I eat them.' He made a great show of piling the vegetables onto his fork and sliding them into his mouth, raising and lowering his eyebrows, like Groucho Marx.

Mitch smiled and bent his head towards the meal.

'Mitch needs a new calculator, Alice. A good one. He deserves it, he's been working hard and has a good deal of talent. A Casio, I was thinking.'

'Dad, he's only ten.'

'Maybe you could bring one back for him from the office.'

'I don't know, Dad.'

'Tell you what, I'll call Abe.'

Abe Lavan had distinguished himself by inventing the rectangular milk bottle. It had revolutionised the dairy industry. Just by straightening the traditional milk bottle's curves, the volume of milk that could be stored, transported and distributed to homes and supermarkets around the country trebled. Alice often wondered how the cows had felt. She wrote to her sister Janet, soon after she got the job at Krista: 'Did each cow have to produce more or did they have to increase the number of cows? Is there a limit to what one cow can produce or, theoretically, can she go on squirting out milk ad infinitum, day after day, as long as she is properly stimulated?' Janet never bothered to address these questions in her reply. Alice thought it would have made an interesting item on Janet's radio show but Janet didn't pick it up, which may have gone part of the way towards explaining why Janet had made something of her life and why she, Alice, for all her triumphs at Oberon, was working as a secretary at Krista through the good graces of her cousin Abe. And she felt so cringing and thankful for it that she made a point of not associating too closely with him at work, which was relatively easy because Abe, in his sixties, was held on as a salesman and was often away.

She thought about Abe while pulling clothes and linen out of the dryer. She warmed her fingers on their heat, folding and sorting them into piles. She could not help noticing that the smallest one was her father's. When the snow stopped she would drive him into town and they would get him something decent to wear. She was pulled up short trying to imagine what to buy. She stood motionless with her hands spread out on a towel. Snowstorms and travel aside, Abe was at work at eight every morning, blue shirt, Abercrombie Fitch three-piece in place – the works, down to the Gucci cufflinks and the Dior aftershave. Would that be the right attire for Herman, a man as they said 'between jobs'? She would have to inquire discreetly about headhunters, which of them would jump at the chance to take on a client whose last employment was kitchen hand in the Nebraska State Penitentiary. Before that? Well, yes sir, a top notch sales executive in his field, promoted to chair of the company. A smallish company, sir, but expanding, though computer software, as you'd know, is competitive, extremely competitive. And one of the creditors, you see, they took him to court . . .

What did Alice dream about? She was ashamed to admit, even to herself, that she dreamed about Randall. She was even ashamed to be ashamed, for who else but herself would she dare to confide in about her dreams? In them Randall was always coming back. He would telephone, or write a letter, and she would prepare for him: she would clean the kitchen, paint the house, paint herself. But then, ineluctably, something invariably would go wrong. Earnshaw would keep her back, so she would miss him; there was no way of telling him that she would be late, and when she arrived home he would have come and gone. She would hear the hiss of an approaching tornado and in seconds the house would be ripped from its foundations and be sent whirling into the air, only to land miraculously upright in some faraway, uncharted country where he could never find her. And this night she did hear a sound, not a hiss or even the knock of wood against the wind, although she woke recollecting a sound somewhat similar, a sound like a door closing against its jamb; and the sound of this repeated itself in her memory, like a counterpoint to the crunching sound muffled by the unrelenting drifting of the snow, in the endless blizzard which was keeping Randall away. For all of it, she realised with some embarrassment, was yet another extension of her dream. One more stage, one more hopeless enactment of its theme, like the endless halls and foyers and anterooms she had travelled through inside the dank stone walls of the Nebraska state prison.

Still, there was a sound.

She groped for the switch to the bedlamp in the dark and lay there listening in its feeble pool of light. When she had wakened sufficiently she blinked a few times and slipped out of bed.

There was not much to be seen from the upstairs window. The snow fell like a thin white veil across the sky, but she thought she could hear it even so, flakes of it brushing and dissolving against the glass. She could just make out the bushes lining the path below and the bare upraised limbs of the cottonwood tree beyond. The bushes seemed no more than a row of black dots on the luminous carpet of snow and, squinting to see more clearly, she transformed them into a thick diagonal line across a field of white. She blinked from the strain, and realised that what she first had seen as two rows was in fact three, the third of which, tracking a straight line down the middle, was actually a series of footprints in the snow.

The snow was easing, accentuating the cold. Intermittently, Alice felt a frozen drop or two graze her nose, where the skin contracted and stung as if bitten. The light from her torch danced every which way as she high-stepped through the crust of packed snow. She felt the edges of it crumble as she went, spilling over the sides of her boots, soaking the bottoms of her pyjama legs. She had pulled Mitch's knitted cap down over her ears and the hood of her padded coat over the cap, winding a scarf around that, across her neck and chin. Her breath came out in frozen clouds. When she got to the centre of the path she plunged her own feet into each of the already formed footprints, feeling them grow larger with the additional force and friction. Ahead, under the flickering light of the fluorescent streetlamp, against the still background of the snow-blocked road, was Herman's stooped silhouette. His face was thrust forward and upwards, as though he were waiting for the snowflakes to accumulate in its crevices until their overflow could wash it clean.

'Dad,' she called, in a loud enough whisper.

He had nothing on but a pair of earmuffs, the suit he'd brought back from the prison and the old, balled polo-necked sweater of Randall's he had worn day in and day out since. He turned and saw her and smiled, but his look was a look of disappointment; he reminded her of Mitch when she'd interrupted him in a game.

'I was counting stars,' he said.

'*Counting* them,' she said.

She looked up and, through the dots of subsiding snow, saw the clearest sky she had seen for three days, a broad capacious sky, dazzling with brilliant points of light. She laughed – it was too incredible.

'I thought you were . . . a prowler,' she said.

'Come off it. What prowler would be fool enough to come out on a night like this?'

'If you're fool enough to add up the stars in the Milky Way.'

'I couldn't begin to, it would take a machine. But, yes, I always wanted to try. And it's exciting, getting out – after being cooped up inside.'

'I was thinking that tomorrow we could do a bit of shopping.'

'No, you don't understand. Thanks, but it's not about any of that. You know, I've been lucky, Alice, anyway for most of the time. How I'll never figure out. I came back from that war – you were only a kid then, just a mook, maybe you don't remember. But, I came back. Other guys, standing right next to me, were shot, bagged, like so many wooden ducks in a gallery; or they'd go out in jeeps and be mined. But not me.'

She saw tears brimming in his eyes and his cheeks were wet, though perhaps from the snow.

'Dad, we'd better go back in.'

'No. Wait. Do you remember, when you were a kid, just a tiny little kid, do you remember, the googol?'

'Dad,' she repeated, taking his arm. 'You're going to catch a death of cold.'

He shook himself free. 'A googol. Didn't I ever tell you about the googol?'

She tried desperately to think. Was it a clown? She felt sure it was a clown. With his sad dark eyes and his white winter skin and the baggy clothes and the shiny red patches on his cheeks he looked like a clown, the sad one, the one who was always falling down. Googol, the famous circus clown. His sad painted face and breathtaking antics on the wire. Or was it Grock . . .

'Ten to the hundredth power. One with a hundred zeros. I was telling Mitch about it the other day. Once it seemed such a big number to me, just as it did to him. "Almost infinity," he said. Only Alice, it isn't infinity, and even a googol*plex* isn't infinity. Even though there are so many zeros that it would take all night to count them all, so many digits that only computers can handle them, it's not infinity. When you are young you think you can go forever, but you can't.'

'Oh, Dad.'

'I want you to know,' he said. 'I want you to know what I thought about, day after day, an eternity itself, in that cell.' His spiked hair seemed to have frozen to a cockeyed aureole in the cold. 'Take a series of numbers, any series of numbers, the Fibonacci sequence, say. Two, three, five, eight, thirteen, twenty-one, thirty-four, fifty-five . . . You think it could go on forever, an endless line; and maybe it does. Maybe the universe goes on forever . . . Here, let me show you.'

She gasped as she saw him lower himself to his knees in the snow. As he sank the snow reached to his middle. She saw the edges of the hole he had made crumble; if she hadn't seen him descending she might have taken him for some autochthonous creature emerging from under the ground. He stretched out an arm, circling it momentarily in the air, and began drawing with his finger on the fine film of powder covering the stiff, older snow.

'You can go from n to N, and there will be an infinite number of prime numbers in your path, numbers with no divisors, numbers you've never come across before. Like mines – tripwires to surprise you in your path. And just as the n goes marching towards infinity, so do the number of tripwires increase, until one day you come to the big one, the one that will blow you apart.'

He rose, with difficulty, from his knees and she hesitated to help him, sensing that it would be wrong, so wrong, to treat him at that moment as though he were powerless and weak. He brushed off his clothes and silently the two of them stared at his crude equation in the snow, the outline of the n fading in liquefaction, as was the N and the arrow, crumbling, between them. Staring, Alice almost forgot to be cold; and imagined herself in the heat of summer, watching castles dissolve in the sand; and it all seemed so beautiful that she remembered hearing once that eternity is the moment, and realised, suddenly, with an unshakeable certainty, what this meant, and how wrong men had been to construct an infinity that meant something else.

'Theoretically it could go on forever,' Herman said, noting once again the deepening timbre of his voice. 'But we don't live in a theoretical world.'

In the morning Mitch charged into Alice's bedroom looking for his cap. He found it where she said it would be, on the trunk at the end of her bed, though it had been hidden by the bedclothes she had flung across it when she got up. He slipped it on as she had, down over his ears, and ran downstairs, into the kitchen and down into the basement. He came up with the spade and ran outdoors. She watched from the kitchen window, sipping her coffee, as he thrust the spade into the snow and started shovelling it off the path. It looked easier than it must have been and she felt quietly proud to see him work away at it, lifting the spade and tossing the bluish-white lumps to the left, then digging in again and tossing the snow to the right. His face was flushed and he'd screwed up his mouth, and stopped briefly once to push back the cap on his head. He was going at it so furiously that she wanted to call out to him to slow his pace, that he could come across a rock or something hidden in the snow. And remembering the night before she thought of tripwires, and tried to imagine how it would be if the whole yard had been mined, secretly, under the snow, and all the yards and streets and alleyways and intersections and freeway ramps and parking lots, from her house to downtown Omaha, and beyond to the packaging plant, and the drive-in movie theatre she used to go to with Randall when Mitch was a baby. All of it wired – secretly, like her heart. She watched Mitch now, at that precious point in boyhood that would vanish as quickly as the winter's snow, and felt that tug again in her breasts.

Yom Kippur in the Cornfields

Every year in early September Janet Marcus booked a room at the Palace for herself and her sister for the Labor Day weekend. Do you know the Palace? Do you know San Francisco? I remember both well. The Palace must be one of the oldest hotels in the city and I'm told it's still there, a Sheraton now, but gaudy and blowzy as ever. My mother and stepfather took me to San Francisco the summer of my thirteenth birthday, and we stayed at the Palace because my stepfather believed in everything being just so. We had a small celebration in the Garden Court – the wild west's first atrium you could call it – and I remember the high, glassed-in roof and the hanging geraniums and the wonderfully flouncing, bristly palms. There was a cake, compliments of the management, and the maitre d' came over to our table to offer his congratulations and I may be imagining this, but I think there was a string quartet as well. Not for me, of course, simply part of the general ambience. I remember sparkling white tablecloths, sparkling silver cutlery, sparkling wine goblets and water goblets, and salads, oh, such salads: huge crystal bowls filled to the brim with crisp leaves of romaine and curling endive, glistening with oil, and echoing in their greenness and arabesques the dark green iron stanchions holding up the soaring glass roof. The management, on learning of the occasion, insisted on giving me a suite of my own, and quite a big fuss was made of removing the folding bed from my parent's suite and opening a door to the adjoining one. And what a suite it was. The decor was incredible: pure rococo, altogether breathtaking for a girl of thirteen years, with at least nine of them relentlessly exposed to MGM costume dramas. The walls were papered with a light beige or ecru silk, the woodwork was a tasteful off-white. There were dim, gold, candleholder wall lamps. There were elaborate plaster roses on the ceiling and curlicues of leafy vines, all picked out in gold. The satin bedspread was pink, as were the drapes, and, yes, I had my own black marble bathroom. All of which was grand, more lovely and feminine than I could ever have conjured up myself, the MGM influence notwithstanding, but when it came to *sleeping* in it, well, I couldn't sleep at all. The lights thrown up from Market Street below made eerie shadows of all those folds and curves and curlicues and I was terrified. And I was reading *Jane Eyre* at the time, which didn't help.

So enough already. The whole point of this elaborate digression is to give you an inkling of the kind of weekend Janet and Alice gave to each other, not just once in a lifetime, but every single year. It started when Alice had her divorce. She was so miserable there seemed no consoling her, and Janet, who had never married, was assailed herself by a fearsome combination of anguish and sorrow for her sister, and a tenacious guilt for the schadenfreude she always felt whenever a marriage went under. And perhaps this was all the stronger because it was her sister. Who knows?

But in order to get the flavour of the story, you need to know something about Janet. Janet left Omaha for San Francisco almost as soon as she left college, and at the time I'm writing about had a job in public radio, a hands-on job: producing, presenting, the works. She sat at the mike and enjoyed the frisson of speaking to that unseen audience (which she numbered at one or two million but must have been far less) and my hunch is that she enjoyed creating her shows even more. She liked the idea that she was shaping opinion. She relished getting up each morning at five, poring over the early editions of the papers, her fingers black at the end of it with the ink from the newsprint straight off the press, and she got to the station earlier than anyone else, planning the programs and writing up lists of interviewees for her assistant to ring up later in the day. People in the family used to wonder why she hadn't gone into television (they were modern in our family, God bless them, and never were caught worrying why she hadn't married, at least out loud) because Janet was beautiful, genuinely so, with Bubbeh Ruchel's creamy skin and splendidly rich red hair, and it seemed a shame the way she hid herself. But Janet didn't see it like that: she thought radio was the pulse of the community, and when she talked about this sometimes, if she happened to be drawn into it by someone – namely Alice, or me – her words had a vaguely messianic quality, which made us hoot and laugh. Partly because ordinarily Janet was so hard-headed and practical, and partly because it was *radio*, I mean.

The particular weekend I want to tell you about took place sometime in the early eighties, don't ask me the exact year. What I do know is that Janet had been living in San Francisco for some time, had carved out a name for herself, had acquired an apartment on Telegraph Hill overlooking the bay, where she could easily have put up Alice, but the whole idea was this idyll at the Palace. Just the two of them, wallowing in its grossly Vanderbiltian, fin-de-siècle/Louis Quinze mélange. I like to imagine their wallowing in my room, taking turns to soak in the raised black marble bath, or leaning out the overdressed windows to take in that view of Market Street, but it's hardly possible that the room remained even then as it was when I was its quivering occupant. The scene would take place in a more understated setting, more on a par with the suite my parents had: a solid, panelled opulence with none of the frou-frou granted me, but lent instead the lean, almost steely tone that we associate now with the eighties.

So. Let's say it was the afternoon of the second day. The excitement of seeing each other had settled somewhat, the pleasure they took in planning their ritual, enacting each step and savouring it, comparing these with earlier enactments and proposing improvements for the future, was still humming through them, but old buried tensions were surfacing. Take Janet's irritation with the drifts of used tissues Alice left everywhere. Before Janet's eyes they gathered, they mushroomed, they billowed, propagating like strange, sporing, swaying saprophytes, not only in the bin in Alice's bedroom, but in the ashtrays in the living area and on the green terrazzo benchtop in the bathroom. Not even the daily clean-up by the Salvadorean maids could staunch the flow. It was an assault on Janet's manic sense of order.

Janet knew everything and everyone. She had introduced Alice to Wynton Marsalis at The Oasis once, and was on first name terms with Linda Ronstadt and Jerry Brown. Wherever they went

Janet took the initiative, negotiated with waiters, ordered the best Napa Valley wines, rang for the theatre tickets and scared Alice out of her wits tootling them over San Francisco's hills in her late model Japanese car. To Alice it was a ludicrous replay of the bullying she'd endured as a kid, the fate meted out to a younger sister who retaliated the only way she could.

'For God's sake, Alice, you're destroying whole forests!'

'I have a cold.'

'You should be taking vitamin C.'

'I have been taking vitamin C. I'm fine. The cold's gone. I have the remains of it though. A lot of phlegm.'

But we shouldn't make too much of this for, then, that night, after they'd returned from the theatre, Janet was pricked by a sisterly insight, compounded yet again by guilt. She cared about her sister, Alice and she were special, all these years a pair. They were sitting in two armchairs in front of the window having a nightcap, the lights from Market Street wandering over their faces as they drank. 'Alice, I'm sorry. You've been crying.'

Alice started at this, and smiled. 'Crying? No. Why should I be crying?'

'Randall, I suppose.'

'Janet, really. That was so long ago.'

Relieved, if confused, Janet took a gulp of the wine, a vintage red from a family vineyard near Yountville. 'What's he up to now?'

'I haven't the foggiest.'

'What about Mitch?'

'He's fine, great.'

'He doesn't miss his father?'

Alice shrugged. 'That's hard.'

Janet reached over and gave her sister's hand a pat. It felt soft and smooth, and incredibly vulnerable. 'You should talk more about it, you should. You've always bottled things up.'

'I have? I've sure done a lot of blabbing to you.'

'But think what it takes! A first class bastard, who you'll have to admit made your life one big fat misery for years, up and leaves you, no money, no help with the kid. *Then* you say something. It was all very mum before then, but you certainly had plenty to say.'

'Maybe. Only it didn't seem so bad at the time. Go on, you can wipe that look off your face. It didn't. It honestly didn't. It's only now that I realise I was unhappy. But at the time? It wasn't so simple . . .' Alice took another tissue from her pocket, wiped the bottom of her glass of Mt Veeder cabernet, and placed it with the tissue under it on the table at her side. 'There were days that seemed as black as anything, but they would go. And some days were fine. And they were the ones I remembered, the ones I missed. At least at first.'

'Marriage shouldn't be like that.'

'Oh no? So what makes you the expert?'

Janet was quiet for a moment, then asserted, 'Mom and Dad. Bubbeh and Zaydeh. Aunt Miriam and Morris. All of them. They were good to each other. They were close.'

'Janet. It was a different world.'

'I don't know. Was it so different? Or have we made it so?'

Alice laughed. 'You're telling me that I shouldn't have married a goy?'

'You should have known there'd be trouble. And the family wasn't all that thrilled – that alone would have made it hard.'

'If you want to know the truth,' said Alice, 'it made it good.'

'Good? Alice! What are you saying?'

'Well, what I'm saying is that it was all *too* close. Anyway, for me. It felt like everyone was watching, every minute, watching me grow, like I couldn't have any secrets, no misery, no puberty, no *happiness* even, that I could call my own. It was theirs. All the hugging and squeezing, the look of pride that they'd get in their eyes – come on, you know what I'm talking about. To be their naches. And more. God, they ran the whole show, with *love* they ran our lives. If you married the right boy, there were presents – how many presents? An apartment, the honeymoon in Europe . . .'

'For some, Alice. Dad could never have coughed up that.'

'Believe me, he would have tried. He would have borrowed however much it took, from Abe if he had to, or Harry, or Sid. Fortunately, we never put him to the test. You've reacted too. In your way. No. I'm glad. It was a tyranny!'

'No,' said Janet. 'It wasn't like that,' she added quietly. 'It wasn't like that at all.'

'Look how they ran that town. Remember Yom Kippur?'

'Sure I remember Yom Kippur. Every year.'

'No, I mean that one Yom Kippur. The year that Evelyn was there.'

'Evelyn? I don't remember that.'

'Of course you do. It was the year Bernice got married and Evelyn was staying with us while they went on the honeymoon. God, it was the Labor Day weekend, the wedding, and we were flower girls and we could hardly get her to put on her dress.'

'Evelyn was a brat.'

'Be kind, Janet. She had her reasons. But when Bernice and Sid went away it was the three of us, only I don't think Evelyn went with us to school. She stayed with Mom and came with her in the afternoons to pick us up. I don't know what they did in the day, but I remember Mom trying to get Evelyn to stop biting her nails, putting that awful tasting stuff on them and telling her grisly stories about burst appendixes. About the doctors finding pennies and buttons and scabs and masses of bitten nail.'

'God, Alice!' Janet laughed. 'How can you remember all that?'

'I'm surprised you don't. Anyway, it was the holiday season, Indian summer and very, very hot. The corn was being harvested. And the leaves on the trees were turning and crackling in the heat. Little snaps of drying leaves, little tsk-tsks as you walked past. And Evelyn was very naughty. She would climb a tree and hang by her knees on one of the branches, and swing and jump down – her knees were a mess. She was always wanting to do things like ring people's doorbells and hide, or call random numbers on the telephone to see who would answer. We spent a lot of time running through the sprinklers to keep cool, and making lemonade. Don't you remember? And how we fought about how to make it?'

'We hardly ever fought, you and I.'

Alice smiled again, and studied her sister's face. 'Oh, but we did when Evelyn was there. Because you said you made pink lemonade with vegetable colouring and she said you mixed the lemon juice with jam, and there was this terrible yurid and Evelyn threw the knife we were cutting up the lemons with at you.'

'God! I've repressed it all!'

'And Mom sent her to our room for punishment and she cried and said she wasn't her mother so she wasn't going to do it, and I hoped she would get slapped or something, but Mom just looked at her, and took her in her arms.'

Here Alice stopped to drink a little of the Mt Veeder wine.

'Well, it was very hot, and humid, as only a Omaha summer can be. Only there wasn't any airconditioning then, maybe at the pictures, but certainly not at home.'

'No,' said Janet. 'We had fans.'

'And it was Yom Kippur. Everything shut down.'

'Maybe in that part of town.'

'So that was the part that mattered – where we were. The blinds on the windows were closed to the sun, and in the streets was this breathless silence, only the quiet snapping of leaves on the great thick elms, and inside the temple it was almost the same, because in the women's gallery there wasn't the usual chatter, the voices of the men intoning down below rose in the hush, but Evelyn couldn't stop fidgeting, and kept leaning over the rail and finally Mom relented and whispered we could go, go outside that is, because Evelyn must have been driving her nuts, but God I was happy too to get out of there, not too far Mom said, and we had to be quiet going down the stairs. You must have been relieved as well, because you didn't have to come with us, or maybe Mom told you to keep an eye on us.

'Anyway, we would have been a lot smarter staying inside. The heat was unbearable. We walked a few blocks thinking of what to do with ourselves but even Evelyn was defeated. The heat must have zapped the last shred of her bratty ingenuity. There was no point in knocking on people's doors because they were all at schul. We had no money and even if we had all the stores nearby were shut. Besides, it was Yom Kippur and even if we'd wanted to eat, sure as shooting you wouldn't have let us. So what did we do? We walked. And we talked about God . . .'

'God?'

'Where He was, if He was everywhere, watching us, knowing what was in our hearts, like He had X-ray vision or something, and you know, Evelyn, she didn't laugh. I kind of expected her to, because of the way she was, but it was you and she mostly talking and I was left out, which was quite a reversal of the norm, she and I ganging up on you . . .'

'I do remember that!'

Alice gave a wry smile. 'Always, of course, with Evelyn as the instigator.'

'You seemed willing enough.'

'But this day it was, as I've said, Evelyn and you. And I remember how she told you that she wanted to be perfect for Him, and how she did try but it wouldn't work, it never worked, something would always go wrong, and you said it was her temper, everyone remarked on her temper and when they did it would only make her wilder, but this day she agreed and she was so quiet and so sad about it that it sent a kind of shiver through me, as if she were abandoning me somehow and suddenly I was all alone and exposed to the glare of that sky pressing down through the leaves of the elms, and it was too hot even to climb them. I don't know how far we walked but finally we stopped, on a street that was curiously bare of elms, and the three of us sat like waifs on the curb, wiping the sweat from our faces. We were too hot and tired to be hungry, but we were dying of thirst, and after a while we did try ringing bells and knocking on doors though we knew no one was home, because *everyone* was Jewish, we thought, and maybe I thought God was punishing us for all the tricks we'd played but I began to feel very scared. And then I began to worry because you weren't supposed to drink on Yom Kippur, so even if someone were home and gave us something we wouldn't be able to drink it, even water, and I think I started pestering you, asking should we drink water, maybe this was a test, and that's when Evelyn and you got angry and told me to shut up. And I started to cry, which seemed to infuriate you all the more. I can still hear you, both of you, your faces were pink and sweaty with the heat, and my own cheeks burned as my tears washed over them: shut up, Alice, shut up. But for some reason I couldn't, I suppose I was too tired to stop, or it could have been boredom that made me want to claw at that awful silence in the morning's glare, at the same time I was so scared. And it's clear to me now that I was stirring up something fearsome in you, because I don't remember how long it took, but it was in the middle of my bawling that you hauled off and slugged me, well, slapped me, right across what was by then my disgracefully snotty face.'

'You're imagining that.'

'No, I don't think so. The trouble was that I was making Evelyn and you afraid. What with her wanting to be perfect and you . . .'

'Me?'

'Well, I guess you thought you already were. But you were thirsty and you wanted a drink and I was reminding you that it was verboten! God, when I think of it. The three of us, like refugees from Sing Sing, and you, you were so wild. Any other time Evelyn would have made a big deal of it, sticking up for me, but my crying was bugging her, too, and she was too relieved when I stopped. Because I did stop, with the shock!'

Janet blushed, and ran her hand across her brow. 'So what did we do?'

'I don't believe this. The whole point of the story! You honestly don't remember?'

'No!' Janet was giggling now. "What am I supposed to remember? We didn't eat you. Although at times I wish we had!'

'I'm not sure who first thought of it. Probably Evelyn. It was so simple – I can't imagine why we hadn't tried it before. But one of us, okay, I don't want an argument, say it was Evelyn, marched up to a tap in one of the yards. She turned it on and bent down with her mouth right under it and waited. She turned it further, and waited. She turned it so it couldn't go any further and still nothing happened. Then you tried. Same thing. So we figured there was something wrong with that tap so we went to the next yard. Same thing. And to the next yard, and the next yard. All of us trying, wrenching one fercockte tap after another as far as it would go, poking our tongues up the spout for any trickle of water and sometimes there was just a drop, but any further than that they were dry as a bone, every single tap on every single street we went to, block after block, all the way back to the schul.'

'Yes . . . It's coming back to me now.'

'Makes you think, doesn't it?'

'Think? About Evelyn?'

'The power they had. How they ran that town.'

'You mean they closed the mains?'

'Sure. What else? It was Yom Kippur.'

'Alice.' Janet rubbed her forehead again and shook her auburn curls. 'No. Definitely no.'

'I tell you, we were terrified. The sky. The davening when we got to the temple. Zaydeh. Dad. Morris. All those old men with their beards. I don't think I thought it was God, at least on His own. No, it was them.'

'It couldn't have been. That's crazy. Maybe as children we believed that, but you can't believe it now!'

At this point Janet got up from the chair. In the space of a few seconds she gathered the two wine glasses from the two little side tables, and the one or two tissues that were lying about, and carried them over to the bar. Then she went to the window, gazed out at the zigzag of neon for an instant, and turned to face her sister.

'Honestly, Alice. Sometimes it's hard to believe we grew up in the same house.'

'Well, why else was there absolutely no water in any of the streets that day, not a trickle, not a dribble, not a drop!'

'It was a drought. The pressure was down. They forgot to pay their taxes. It could have been anything.'

'That's not what Mom said.'

'She told you the schul got the town to turn off the water supply because it was Yom Kippur?'

'Not the whole town . . .'

'I know, I know, only that part. Alice, what kind of amazing powers do you think those guys had? I mean, now, maybe it's different. But no city hall in 1946 in Omaha, Nebraska or, Council Bluffs, Iowa or anywhere else in the Middle West would have agreed to such a thing. A handful of Jews in the cornfields. They could have been Hottentots! Don't you know how they were despised?'

Alice stared at her sister, surprised by her sudden vehemence; it was a glimpse of a passion that she had only the rarest hints of: the miracle of radio – and that slap in the street under an implacable sun.

'I can't understand how you can go on living there.'

'Omaha? It's home.'

'You must have heard about the Klan, don't tell me no one told you about the Klan and what they did to Uncle Morris. How they burned down his store and would have lynched him if they had the chance.'

'That was a long time ago.'

'You think it couldn't happen again?'

'It was the Depression, Janet. He ran out of food.'

'Yeah, and it was all fine and dandy while he was feeding the town. But the minute he ran out what was he? A dirty Jew.'

'There were others. The ones who helped him get back on his feet.'

'He never was the same again.'

'You're looking too much on the dark side.'

'Underneath, Alice, it's all dark.' Janet held her sister's gaze with a look so intense, a deepening of the grey in her beautiful round eyes so like the darkening current of a river, that Alice caught her breath. 'And, God only knows,' Janet added, 'we've been the lucky ones.'

'Janet, please. However did we get on to that?'

Janet paused, reflected and, for the moment, put her allusions aside. Alice was right: it was shameful to let all the sufferings of the Diaspora creep into every argument, colour every observation, season every joke. But her fierceness would not be checked; all she could do was turn it back. 'It's ridiculous! What about all the people there who weren't Jewish? Were they supposed to fast on Yom Kippur? How could Mom have told you such a thing?'

'Well, maybe she just let us think it. Maybe she wanted us to think it. But, no – you're putting words into my mouth! I distinctly remember climbing up the stairs into the women's gallery and looking down on the rabbi at the bimah and the men with the Torah and our mother fanning herself, and nodding, whispering that on Yom Kippur *everything* shuts down.'

'Oh, God, Alice, you are really nuts!'

Then Alice got out of her chair, and marched over to the phone.

'What are you doing?'

'There's only one way to settle this,' Alice said, rummaging through her bag. She squeezed the receiver between her shoulder and her ear and flicked through the pages of a small plastic address book. 'I'm calling Evelyn.'

It was about four in the afternoon when the phone rang. I was sharing a house in Glebe then with two academics, reformed drinkers working steadily and seriously on their careers. My room, the cheapest, a converted sleepout, was at the back, beyond the kitchen and, as luck would have it, some distance from the phone. But because of my work it frequently rang for me, and was at the time the source of rising domestic contention. Natalie, at the front of the house, heard it first, answered it, and was about to be rude when she realised it was a call from overseas. She was annoyed and disappointed when it became clear who it was for – Natalie and Dawn both were angling for overseas publication – and she stomped down the hall to the kitchen, where she couldn't have failed to notice that I'd left the dishes from breakfast and dinner the night before soaking in the sink, and barked out something about my being wanted on the phone – again. It was early spring in Sydney, but the house was draughty and cold and creaked and groaned like the old wooden hulk that it was, and I ran through the chill in the wake of Natalie's thumping footsteps. I picked up the receiver just as Alice was about to put hers down. My hello stayed her hand.

'Evelyn? It's Alice.'

'Alice! What's wrong?' Distance thrusts the most dreaded images into your head: Bernice mangled in a car crash, or suddenly felled by a lurking thrombosis . . . But Alice was too het up to think of this, and I was too frightened to be any more explicit.

'We're having a discussion, Evie.'

'Who? Who's having a discussion?'

'I'm in San Francisco. With Janet.'

'Oh! How's Janet?'

'She's fine. Everyone's fine. But we want to ask you something.'

Janet pulled the receiver from Alice's mouth: 'Hi, Evelyn. It's not me, it's Alice who wants to ask. Did we wake you? What time is it there?'

'You got my housemate. But it's okay, fine, it's late afternoon, it's great to hear from you.'

'Evie, it's Alice again. What we want to know is, remember the time you stayed with us when Bernice went on her honeymoon? And it was the high holidays and Mom let us leave the synagogue on Yom Kippur?'

'Yeah. Sure. And there was no water.'

Alice turned to Janet. 'See? . . . Well, can you remember what Mom told us went we got back?'

'She said what she usually said, that I looked a mess.'

'No, no. About why there was no water. Didn't she tell us that the town turned off the water because it was Yom Kippur and no one was supposed to drink?'

I needed a moment to grasp the implication of all this. Experience had taught me to be careful. 'You're arguing with Janet about that?'

'She says it wasn't possible.'

'I don't see why not. Anyone can open a manhole and turn off a main.'

'Did you hear that? Evelyn says anyone could have done it. They wouldn't have had to ask. I don't know, Evie. Why is it that you can always come up with the answers? Janet and I have been arguing half the night.'

'It's a funny thing to argue about.'

'I'm telling you, Janet was fuming at the very suggestion.'

'Fuming? Why?'

Alice hesitated. 'I'm not sure. Anyway, thanks for clearing it up.'

'I'd like to, but I don't really think I have.'

'What do you mean? You just said . . .'

'Yeah. But there's a problem. Do you remember that sky? And the faces of the congregation when we returned? I don't think we would have told them, Alice. We would have been too ashamed.'

I've often wondered about Janet. On the surface she seemed so perfectly poised, in control of her life as neither Alice nor I ever were. From the time we were little she knew where she was going and how to get there. But where, in the end, did she go? Hiding her anger or fear or whatever it was behind a radio mike, so no one could get too near her. So whenever I think of that story I think about how deeply the past has wounded us, each of us, in her way; and it has to be said in her favour perhaps that Janet never flew as far afield as I did. After the last click, that tiny toll of separation, not unlike the clicks of those dying elm leaves long ago, I stood staring a while at the telephone, and then for some reason walked out the door into Sydney's blustery sunshine. An ordinary day, a spring day, with the smell of daphne and exhaust whirling in the street, and the terrace houses opposite hunched over the footpath, shabby and gentrified together, their window-eyes closed to the grime and dust. And I remembered, from that phone call, that this would be the month of Tishri, the month of Yom Kippur, the holy month, the month that begins with Rosh Hashanah and ends with Simchat Torah, and I guessed that in some years at least, the Labor Day weekend might fall in it too. The penitential season, the harvesting of corn. These were things I hadn't thought of for many years, and I felt both lost and elated somehow, both together, at exactly the same time, for if it hadn't been for that phone call, how else would I have known?

The Grove of Asherah

My grandmother, Miriam Lavan, died the year the Russians sent a woman into space. She was neither surprised nor disdainful of this: 'There will always be miracles,' she said, 'and their blessings will always be mixed.' They moved her bed into the parlour, which had the best view of the fig tree she loved. It was summer when the woman made her orbit around the earth, and summer in Council Bluffs; in Sydney it was rainy and cold; and though we had expected it for many years, it sent a chill through my heart to hear long distance that my grandmother was dying. I caught a plane, just in time.

I was shocked that summer to see the parlour was so small; my memories were of a room much more spacious and exalted. No wonder my mother and cousins had such a time cramming the bed in, and positioning it so that the foot was flush with the window, forming an impossibly narrow passage for them between the bedhead and the opposite wall. A thin, rectangular room, it had just enough space for the bed, a couple of easy chairs, and the television set squeezed into the far corner. The bed, on the other hand, was high and wide, a barge of fragrant mahogany afloat on the stagnant summer air; and on it was piled such a thickness of blankets that my grandmother was scarcely to be found. She was cold in that stifling heat, and so tiny and withered then; her hair, though still black, had lost its blue fire, and her skin was as dry as a page in an ancient book. It seemed that all that was left of her were those eyes, burning from the pillows, even larger, rounder and blacker than they had been before.

All day they watched the green light hovering at the window, so alive with the buzz of insects: wasps and March flies, gnats and bees. The branches of the tree spread in a mass of loops and curves, some as delicate as lacework, some as thick and graceful as elephant trunks. Ivy climbed from the base and covered the centre branches, and the leaves of the fig itself glittered dark and sharp. Through the shimmer of the flyscreen and the heat's haze this richness of growth glowed like an illuminated map, and all day long, when there was no strength in her for speaking, the gaze from those great black eyes wandered through its rivers and byways.

My mother spent many hours in the kitchen, preparing small meals in the vain belief that, if modest and tasty, Miriam could get them down. My cousin Alice swore by chicken broth, it was what she fed her own mother, Miriam's sister Zipporah – Zoe in America – in her last days. There were many pills and potions to keep track of.

I was sobered, too, by my mother's appearance. She had bleached her hair, and straightened it – it burst from her skull in the shiny blonde bouffancy of the day. She looked smart; she was working again, but she had hardened since her divorce. She entered the parlour balancing trays with soup bowls and medicines as she squeezed through the passage between the bedhead and the papered wall. It was only when she was in the room that the television went on; she was restless, abstracted, displaced. 'Come on, Ma,' she would coax my grandmother, 'just a taste', and her eyes would cloud and she'd set down the tray on the new shaggy carpet and sit for a time in one of the easy chairs, her lacquered hair brassy in the window's green light, the bluish lights from the television waving soundlessly across her painted face.

Sometimes we read to Miriam, from the paper, or some passage from Dickens or Willa Cather. Bernice read beautifully but this was my job in the main; Miriam enjoyed the new clip to my sentences that I had picked up in Australia. Like most Eastern Europeans my grandmother had a great admiration for anything British, colonial included, blurring the distinction; to her I had acquired a civilised touch, an enviable gloss. But I like to think that it was as a listener that my presence was most valued, the role I had played in my childhood when, for some reason or another, Bernice couldn't manage both me and her shows, and she sent me to stay with my cousins or, if Miriam were well enough, with Miriam herself. And even then, in the lime-green heat of her dying, when the low-lying sun made the tree all that much brighter, or in early evening, when the gnats grazed the flywire and the arabesques of the branches became dark and mysterious against a lavender sky, she would tell me stories again, the old ones that by my knowing required the minimum in telling, so that in short shallow breaths like the quick strokes of an artist her meaning was instantly, subliminally shared. There was the story of the lost woman and the sapphires hidden in the hearth; and her stories of trees, or what I took to be trees, but now I know as the tree of life itself, with its descending sephiroth, all ten of them, the emanations of the Ein Sof, endless, unknowable, zigzagging down like sap through its branches and flowering in each of those bright blossoms until the last one, the world itself: all that we can smell and touch, hear and see. Who would have seen in Miriam such a neoplatonist? But all this with a wryness, a belligerence even, a spirit wrestling, in a kind of delirium I suppose, that made it so difficult for us, for me. And the papery lids would drop over her eyes and the room was silent but for the beat of gnats on the flywire and the rattling whistle of her breath, and then, some minutes later, more stories, more women, more trees; fragments of lucidity as bright as the sapphires of her story but scattered, as when they tumbled from the broken string. She coughed, caught her breath, and so it would go.

But one night she seemed to rally. She could focus her thoughts, and if these were more prosaic than they had been, I was grateful to receive what appeared to be a simple set of instructions for a change. She asked me to go upstairs to her bedroom and get an envelope from a drawer: 'one of those old ones', as she described it, of thick manila and secured with a string wound round a cardboard tab. She had me dump out the contents on her blankets and she rummaged through the yellowed clippings and documents and photographs with her fingers until she fell back exhausted on the pillows. 'It's a photograph, kindele. Of a young woman, in a tweed coat. See if you can find it.'

I plucked out all the photographs I could find and heaped them in a pile: the formal ones of the entire Kozminsky clan, with Zaydeh Lev and Bubbeh Ruchel in the centre and all their children, and grandchildren and great-grandchildren – my cousins and me – gathered round (in one, I am squirming in Bernice's lap); one of Miriam herself in front of a fountain, in a dark dress and a flapper clôche and twisting a long strand of beads. There were publicity stills of my mother at various stages of her career, the half-profiles tilted against waves of pale silk, a shot of her in a bathing suit on some yacht; there was even a pose of a three-year-old Evelyn helping her mother baste a Thanksgiving turkey, mother and daughter at the oven, mortifyingly phony, from the smiles to the cardboard bird. But a woman in a tweed coat? I sifted through the pile again, shuffling the photographs over the counterpane. Then my grandmother held out her hand for me to hoist her up, and when she was high enough to survey the contents of the envelope again her fingers scrabbled over a packet of papers tied with a strand of knitting wool.

'There.'

The photograph was stuck between two letters. I handed it over and Miriam inspected it, gave a satisfied nod and handed it back. 'Her name is Bella,' she said. I was puzzled. I had never seen this woman before, and the picture – well, it was like a parody of one of Bernice's early publicity shots: the careful make-up, the craftily constructed pompadour – but there was the shapeless coat drawn across the woman's chest and held in place by an ancient leather belt, the kind that might have been used to hold up a peasant's trousers. Who was this odd woman? Certainly not a relative.

'I had a friend. Lena Edelson. You may not remember her – she died a couple of years ago. And who would have thought,' my grandmother said, managing a weak chuckle, 'that Lena would beat me to it?' She paused, reflecting on this perhaps. 'Where was I? Ah, yes. Lena. This woman, Bella. She is related to her.'

'But this is a very old picture.'

'From my point of view, not so old. And in any case it is the only one I have. But you see the letters there. Look. The last one.'

The postmark was in Hebrew.

'Turn it over.'

On the back, in English, was the return address. Israel, Haifa to be exact. A street in a place called Haifa. A port for refugees, but where they were often turned back. I had seen this in a movie once, the movie based on a novel . . .

'It would be good,' my grandmother said, 'if you could go see her.'

'Me?'

Miriam nodded, the stiffness of the motion making her appear more than ever a fragile doll. 'I would like it to be one of us. I would have liked it to have been me. But you know, kindele, it simply wasn't possible.'

'What about Mom?'

'Your mother, you should forgive me, she's too much of a Yank. She thinks everything happens in this country. In New York – or worse, that gehenna Hollywood. You are the traveller.'

I stared at the envelope for a moment, gave a slow, considering nod, then put it in my shirt pocket.

My grandmother smiled. 'She revels in the world, your mother. That is her gift. But you are the traveller. You hear me, kindele? Not a tourist – a traveller.'

Traveller. My grandmother died shortly after, and I flew back to Sydney. Which, in truth, was all the travelling I could stand. What was it that I sought in that distancing? A shifting of images, one floating over another, so that in the end I could impart to them the connection, the commonality, the identity that I had been looking for all the time? But if it had been too hard to be different, why did I put that difference to so severe a test? There was that fig tree, saturated in the summer light, and the giant, muscular figs round the ovals where Paul and the other men tangled in their scrums, and the fig in the park at whose base I sat and wept after I left him. One tree, many trees. My strange flying grove, the branches intertwining. Their images float in the air, above, below, and across each other, until they lose their specific shapes and acquire new, geometric shapes: flimsy, inconstant, tossing in the wind like kites. And just outside my window stands a telegraph pole: splintered, grey with weathering, the ceramic bells cracked on its crossbars, its wires taut like kite strings, fizzing with life; a strange tree with stranger fruit, which my grandmother in her time took for a miracle, but mixed, because there were so many voices that it couldn't reach, whose numbers, unanswered, kept up a shrill, plaintive ringing.

How cold Sydney can be. I had never expected that. The houses are made to withstand a sultry heat, but the winters sneak through the cracks in the flimsy walls and snap-freeze your bones. And there's the rain. As I write I watch the telegraph pole through the water slithering down the windowpane, distorting its trunk so that it looks broken in parts, perilously balanced like a child's tower of blocks. It had always rained, since the time I first arrived; that was unexpected too. Australia is a dry country, I'd been told, but no one mentioned the rain. Maybe it falls in the wrong places, where it does no earthly good, but coming from the hot, littoral desert of Southern California, I had never seen such rain: blinding silver sheets of it, so that running through them you would think that the sky itself had tilted and the water was falling in one great wall. And by the middle of the 1980s it seemed it was raining all the time. More rain and different rains. The same old downpours, but quick, face-licking showers too, and monotonous drizzles that seemed to suggest by their dreary persistence that living in the world was getting more and more sordid and impossible. Global warming, people said, which would have been plausible if it weren't for the fact that it was also unusually cold. Rainy and cold – have I made my point?

Things at work mirrored this bleakness. I was working on a drama series, low-budget but serious, something different for me. Until then I had concentrated on the light stuff, my specialty being the slick, fast-paced dialogue needed to give an appropriate zing to the comedy sketch shows or offbeat whimsical thrillers the corporation was churning out at the time. So what induced me? Say it was the rain and the cold of the season, say it was the polar ice caps, say it was advancing, spinsterish age.

The writers met in a draughty warehouse in Ryde, swilling coffee from styrofoam cups, and came up with a story line that managed to postulate all that the eighties were not. The producer – get this – wanted us to create a character becoming politically engaged. We spent hours thinking of issues that might tilt her (for there was never any doubt that our hero would be a woman) out of a self-satisfied, sybaritic yuppiehood into a lost world of great and noble causes. A risky if worthy undertaking. The very setting of these wildly romantic story sessions indicated our position. Stowed away in the network's least luxurious premises by far – a portable box of a room made of thin sheets of varnished plywood our only protection against the buckling tin and hanging wires of the warehouse – we saw quite well that for those of us who had them our careers were on the line, while others knew in the deep dim regions of their hearts that they wouldn't have been hired if the project hadn't been quite so marginal. The producer rationalised this by boasting that he needed talent 'unsullied' by the industry, which must have been another way of saying that he had limited his choice to fools and desperadoes.

After much searching we found our issue: the twenty-odd-year-old struggle of West Papuans for independence. It was dramatic. As we were sugaring our instant coffee with the network's plastic spoons, the guerillas were waging a war in jungle just to the north of us, the guile of the OPM pitched against the crushing momentum of the Indonesian army. There had been great injustice: the former Dutch colony had been seized by the Indonesians at the moment of independence and renamed Irian Jaya. The area was being relentlessly colonised in a program called transmigrasi, involving the torture of resisting West Papuans and the steady suppression of their culture. And the Australian government, so quick to condemn human rights abuses in other parts of the world (and later to send troops in a trumped-up exercise in the Persian Gulf) did nothing. While we deliberated, OPM members seeking asylum in Australia were being refused.

Once someone raised it there was no argument. For me, perhaps, it stirred long suppressed memories, more responses than memories, the images too deeply buried, though I recognise them now and can acknowledge their power – images of tyrants and resistance, and people floundering in boats on treacherous seas. The other writers were galvanised too. This was the cause that could not fail to rouse an audience, or to ignite the sleeping passions of our heroine, a radio journalist like my cousin Janet in America. Settled. Clinched. And with hindsight the choice was inevitable; there were few other situations which could have so closely paralleled our own.

Big power shifts were taking place outside the warehouse. The board appointed a new network chief, noted for a ruthlessness not unlike an Indonesian general's. And, like guerillas, we made the show. We met with OPM members, gave some of them roles. We wrote day and night, and rewrote as the directors were shooting. My phone never stopped ringing with desperate requests to change outdoor scenes to ones that could be shot in the studio because the trucks for outside broadcasts would be suddenly and mysteriously re-scheduled. The network chief appointed a new head of drama, a woman burning for success, a woman who was a version of our heroine, that is, before we had set about enlightening her. The new drama head didn't like the program at all, the big chief liked it even less. The show was screened around midnight, whenever the rugby re-runs happened to end. And there was no promotion, on screen or off.

Television. A mixed blessing, as my grandmother would have said, must have said, at one time or another. Huddled in front of the radiator after midnight, a blanket flung over my shoulders, I would watch the show. The music – reedy, suspenseful – lent a wistful dissonance to the action, a dimension that we, the writers, had only permitted ourselves the slenderest intimation of while we laboured; and the casting of the actors and the colours of the sets were a hair's breadth askew from what we had wrested from our own imaginations and set down on the page. The producer had wanted a documentary look, and in parts he had achieved this, but mostly the production had the watery, chartreuse tones of low budget video, a result, though he had wanted to avoid it, that somehow enhanced the overall effect. But I had the sensation as I watched, week after week, alone in the cold, that these colours, with their sad, grotesque, neon vulnerabilities, were bleeding from the edges of the screen, sloshing over me and the furniture as they swam into every corner and crevice of the room. It was the loneliness, I suppose, or, more precisely, the slow certain knowledge that all around the city only a handful of souls would have been sitting like me, toasting their shins in front of a heater, braving the cold for the sake of real, risk-taking drama, and that these were the actors, the directors, the producer, the writers, some OPM fighters, and a few stalwart friends. It was, indeed, a long way from comedy.

My own friends, though not altogether comprehending the depth of my sense of failure in all this, were supportive. But their actions betrayed their true position, and only reinforced the conclusion I had reached through the weeks of solitary viewing and, before that, from watching the rain: that for all their apparent glitter, these were truly sad times, and that we, with our daring – the producer, the writers, the directors and actors, like the OPM whose story we wanted to tell – were like survivors of a shipwreck washed up on a desolate rock.

'I'm going to move,' I told my friend Dawn, who had shared a house with me once. 'Away from Sydney this time, maybe to the country. I'll get a job typing for some country solicitor. I've done a lot of bookkeeping, typing. It's good, clean, honest work compared with this.'

And listening to me, my friend shrugged. She took a handful of her corn-coloured hair and secured it with a clip. She too had abandoned extreme gestures. 'What's that going to do? Why can't you just take a holiday, like anybody else?'

Good advice, which as it is with most advice, I intended to disregard. Despite everything, I still was drawn to romantic, dramatic, in all likehood futile gestures. I went home and began to pack. I took the boxes of files and papers off the shelves and plomped them in the centre of the flat. I pulled my clothes out of drawers and off racks. And after I'd got this far I sank down on the bed and stared at the pile in a state of such inertia that it didn't seem possible that I could ever move it, out to the bush or anywhere else. I lay there for many hours, perhaps days, the time anyway that it took for defeat to finally settle and spread through my bones, until I was up again, meekly slipping the clothes back on their hangers and into their drawers, and the boxes back on the shelves, readying myself for another fateful call to my agent, and all the while sifting through these objects that in my self-pity I saw as no less than the sum of my fruitless life. Scripts and sketches and plays, old essays, photographs, letters. And this is when I came across it – the letter that my grandmother had given me so many years before.

A miracle? At the time I wouldn't have thought so. I fingered the envelope, guiltily, for I knew even then that notwithstanding my penchant for grand failures, the small, scarcely noticed ones are the most telling. She had trusted me and I had let my grandmother down. I turned over the envelope, several times before opening it, which, because the paper was brittle, I did carefully, sliding out the pages with a sinking feeling and pressing them flat against the shelf. A dull, dogged winter sun struck the ceramic bells on the telephone pole and nudged the rain-spattered glass of my window, and with it I could construe a patient formality in the letter, though the pages were filled on both sides with the loops and humps and wayward squiggles that I remembered from my childhood as Yiddish but couldn't read. The writing on the envelope, though, was in English; the return address that street somewhere in Haifa. Somewhere, too, I remembered, was a photograph, and I searched through the box until I found it, and held it closer to the window's light. For several minutes my glance swept back and forth like a metronome, from the Yiddish on the onionskin pages to the photograph, with its white fretted border and its subject's defiant gaze, until I laid both of them, the letter and the photograph, side by side on the shelf and stood nodding at the sunlight refracting through the beads of rain.

Holiday, holy day, a soaring through space and time.

It was Sukkoth, the harvest festival. All over Israel people had put up makeshift tabernacles, booths of olive or willow branches, roofed over with the withering leaves of palms, and lavishly decorated with fruits and flowers. I saw them in yards, on balconies, in the parks and in the streets, their fragrances mingling with the smells of petrol and dust. These rude huts were where the faithful and the not-so-faithful ate, and sometimes slept, and children played, with only the rustle of the palm fronds between them and the stars and clouds. Built to commemorate the forty years of wandering after the exodus from Egypt, when Moses was leading his bands of dispirited nomads to the promised land, they had a look of innocence about them, the touching look of lopsided trees. And here, in Eretz Israel, in the middle of the Intifada, perhaps they served as sobering reminders that in some ways it is better to wander than to arrive.

In Jerusalem a giant communal sukkah stood in the forecourt

of the synagogue. Hasidim in long, black, scarecrow coats and fur-ringed hats sat at long benches and ate lunch from plastic containers before davening at the Western Wall, and all around soldiers in uniforms of the same dusty green as the palm fronds were keeping a tense peace with their guns. I watched all this on television as I sat in the lobby of my hotel, perched half-way up the slope of the mountain of ancient Samaria where Elijah slew the idolaters – the prophets of Asherah and her consort Ba'al; looking down on the Persian Gardens and the Ba'Hai Shrine and the wide glittering bay that separates Haifa from Acre. The lobby swarmed with visitors, the men like some of the men of my childhood, hirsute as bears, and like bears in the way they moved, striding in and down to the bar; the women following, with lacquered hair and wearing jewellery with their resort clothes; the timid daughters, the handsome sons, the cheeky boys; laughing, kibitzing; rejoicing in a festival I had no memory of at all.

I was keeping my eye out for a woman who had described herself as greying and, with a short burst of laughter, 'far too heavy for my own satisfaction'. This was not my grandmother's correspondent – Bella Palchan had died four years before. But her daughter, a widow, having inherited her parents' house, was living at the address I had written to; and replied, in English, in the same warm impeccable style I had detected somehow in her mother's Yiddish, that she very much looked forward to my visit. I had enclosed a photo of myself, but all I had for her was the description she had given later over the phone, and I struggled to keep in my head a plump, good-natured, haimisheh woman; in any case, a woman who could laugh at herself. But for all my effort I persisted in searching the crowd for the woman in my grandmother's picture, her sad pompadour and ratty tweed coat and her bold, wounded stare. She would have been miserably hot in that lobby, hotter outside in the sultry September air, but I couldn't rid her of the coat, or myself of her. But when her daughter tapped me on the shoulder she presented so strong a picture herself that all this was dispelled.

By now I've begun to suspect that it is pointless to give descriptions, of oneself or anyone else. But to my eyes then Bella Palchan's daughter Dvora was tall, and had her mother's dark hair, with a few, almost invisible strands of grey. It hung in two sheets from a centre part, falling on a forehead that swept high over a strong, cleanly sculpted nose. She was dressed simply, almost severely, wore little jewellery except for a handsome gold necklace, a heavy-linked chain, and the weight she complained of – chiefly in her breasts – she carried well. She reminded me of pictures I had seen of Cleopatra, taken from coins and statues; but Dvora – I knew of no statues of her. Dvora, Deborah, the one female judge, who dwelt in the desert under a palm tree. And in a voice full of the power and harshness of Hebrew she exclaimed, 'Evelyn? Sorry, I nearly overlooked you! You're not . . . what I expected.' She laughed, though, with bright warm eyes. 'What did I expect? Australia. Who knows?'

I followed her out into the blinding sunshine to her car, a new, natty, bright blue little Ford, which she drove expertly through the old winding streets towards Mount Carmel's summit. The flat-roofed, buff pink houses, some of stucco, some of stone, seemed not so much to cling to the mountain as to grow out of it, like the cypresses and casuarina and scrubby oaks. Oddest of all were the jacarandas, and the gums that we could see later down on the plain, the latter a different, sour, yellowish colour, I guessed from the chalky soil or perhaps from the effort to grow, their leaves drooping in the swelter yet drenched in the omnipresent dust. There seemed to be some balance achieved – or strived for – between the coastal humidity and a grinding, implacable dryness that brought to mind the antiquity of the land: a distillation of the same salted agedness as Australia's.

The car zipped up the mountain in fits and starts and Dvora stretched her hands when the traffic slowed and she could take them off the wheel, filling me in about the correspondence that had taken place between her mother and my grandmother. 'It began because she had tried to help Mother get to America, and, you know, she was successful. Or her friend was, Mrs Edelson, who was a distant cousin, and was willing to be her sponsor. But maybe that was not enough, so she enlisted your grandmother – Miriam? – to help.'

'That's right. Miriam Lavan.'

'Yes, I have some of the letters.'

'I think she would have liked to have done more. But she was a sick woman – most of her life. For long periods she was confined to her house.'

'Oh, they got her the papers all right. But Mother, you know, she had met my father by then and it was not so easy for him so they came here instead. But that, you know, was not easy either.' She clasped the wheel with her hands again; the traffic for some reason had lurched into the final leap of its ascent.

'You must stay. You can see, I have plenty of room.'

Dvora offered me what had been her father's study, a small room in the front of the house with a desk and a convertible sofa and two windows, barred and shuttered as the windows were everywhere, looking out on her modest patch of garden. Her father had studied engineering in Europe but here he had specialised in hydrology, working on the network of pipes bringing water to the northern cities and the large conduit that draws it from Lake Kinneret and carries it as far as the Negev. He had written a number of texts on the subject for which he received some measure of renown and the additional income to build this small detached house in Ahuzat Samuel, one of Haifa's more prestigious suburbs. Dvora pointed out these books, which occupied a space on the wall-length shelves with many other Hebrew books, possibly on the same subject. But there were as well books in English, German and Russian, Polish and Hungarian, Yiddish and Rumanian – a welter of language that, silent, repeated the babel that had confronted me in the streets outside. 'You're a writer,' Dvora said, handing me a towel. 'You should feel right at home here.'

The Palchan house sat on the spine of the mountain; the buildings in front of it, mostly blocks of flats, obscured any glimpse of Haifa's bay, but at the back there was a terrazzo-tiled balcony, whose metal shutters, so hot to touch, opened on to a fine view of the Mediterranean. On clear days, Dvora insisted, you could see as far as the cliffs of Rosh Hanikra, but the sky, though bright, was rarely clear. The eye travelled downwards, over the stony white soil of the mountain, sparsely treed with clumps of bedraggled pines and stunted native oaks, lighting on the red-tiled roofs of a few new houses before reaching the stern, undeviating line of the waves, the horizon blurred. And there, on Dvora's balcony, it was as though you could feel the mountain rise from the coast like a loaf, a round, hard-crusted, hollow Italian loaf dusted with flour, like the ones I bought on alternate days in the delicatessens in Leichhardt; and the strong light all around seemed dusted too, everything drenched in a shining haze. On the neighbouring block Arab workers were building a house which would cut off much of this view, a huge stucco house for a family of fundamentalist Jews. At every permissible break in the regimens of Shabbat and Sukkoth their jackhammers thudded and squealed. Dvora raised a fist each time they started up, for every day that the Arabs worked brought her closer to the house's completion, to the shaving off of her view and daily friction with her new neighbours. 'You think that will be the end of it?' she wailed. 'These fanatics stick their noses into everything. They will be watching my comings and goings like hawks!' Numbers of these religious families were moving into Ahuzat Samuel. I saw them in the streets, in the busy shopping mall; the men in the yarmulkes and sneakers, the women in their ill-fitting wigs. 'I want to knock them off their heads every time I see one,' Dvora cried.

At night on the balcony, as we sipped thick Turkish coffee and swatted the mosquitoes, watching the stars and the lights of the scattered houses on the steep, Mediterranean side of the mountain, and the pinpricks of light out to sea, her mood was more pensive but no less aggrieved. 'The pity is, they're running the show now, these fanatics. And what do they know? They don't go in the army, they don't pay tax. They just make the rest of us suffer, for their outworn beliefs.'

Down below on the shore, on a night perhaps like the ones I spent with Dvora, with a tiny wind barely lifting the sluggishness in the air, her mother and father had waited on some rusty tramp steamer, to be picked up in the dark by the Haganah's dinghies, risking capture by the British who would tow them round that one hook in the coastline that formed Haifa's bay, and send them back without even the courtesy of landing to Europe, or Cyprus, Mauritius or wherever. 'My parents were lucky. Luck, that's not the word. And no sooner had they landed than they were smuggling in immigrants themselves. Ach. What do these zealots know, with their wigs.'

Inside, the house was full of mirrors. So that during the day, when the heat was its most intense, and the shutters were clamped to keep it out, a silver glow flickered here and there, in an illusion of ever expanding space. Dvora would rise from her siesta and pause before one of them, lifting the straight dark strands of her hair with her fingertips and letting them fall with her breath, and I, unaccustomed to sleeping in the middle of the day, and walking through the door after wandering addle-headed in the heat, would catch her at this, tuning my nostrils to the faint pungent scent of her sleep. She would peer at her face in the mirror then, brush her eyes, and pat the sides of her head. 'In Australia you stay younger because there's no stress.'

She spoke about it constantly, the stress. 'We are a hard-living, hard-driving people. Because any day—' She drew a finger across her throat. 'Who knows?' She worked as a counsellor at the high school directly beneath us on the coast, near the naval facilities and a couple of Arab villages, and she spoke with authority. The children she cared for would soon be going into the army, for three years. They had no choice. It might take them to the Gaza, the West Bank or Lebanon and 'actions, believe me, that many of them would rather not be part of'.

Dvora was on long service leave but spent some of the time at the university where she was enrolled in a short course for counsellors. This, I presumed, was to brush up her skills but, oddly, I didn't think to quiz her on it and, odder still, she, who was hardly backward in offering opinions or information, didn't say much about it. The few days I'd spent with her had reduced me somewhat, at the same time that they greatly expanded my knowledge; no longer merely a tourist, I had become part of a relationship, but it was not, of course, an equal relationship, for not speaking the language I came across as having the limited understanding of a child. And as one might warn a child, against accepting lollies or lifts in cars from strangers, she attempted to teach me the basic, contradictory routines for survival. For example: although it was safe enough even for a woman to walk the streets alone at night, it very much depended on what streets;

and one could shop in any of the Arab villages along the coastal road, but if one got out of the car it was better to lock it; and one was wise to avoid certain towns, ironically Bethlehem and Nazareth the worst of them. But a bomb, an attack could happen anywhere; I learned to open my bags for inspection with studied nonchalance (or was it fatalism?) before entering a theatre or a supermarket, and to avoid and report any unattended parcel. On a trip to the caves at Rosh Hanikra, in fact, on the Lebanese border, we were stopped at gunpoint by a khaki-suited army reserve officer with a salt-and-pepper moustache and a burgeoning paunch, who made us wait with the crowd swelling in the parking lot until a detonation expert came to inspect just such a parcel left on the verandah of the kiosk. I didn't feel safe until we had descended in the cable car to the caves, and the murmur and crash of the water could calm me.

But it was more than that. Even when I was out in the streets alone, during Dvora's siesta, when I would roam through the near-empty streets and the airconditioned walkways of the Merkaz, trying to piece out the Hebrew on the signs, or on the one or two occasions when she had business to do in some office downtown and I would push through the throngs in the old market, jostled in turn by Russian Jews, Yemenite Jews, Indian Jews, Ethiopian Jews and Arabs, too, haggling over the cucumbers, the aubergines and tomatoes that Israelis use for the salads, and the delicate, perfectly yellow, perfectly shaped miniature pears that caught my eye, it would be her voice I would hear through the babel, clear and melodious if harsh, informing, instructing, nudging me towards the bargains, lending me words as valuable as shekels to clinch the deals. Kayn. Loh. Na-hon. Buh-va-ka-shah. Slee-kah. To-dah ra-bah. La-heet-ra-ot. Buh-say-der. I would plan my day according to her day, sift my impressions through her eyes, cut my ideas to her cloth. Or so it seemed.

How different, I thought, Dvora was from her mother, or what I had gleaned of her mother from Dvora's references to her parents. But if she had said nothing I suppose the house would have told the same story. Even in death her father dominated: I slept in what had been the only spare room – his study, on the narrow bed surrounded by the floor-to-ceiling cedar shelves of his library, and when the mood took me I sat at his spacious desk. One could only admire what he had made of himself, in spite of everything, and Dvora must have adored him, for the same reasons. His spirit seemed to hover over the small house on top of the mountain, and mingle with the ubiquitous luminous dust: the spirit of a man who had brought water to the desert and made it bloom, however tenuous or ephemeral the flowering, was something to marvel at, to swell one's chest with the miracle of transcendence, his tall confident daughter the living proof. But the mother? What had become of her? 'It is a sad, difficult business,' Dvora explained one night as the two of us stood at the sink preparing vegetables for dinner, 'for a country to have so many people who have survived the trauma. Some are strong, that is their nature, they would have survived anything. But some, maybe, it was, how do you say it? . . . a freak occurrence, luck . . .'

'A fluke.'

'Nahon, a fluke.'

'But to have come through it . . .'

'She was, you know, like an invalid. Except there was nothing, really – and everything. Sometimes . . For weeks, sometimes, she used to sit alone in here, in the dark. The shutters all closed, also in winter. I think she was very . . . tired.'

First of all – and it is amazing that such a simple fact and its import had escaped me – there was the language. Most men, when they made their aliyah knew that language, if not the Sephardic version officially adopted when Israel became a nation, then close enough. But how many women would have? 'The pioneers – those who came early in the century, well they made a point of it – it was an essential part of their Zionism, but even then it was hard. But those who came later, the refugees . . . Mother had a facility, but Hebrew is hard.' Moreover, Bruno Palchan the cheder boy had grown up to be a partisan, and escaped the camps; his wife carried the memory and, worse, the shame. 'That is something that never goes, maybe,' said Dvora, sprinkling salt on the rings of aubergine. 'My mother had to bury herself in a pile of corpses.'

Twice I accompanied Dvora to the university when her class met. The first time I wandered through the grounds and after a spell of this checked my bag and whiled away the time in the library, reading books on the history of the region: Haifa itself and, long before the city existed, the ancient kingdom of Samaria, in this, the stony land of Canaan. The university also perched on the crest of the mountain, only a couple of miles to the south of the Palchan house, in a grove of pines and the curious, stunted, bushy oaks that two years later were ravaged by fires set by the Palestinians. But my perambulations were inordinately peaceful, misleadingly so, in a place that had rarely known anything other than conflict. The university year had not yet begun and the campus was all but deserted, apart from the cheeky little multi-coloured bee-eaters flying out of their tunnels and puncturing the air with their calls. And the second time I visited the museum of archaeology in the basement of the university's main building, a monster of a tower sticking out of the mountain like a giant domino, a monument, according to Dvora, to the megalomania of a former Haifa mayor.

I descended underground in the rapid lift, the only visitor. The caretaker, a bald, pudgy, elderly man who took my bag with a gentle smile, left me to fend for myself in the windowless rooms. The displays were set out in glass-fronted cases that ran the length of the walls. There were grinding stones and fragments of pottery, clay figurines, coins and stone weights, stylised bronze statues and gold jewellery, cuneiform stelas and cylinder seals, bowls and chalices, growing ever more elaborate as the eras marched on; and I, too, must have walked too fast and too far, for if the basement was airconditioned and cooler than the campus above, the lack of windows produced a suffocating feeling, and the glare of the lights against the white of the display cases was hard on my eyes, and I sat down to rest on a black Naugahyde bench rivetted to the tiles on the floor.

I thought then of Rosh Hanikra, and how the same white light that shimmered outside shone bright cleansed of dust in the caves, and there too it had been blessedly cool. But I could breathe down there and felt secure somehow even as the waves surged and slapped the walls, and our voices flew in the space, lighting on the rocks like birds; whereas here, as if there were another side to it, I felt stifled instead of safe, as if the weight of the tower above was pressing into the mountain, as a tombstone would on a grave.

I stood up rather too quickly, paused to regain my balance, and found myself staring ahead at a statue of a woman with huge, thrusting breasts – Asherah, Ashtoreth, Astarte – there were half a dozen representations of her that I had come upon thus far; but this one, the last one, had been given the inscrutable face of a bird, and her wings, though cradling her monumental breasts, were clasped stiffly to her sides.

That night we were joined by two member of Dvora's class: Riva, from one of the outlying towns, and Shoshana, who lived in a kibbutz south of Jerusalem, and had risen early that morning to catch the bus to Tel-Aviv and another to Haifa. Two energetic youngish women, much like Dvora, though Riva was stocky and somewhat matronly, with tightly-curled iron-grey hair and short, slightly bandied legs that added to her sympathetic, no-nonsense air. Shoshana was different again. Her pale eyes set in a square, freckled face gave her a look at once handsome and ethereal, but she wore her long hair, a pale, reddish shade, pulled straight back from her forehead, and her mouth had a curious set to it, as if she had been disappointed in something once and was waiting to be shown that she'd been wrong. The three of them were planning a project for the coming school year, some kind of course, and began work on it straightaway, consulting excitedly in Hebrew, scrabbling through pamphlets, books and notes spread out on the metal table on the balcony, and they didn't break until around ten. They asked me to join them for a meal and we all left the house for the Merkaz, passing through the streets where families were stalking that elusive night air, and a woman in a wig and a shiny black dress walked a yellow dog. Here and there lights twinkled in the branches of a sukkah. Up on the main road the shops had just closed and people were getting into cars, Yemenite songs bursting in short raucous blasts from their radios, and the buskers in the square were gathering up their instruments and ground cloths. We crossed the road and bought shawarma and falafel from the stand, and ate them at a table under an umbrella, our faces and Dvora's golden chain lifted from the shadow by the hanging lights, and in between flurries of talk about their jobs they asked me, and I told them what I could, about

Australia. I said it was not the easy place they supposed, that though there was much about the lack of pretension that I liked, a ruthlessness lurked under it (*a shark in the shadows of the sun-dappled surf*, I thought, but didn't say). I said that the people were afflicted with a fear that they didn't count, a fear seared in their history, a disease of the soul, manifested in some by an overweening ambition while most were given to dulling it with booze and ridicule and drugs, though maybe this was changing and maybe it was getting worse. I said that it was nicer than America where I came from but was getting more and more like it, that the country had had its chance once and blew it. I told them about the nomadic Aborigines, their closeness to the land, and how they had been robbed of it. And as I spoke I wondered who these woman might have identified with: the soul-afflicted majority or the ill-used Aborigines. But though they were utterly fluent, I sensed it was a strain for them to converse at length in English, at least about things like this. We walked back, and they settled in for another bout of work.

In the morning they were still there. Well, Riva had taken a taxi home, fed her husband, showered, and was back before I got up, and Shoshana had slept on Dvora's couch. And how they threw themselves into it! I could see them from the kitchen on the balcony: haranguing, guffawing, gesticulating, Shoshana leaping up from her chair when it all became too unbearably tense, and pacing the dusty tiled floor, her long reddish ponytail flicking like a whip across her back, till Dvora or Riva would laugh and cajole her into her chair. From these gestures and their voices I grasped that Riva was indeed a mameleh, concerned, talkative, kind (so I was astonished to learn later that the stroppy spirited Shoshana was in fact several years older); Dvora warmhearted but stern; Shoshana petulant but wise; all this while understanding next to nothing of what they said. Yet I found everything about these women beguiling – their dedication and energy, the fierce concentration on their faces, the rapid concatenation of their speech. To keep myself from staring I had to force myself to retreat to the study, where I began wondering again about Dvora's mother, and my grandmother, those invalids; and in that austere room lined with the hydrologist's bookcases the horrible image came to me of a woman struggling for breath in a pile of corpses, and a burning blue spark in her that, in the enveloping stench of it, was keeping her alive.

I got myself ready to get some cash while the banks were open, but just as I was lifting the spare keys off the hook near the front door, Dvora called out. 'Evelyn! You're the writer. Come and help.'

'Sit down,' Riva said, giving me her chair before grabbing another from the table inside. But the jackhammers next door had started, so it was decided that we all would move in from the balcony.

'We are devising a program for sex education in the high schools. A good one, how do you say? No punches held,' Dvora announced. Her eyes were beaming, and so were Riva's and Shoshana's.

'AIDS, herpes, pornography, homosexuality,' said Riva.

'Orgasm,' said Shoshana.

'But what we need is a catchy title – something that will interest the kids.'

Their eager faces threw me into a state of deep confusion; in defence I started to laugh. But those years with the corporation saved me and, plunging myself into a story session, I responded quickly, tossing up the first thing that came into my head.

'What about . . . Three Cheers to the Earl of Condom.'

The women glanced at one another. There was a long pause, and then, 'Slee-kah. Who is he?'

'The physician to Charles II. The condom, sheath, French letter – it was named after him. Now it's for AIDS, but he invented it to keep the king from getting syphillis.'

'Oh.'

Shoshana's look was disdainful. 'We have to get the teachers behind it too.'

'Yes. Respectable . . . but compelling.'

'Just the job for a so-fayr, a writer, no?'

'Something catchy,' Dvora repeated.

My cheeks burned; my mind a cavernous blank. 'How should I know? Reproduction and Responsibility – something like that. Does it alliterate in Hebrew?'

'Acherut . . . le Yetzira Michadash?'

All three burst out laughing.

'That's terrible! Even in English,' Dvora cried.

'Don't you have sex in Australia?' said Shoshana, flipping her ponytail over the pad on her shoulder.

'Me?' I laughed. 'Sometimes.'

This last remark, innocently supplied, seemed to pull Riva up sharp. 'Sometimes? With all those wonderful men?'

'Yes, Australia. For every woman at least two men.'

'Well maybe once. And anyway, you can't imagine what Australian men are like!'

'I don't think we'd care,' Dvora said.

'You see here, there is a such a shortage. Husbands, sons dead, fighting in wars. Or because of wars. So women of our age,' Riva explained, 'there are many alone.'

'You mean that?' said Shoshana to Dvora. 'After the last one? He was a manic-depressive!'

'And who could blame him? Who wouldn't be a manic-depressive?' said Dvora.

'We are a nation of grieving women, *randy* women,' Shoshana said. 'God, they are making a noise. Can we close the shutters?' She strode over to the balcony and pulled them to, and suddenly we were aware of a blissful softening of the jackhammers, and our eyes, too, were relieved in the dimmed light.

'I thought the women fought too.'

'And that,' said Shoshana, striding back, 'is a myth. Army service is strictly non-combat. Oh, there were women in the Palmach, but take it from me, a handful would have actually fought, or died in battle.'

'You would have wanted that?' said Riva.

Shoshana, sitting down again, shrugged.

Over a lunch of hummus and cheeses and buttermilk and salads, the conversation resumed. The jackhammers had stopped but the shutters remained closed to keep out the heat, and sunlight ran back and forth in the cracks, like an uninvited guest begging to be let in.

The light in turn flashed and ricocheted on the mirrors.

'It isn't easy,' Riva said, smearing goat's cheese on a slice of challah. 'These kids have the feeling deep down that they'll have a short life. They want to live what they have to the full.'

'This is nothing new,' said Dvora.

'Loh . . . But maybe it's more intense. Or confused. And there's HIV now. And if you got pregnant in the old days that was okay. When I had Michal and Amos,' Riva said,' they lived in the nursery. The kids were looked after. They belonged to the community, the kibbutz. But now we think that's wrong, to have someone else look after your kids.'

'The cult of the woman, we've got.'

'And the Sephardim, they're the worst. They know nothing at all,' said Riva.

Shoshana swallowed some cucumber and waved that aside. 'The girls don't want to be like their mothers, one kid after another. They've seen how awful that is; they don't want that for themselves.'

'But the Likud. They may *want* us to breed. As if there's some race with the Arabs,' Dvora said.

'Don't fool yourself. With Jewish men, we're not much better than Arabs.'

'Shosh!'

But it was siesta time, and Riva left it at that. We cleared away the dishes, and Dvora went to her bedroom, Shoshana took up her position on the couch, and I gave Riva my bed. The three of them fell promptly, like children, to sleep. The jackhammers had stopped and the house was very still; it was as if a host of little animals, furred and sleek, rabbits, foxes, lizards, chameleons, had burrowed deep into the bosom of the mountain, and all their fussy energy grew quiet. I filled in time reading, attempting letters, baking on the balcony (the metal shutters now were radiating heat), trying to come up with the slogan the women wanted. But the truth was that I had no heart then for slogans, or for writing of any kind. I wasn't sorry that I'd made a fool of myself, that I couldn't think of anything funny or flash, that my adspeak was gone. But what was to take its place? I'd had my bout of sincerity and compassion and where had that got me? But irony was failing me too; I no longer even knew exactly what it meant, except, that it seemed that in each place I found myself there was a special variety. So did this mean that no one could laugh at anyone else's jokes? And if they couldn't laugh at their jokes, could they feel their pain? The women peacefully sleeping (although Shoshana gave out a cry and a whistling little snore from time to time) could have little idea of my turmoil. To them, I supposed, a so-fayr was simply a person with a facility with words.

They awakened with the whine of a saw next door, jumped up and started immediately to work, and kept at it until Dvora stood up and stretched and announced that she needed something more to eat.

And again, around the table collapsing with food, we took up where we left off at the last meal, Shoshana getting angrier and angrier, Riva trying to calm her down and only infuriating her more, Dvora doing her level best to arbitrate. All three, from the strain and their excitement, would lapse into Hebrew, but remembering me, pulled themselves up short.

'Maseiha, asiva, nu? It's been masked, a disguise. So we were to have 'complete and absolute equality'. That's what it says, it's in the constitution. Men and women, absolutely equal. But three years later, what do we have? All this is undermined, in that farce of an Equal Rights Law, so-called. I tell you, we caved in pretty soon.'

Riva struggled for patience, lacing her fingers together so tightly that the knuckles were white. 'It was the men, they were fighting the wars.'

'Stop it, Riva. It's blackmail. That's how they get away with it, every time. If there weren't any wars they couldn't get away with it.'

'And who causes the wars? The Arabs want to wipe us off the map. The ink wasn't even dry before they were attacking!'

'It wasn't the Arab women who were attacking.'

'Loh, they were just egging them on.'

'Like children we were treated. Not even allowed to work at night! And tell me, dear Riva, how were you employed on your kibbutz? In the vineyards? In the fields, driving a tractor? No, don't tell me, I'll guess. You were peeling potatoes one month, and maybe the next you were scrubbing in the laundry.'

'They had to accommodate the religious parties,' Dvora explained to me. 'The state was not allowed to interfere in marriage and divorce.'

But between the two others the argument raged. Riva had unlatched her hands and was shaking a fist: 'Would you say, Shoshana, that you don't do important work?'

'No! Because my work is outside the kibbutz, and things are organised a little differently now. But you know as well as I do that when there are sheets to be washed the women are the ones who are washing them!'

'And should the men? Look, your own Jocha. And Dvora's Itzak . . .'

'You want to make me sound cruel and hard, but you cannot alter the facts,' said Shoshana, lowering her voice.

'Shoshi, women have a beauty, a warmth, a commitment to life. Why lose that? Who wants to be out in the fields all day so you can end up with rheumatism and looking like a prune? For the pioneers, maybe, but no one wants to do that now.'

Dvora got up from the table, walked over to the balcony and, with a loud scrunching, raised the shutters high. A rare breeze entered the house and she leaned out to catch it full on her face. Riva and I collected the coffee things and moved them over to the metal table. It was dark; the workers next door had left; a chorus of crickets replaced their hammers and saws. Riva had made a seed cake and started slicing it and lifting the pieces onto plates, but Dvora stayed at the edge of the balcony and Shoshana stayed sulking inside.

'You know the story of Dvora's Itzak?' Riva whispered. I nodded. There had been a raid over the border, not far north of the caves. He had been on reserve duty. 'And Shoshana's Jocha? He was much older, he fought in the War of Independence. And, you know, he had a heart attack, at the front, but there wasn't any way for him to get back. So he walked, maybe ten, fifteen miles, and they treated him. But he was never the same. But, you know how men are, he wouldn't admit anything was wrong. He did his share, what he always did. Then one day – pouf – he was gone.'

'Boyee, Shoshana,' Dvora cried, coming towards the table and the cake. 'We'll have to finish this, or Riva will be hurt.' She sat down, her chair scraping harshly on the tiles; as soon as she left the full strength of the breeze her cheeks became flushed, and the first sip of coffee exacerbated this. 'You must understand,' she said, turning to me, 'that for all our achievements we are a poor country, really. Always trying to do too much. It's not like it was for you, in Korea or Vietnam, with ice-cream for the troops. So when Jocha died, well, it was a miracle that he lasted so long.' She took her fork, cut into her bit of Riva's cake, and slipped it deftly into her mouth.

'Shoshana would like to believe it would be different if women were in charge,' Riva said.

'Maybe's she right.'

Dvora laughed. 'Look, so-fayr. We had Golda, and Golda went to war. And believe me, she was no fighter for women's rights. She was one of the boys.'

'Have some more,' said Riva, and I said yes, knowing by now that to refuse was to give grave offence.

'Shoshana, boy*ee*,' Dvora cried. 'There won't be any left.'

Riva poured a second round of coffee into our rust-red earthenware mugs. Sated, Dvora sat back in her chair, her large breasts thrust forward, her arms dropped wearily to her sides. And I was also weary, plagued in spite of myself with my failure to come up with a slogan, with questions about what it was to be a writer, that it might have something to do with finding the connectedness of things, challenging or at least subverting all those notions of originality, individuality, nationality, the revelling in particularity that threw a beautiful veil over whatever it was we humans had in common. But the danger in this was that it challenged my very existence as a writer – a sofer – clever with words and creating distinctive characters, building on conflict for dramatic effect, heightening these differences as, perhaps, I was doing even now, as Shoshana stepped forward out of the dark.

'One woman up on a pedestal isn't going to change a thing,' she declared. 'So Golda was Prime Minister. One woman up on a pedestal, while the rest of us struggle with our lot, which isn't even supposed to be a lot, because everyone can see, can't they? – a woman can be the leader of our country. She may not be able to get a divorce, but she can be a leader of our country. It's like worshipping a goddess instead of a god.'

'It might be an improvement,' muttered Riva.

I glanced at her, surprised, but opened for an instant to the possibility. Had Shoshana heard? What might it mean for Riva to feel this? And I grappled with what it was that women held in their breasts, what yearning, what sadness, what bitterness festered there, even in a woman like Riva, even perhaps in the woman who was head of drama back at the network, catching in some revelatory moment that she was hostage to a chimera called success.

'But isn't it a question of justice – of *balance*?' I said suddenly, glancing then at each of the women in turn.

'Would someone please tell me how we got on to this?' Dvora sighed.

'Shoshana again,' accused Riva.

'And would it make the slightest difference,' Shoshana went on, 'if we all were chazzans and rabbis, if *we* were to make the rules – like, say, women now making up a minyan, or calling for it at a different hour, or making it thirteen instead of ten?'

'All this is getting us nowhere, Shosh. Can we get back to work?'

'Yes!' I found myself protesting. 'Yes,' I said. 'Symbols are important.'

But I felt silly with all of them staring at me. 'I mean . . . I find it terribly interesting.'

'It's the sort of interest one can indulge in the Diaspora. For us, we have more pressing things to do,' Dvora said. 'Like making sure too many girls don't get pregnant before they finish school, without robbing them of the little enjoyment they may have. And you, you were supposed to help us. What kind of writer are you, anyway?'

'I honestly don't know,' I said.

'My head is aching, too, from all this English.' But Dvora, who like the other two, could be driven to a pitch of excitement on any manner of subject, could also be contrite. She looked at me with eyes of shame. For being impolite to a guest? 'I'll tell you what,' she said after a moment. In one swift motion she pushed forward her plate with the crumbs of Riva's cake and pushed back her chair. Then she flipped the switch that turned on the lamps in the living room and went inside. On the wall facing the northern window was a small secretaire I had scarcely noticed before, taking it for no more than an ornament, and with the lamplight glowing on the muscles of her neck, her arms and back, and reflected again in each of the many mirrors, Dvora lifted the top of this, stared into it for a moment as down a well, then beckoned me towards her. Inside were a pile of black notebooks; a stack of envelopes tied with string, the top one carrying a hand which I recognised with a stab as my grandmother's; and books: old dusty books, most disintegrating in one way or another. Dvora took one of these, its cover a crumbling red morocco almost detached from the pages, which peeked out from under it in the endearing, depressing manner of neglected children. Dvora brushed the cover with her hand, and the odour of dust and the mustiness of old leather wafted onto the steamy air in the room, unsettling the mosquitoes and gnats. She examined the spine, looked inside at the frontispiece, then closed the book firmly in her palm. 'Here,' she said, with Riva and Shoshana now watching. 'It was my mother's. She dabbled in these things. You know this? It's a copy of the *Sefer Ha-Bahir*.' She placed the book in my hand and gave it a pat. 'A so-fayr should know the say-fayr, kayn?' She smiled, observing me with the indulgent but rather sceptical look that I had come increasingly to expect. 'For this, of course, you'll have to learn Hebrew, but these others . . .' There were books in Latin, English, French, German and Hungarian, and, Dvora explained, parts of the *Zohar* in Aramaic; some plainly bound, some with their covers missing and the spotted, disordered pages torn or creased, some with their leather binding finely tooled. 'Take your pick. They are all, well, rather subversive. My father didn't like them at all. But my mother and your grandmother, to them it was a passion, what they wrote to each other about, for many years – the sephiroth, the Shekhinah . . . they read, they corresponded about this, God alone knows how.'

Dvora dug deep into the desk and let her fingers travel up from the bottom, running them over the papers, the notebooks, the volumes. 'Two dotty ladies dabbling in mysticism in their confinement.' Looking up, she caught the expression on my face. 'You knew about this? You knew about the Kabbala?'

It was as if I was hearing that my grandmother had been addicted to heroin, or had run a brothel from her parlour, in the shadow of that fig tree; and the images the words released were so vivid and preposterous that I laughed out loud.

'I knew the stories. They were bubbeh mayses, grandmother's tales. I never realised they were anything more than that.'

'Bella? She believed in all this?' asked Riva. Shoshana and she were lifting the books out to inspect them, passing them backwards and forwards. 'Here's the *Sefer Yetzira*, in English,' she said, handing it over to me.

'These are beautiful books,' said Shoshana.

'I think you should have them – all of them,' Dvora said. 'To me they are of no conceivable use.' One by one she heaped the books on my arms. 'How do you say it? I am having a hunch. I may have, you know, misread you.'

'But you never mentioned any of this. And it was so . . . so important to them.'

'To tell you the truth, I thought I was sparing you. I thought you would be embarrassed.' She smiled. 'But now I suspect you're as crazy as those two were.'

Shoshana, Riva and Dvora went back to work. They brought out their shiny new pamphlets and books and papers and set them up on the table inside. The breeze had strengthened; for the first time that Sukkoth it was pleasantly cool in the house. But rather than hide away in the study I went out on the balcony again and, leaning on the rail, listened to the women arguing and joking in Hebrew, to the flap of clothes on Dvora's clothesline and, lower down on the mountainside, to the rustling trees that recalled the rush of water in the caves. The lights in the houses swirled with the stars and the bluish lights out to sea; the night was too dark and the air still too thick to discern the horizon. But even in that darkness I was conscious of having scaled a mountain: Mount Carmel, Our Lady of Carmel. I now know, though I didn't then, of the holiness of that mountain. Carmel: kerem: orchard. The grove of Asherah. Shrine of the lady who treads upon the sea. I know many things I didn't grasp then but it was fitting that it was there that I began to learn them. I thought again of Miriam's stories, the stories of the women, the lost women, the story of Dvora's mother was now one of them. It is possible that having learned their true meaning

I love them better, but I loved them anyway: stories of mothers, and the daughters that down the generations were their hope: the Hebrew word for daughter, *bat*, who, the kabbalists say, comprises all the paths to wisdom. The Shekhinah, the Holy Spirit, the bird with clasped wings, the exiled princess without whom the world is given over to evil. And wild old Elijah, prophet of the patriarchs, Jew and Arab, for all his fierceness, first humiliating, then slaying her worshippers, had not succeeded in subduing her entirely. That night I stood on the mountain overlooking the Mediterranean and saw the lights of the fishing boats the lights of the boats to freedom the lights of the tramp steamers smuggling refugees the lights on the boats bringing Papuans to the northern coast of Australia.

The women knocked their course into shape and the next day they presented it to the class. Dvora was pleased; not a punch was held. And they weren't going to worry about a title. 'No point in signalling your punches,' she said. She was driving me to the bus station downtown, and from there was an hour's ride to Tel Aviv, where I'd catch the plane back to Australia. The dusty white light bounced off the bonnet of her Ford Fiesta, and off all the cars ahead and behind us, a blinding chorus of lights reminiscent of the flashes on the mirrors in her house. Tomorrow would be the last day of Sukkoth, a holy day, Simchat Torah, and all of Haifa was on the road, hurrying to their offices in the Hadar or to do their shopping before the town shut down at noon. The burning sun had swallowed the breeze from the night before and we were boiling in our cars. Dvora, uncharacteristically patient, waited with her foot on the brake and her right arm flung over the seat until she could inch the Fiesta forward. The trees were as sad a sight as we humans gridlocked in our cars. While we waited I climbed on my knees and leaned over the seat to check the back for all my bags. When I came up I felt giddy. But in that moment I happened to see a sukkah in a front garden, its flowers bruised and wilting, its fruit long gone; I could almost hear its twigs and branches crackle in the heat. A child was playing in its pitiable shade. She was a pale child, with light brown hair and the luminous, etiolated skin of the children of the devout; she looked as if she had been hidden away for all her three or four years and had never before been out in the sun. The street was so narrow that it seemed she was staring at me, perhaps she was, though at that moment this seemed improbable, more likely she was merely absorbed in her game. The light sifting through the palm branches dappled her white skin and made the silky hair on her head seem to shimmer and ooze like honey. Laughing, she threw herself down on the ground under the sukkah and began rolling around on the prickly grass. She rolled and rolled then stopped, and, looking skyward, lifted her skirt and slipped a hand in her pants. I wanted to point this out to Dvora, but a great diffidence came over me and I looked away. And just then, in any case, Dvora slapped her hand on the wheel and shifted her foot from the brake to the accelerator. At last! We were moving again. With relief I stretched my neck and leaned back against the headrest. All around, the sky, the lights darting off the cars and glittering like crystals on the harbour, was a dome of brilliant white. What rapture, I wondered, was that tiny girl releasing? The rapture of pleasure or the rapture of discovery? In our world, I knew, it is sometimes hard to make that distinction.

Paris

Conversions

Evelyn's mother was an actor. By the time they met in Paris that summer no one in the profession called herself an actress. But how long had it taken? For Bernice over half a century, a whole career, decades of smearing on greasepaint or stepping up to a radio mike or repeating takes on a hot dusty soundstage. The years fluttered by, like the photos in one of those old penny peepshows. Anyway, that's how Evelyn saw them and how she wrote about it in her notebook. *Actor*, she wrote as the turbine hurtled her through the clouds, and under that she jotted down the images: the brazen look of the chorine; the inflated chest and doleful, downcast eyes of tragic heroines. And under these she played with incongruent meanings. *Act*, from the Latin *agere*, to drive, carry on, do. One acts upon. But an actor doesn't, an actor pretends. How then does an actor act upon the world? A writer made a mark, a physical impression on the page. Evelyn was absorbed in these questions, watching her pencil slip a little when the plane bumped onto the tarmac.

Wanderers. She had flown in one leap across the globe. Thinking of this, seeing herself aloft above the mottled earth and landing in Paris now, the notion seemed insane. Globetrotter. Not even a trotter but a bird, a sober-eyed eagle swooping on the world. And here it was: the prize. The best of it. You'll find it all in Paris, Bernice had crowed long distance on the phone. 'Come on,' she pressed. 'Nothing's happening in this town. Who needs an ingenue in her seventies? I tell them I'm a little old yenta and they say I don't look Jewish enough. Hollywood. Maybe Paris will change my luck.'

She led her daughter through it. She treated her to its riches. The crowds at the Pompidou, morning coffee in the cafes, the snake and the crazy red lips in the Chagall fountain. They stayed in a small, elegant hotel in the Marais district and visited the Picasso Museum. Yet somehow Evelyn's responses were muted. She wasn't ready, or maybe she wasn't humble enough to open herself up to the joys of being a tourist, though she could see that Bernice was entranced. Bernice loved it all, everything she could be expected to love, but most of all, and this was less predictable, she loved a small green park a few blocks west of the synagogue. The surrounding houses were solid and handsome and after a day's shopping or sightseeing they would sit in the quiet, watching the late sun's reflection glow in the tall casement windows, before they went through the business of deciding what to do for dinner.

Evelyn suspected her mother of sentimentality. A wistfulness had settled on Bernice's features. Though she knew Bernice had gone with everything from musicians to longshoremen and not long ago a drunk half her age whom she'd met on a stopover in Tahiti, she wondered if she was thinking of another life, the life she might have had if she had used herself wisely. The park was not Bernice. Even in the heat and with the smell of diesel clogging up the air it was too refined. Its bourgeois sedateness was just the sort of thing that Bernice would have scoffed at once. It was the same with the hotel, which neither of them could afford. Evelyn studied her mother in the fading light, her pale green eyes, the sculpted cheeks that spared her from the grosser decompositions of age. Good bone structure, they called it in Bernice's trade.

Evelyn looked at the park, at the velvet grass, the shaggy, overhanging trees. She tried to imagine a man in the shade of one, with a shock of silver hair and smelling of Lanvin in his herringbone suit. Or on one of the other benches, crossing his legs, eyeing Bernice over the top of his newspaper. She almost wished him for her mother. He would take her away to a beautiful provincial castle, in Normandy or Angoulême, and Bernice would be secure at last, warmed by his ardour and his francs till the end. Evelyn suppressed a playful smile and shifted position on the bench, draping her arm over the back of it to get a fuller view. Was there a man? Perhaps there was one after all, someone Bernice was being coy and sensitive about, someone she hadn't told Evelyn about. But that was unlike Bernice, too.

That night at dinner Bernice seemed herself again. They chatted about friends and work and pastimes. They made themselves laugh. Bernice's laugh was loud and warm, Evelyn's more a light chuckle. It was a cheap restaurant in the fifth arrondissement, packed with students from the Cité Universitaire. Bernice spiked her speech with French and, as ever, projected her voice in the crowd. She had a new friend named Connie whom Evelyn wanted to hear more about. Bernice raised her shoulders. 'Qu'est-ce qu'on peut savoir? She's an actor.'

For as long as Evelyn could remember Bernice's friends had been actors.

'What do you do together?' she asked. Writers love stories and Evelyn had always got a kick out of her mother's. But now somehow she felt they were less her mother's, more her own.

'Oh, we go to concerts. To the Academy screenings.'

'Does she live close by?'

'She lives in Ventura.'

'She comes all the way from Ventura to see you?'

'It isn't far on the freeway.'

'How did you meet her?'

Bernice shrugged again. 'On a show.'

'What was it?'

'I can't remember.'

Bernice folded her napkin and took out her makeup case. She was touching up her lips with a brush when suddenly she stopped and put the compact down. 'Wait a minute. Of course.' She let out a laugh. 'It was the show we did for the Mormons, honey. I had to row a canoe on the Great Salt Lake.' She laughed quietly this time. 'It was tough, and boy was I cold.'

'The Mormons?'

'Listen, the Mormons have plenty of money. Why wouldn't they want to invest in a picture? Everybody else does.'

Bernice had the part of a trapper and Connie was a barmaid in a frontier saloon. Connie was good in the role because she'd worked in many Westerns and musicals, Bernice said, starting as a kid in vaudeville. Which did not explain why the Mormons had wanted Bernice for a trapper, but Evelyn had learned to expect the improbable. The film was never released and that at least was normal.

'What does Connie look like?' Evelyn asked.

Bernice's response was subdued. 'Depends,' she said. 'If they want her for a cookie commercial she can turn herself into a bubbeh. But she's great in a comedy, even now. That's been her mainstay. She wasn't like me, she never had romantic parts.'

They left the restaurant before dark and strolled up the Rue Mouffetard. Music poured from the cafes and restaurants, the lights strung across the narrow road sparkled in the dusk and Bernice swung her shoulders to the music as they pressed through the crowd. The shadows and the coruscating light deepened the aubergine tones in her hair. Evelyn had persuaded her to let the grey grow in – it was a pretty grey and softer on her face – but she'd had to dye it again for a job. She was quiet for a while, smiling and swaying to the music. She moved sensuously, like a cat, forward with her thighs – but she was old. Evelyn felt confused by this. She tried to concentrate on the people and the bookstalls and the stands of postcards and teeshirts, but she wasn't seeing these; she was seeing the earth, turning, and with each rotation Bernice was changed and was the same. Evelyn felt that time, that sly trickster, was baiting her, as it tumbled her forward into her own old age. Suddenly she felt sad and tired. She took her mother's arm and led her back down the hill to the métro.

She woke early while Bernice was sleeping. It had been too hot to close the shutters and the sky was light before 5. What a time to come, in the middle of the peak season and a heat wave. Evelyn got up, adjusted the shutters and went back to bed. She draped her arm across her eyes in the semi-dark. No use. Soon she was leaping up again. She pulled a pocket calculator from her bag and a handful of receipts from her wallet. She inscribed the figures from the receipts in her notebook, totted them up on the calculator and in another flourish converted the francs to Australian dollars. Five or six francs to the dollar, seven to eight for the American one. On top of the airfare. She reckoned it was twice as dear from Australia and that wasn't taking the different currencies into account. The numbers danced before her, whirling between the roses on the wallpaper. Evelyn shut her eyes and put her pencil to her teeth. Her thoughts circled back to the park and the wistful expression on Bernice's lined face, the air of make-believe about the great shaggy beeches and the grass. But when Bernice awakened Evelyn complained that the hotel was just too expensive, and, with some reluctance, Bernice agreed to move.

Wanderers

It was an effort to get their bags down to the street. Evelyn had a small sturdy suitcase but a handbag as big as a briefcase; Bernice had a large case on wheels and a lighter nylon one stuffed with her purchases at the summer sales. It pulled at Evelyn's shoulder as she carried it downstairs. They had to wait for the taxi. Boys were filing into the yeshiva a few houses down the block. A black-suited Hasid hurried them on, waving his arms and shouting in a dialect Evelyn couldn't begin to understand. She watched him herd the boys through the iron gate and saw him recede: black bowler, black sidecurls and the arms outstretched like a scare-crow's above a field of corn. The taxi pulled up and she helped Bernice into the back while the driver stowed their luggage in the boot. As he drove the taxi from the kerb there was a growing tumult behind them and they heard the Hasid's shouts and Bernice and Evelyn looked out the back window and saw the kids flying out of the school. There was another teacher with them and the two men shouted at each other above the milling boys, shooing them away from the building with their flapping arms. 'C'est une bombe,' said the driver. 'Une bombe?' The women strained to see. 'Peut-être un mauvais tour, une panique.' 'Les Palestiniens?' said Bernice. 'Oui, madame. C'est vrais.'

They probably lost in cabfare what Evelyn had planned to gain by moving to the cheap hotel she had heard of from a friend in Sydney. Bernice took a long hard look at it, and muttered something surly about it being just the sort of tip you could expect from an Australian. She pressed her lips together so that the high cheeks were more pronounced and started wheeling her suitcase towards the entrance.

The hotel was diagonally opposite a concrete square, with steps down to the métro and a fleet of banlieu buses along one side and a cafe with space invader games and a paper shop and a Croque Burger. The concrete rattled with the sound of skateboards. The boys, African, Lebanese, Indochinese, zoomed to and fro, negotiating curves and turns like skaters or skiers. Evelyn liked the colours of their tank tops and board shorts, and felt for the dark-suited yeshiva students in the Marais.

There was an ancient colour television set in the room and Evelyn switched it on to listen for news of the bomb while they unpacked and rinsed out their smalls and hung them over the rickety shower curtain rail to dry. But there was no mention of it and she mulled over a range of possibilities: that the cabdriver had been mistaken; that he had not been mistaken, but it had been a hoax; that it hadn't been a hoax but in the interests of security it hadn't been reported; that it had been reported but in a city the size of Paris such an incident was hardly news.

They bought capuccinos in the cafe in the square. Bernice took her spoon and toyed with the froth in her cup. In the large indoor shopping complex they came to at the end of a stroll Bernice looked listlessly through racks of cotton slacks and dresses and decided in the end to buy a sailor suit for the grandchild of a friend. Evelyn asked for evening primrose oil at the pharmacy. She got nowhere with the request and concluded that it wasn't sold in France. Bernice helped, although she didn't know what Evelyn was asking for. She was impatient with the sales attendant as they struggled with translations. 'L'huile des primeroses . . . l'huile des primeroses du soir.'

'Oui,' Bernice said. 'Pour les femmes . . . dans la midi du vie.'

'Du soir, madame?'

'Du soir, Evelyn?'

'Look, Mom, I don't think they have it.'

'Ma fille,' Bernice explained. 'Elle habite en Australie.'

'Ooo, Australie, c'est une belle pays.'

'Je n'habite pas là.'

'Non?'

'Je suis americaine.'

'Ah,' said the sales attendant, turning to Evelyn. 'C'est australienne, cette chose?'

'Je crois,' Evelyn sighed.

'Je regrette, madame.'

Evelyn gave up with a smile but Bernice seemed glummer than ever. Evelyn tried to cheer her up by suggesting a gift for Connie. Perfume! The woman in the perfumerie admired Bernice's eyes. 'Vous etes trés belle,' she said. And Bernice replied, 'What for?'

Dirty Dancing

On July fourteenth there was a celebration in the square. The musicians were on a platform next to the entrance to the métro. They were dressed as Jacobins with floppy pointed caps and red, white and blue striped pantaloons. Festive lights were strung around the dance floor. Women danced with men, with women, adolescents danced and prepubescents, toddlers on their own or on their parents' shoulders. Boys and girls chased each other through the dancers and the skateboards clattered over the concrete. Workers drank beer outside the cafe and munched the frites from the Croque Burger. The air seemed to beat with generation, procreation: a coarseness and release of spirits that brought back elements of Evelyn's own childhood. But Bernice turned to her and said, 'Remember how I used to sulk because you hadn't given me any grandchildren?'

'You?' Evelyn laughed. 'You never wanted to be a grandmother.'

'I did once. For about a second,' she was quick to add.

As it got dark more young people came, and an older couple crossed the road into the square, bought drinks at the cafe and sat down at a table near Evelyn and Bernice. Everyone seemed to know each other, from the primly dressed wives of the men at the bar inside the cafe to this oddly anachronistic couple, the man in a zoot suit, the woman in gold lamé. 'All got up,' Bernice muttered, 'like a pair of superannuated apaches.'

The couple finished their drinks, crushed out their cigarettes and pranced off among the dancers. The man took his partner by the waist and they glided into a foxtrot, oblivious to the rockers and the kids running in and out. Evelyn found herself grinning, but Bernice was impatient to leave.

They were squeezing their way past the platform with the band when two men intercepted them. Almost before she realised it

Evelyn was with the taller one, shuffling with him on a tiny section of the concrete. Now and then she looked up at him but what French she had had disappeared. She had also lost Bernice. In any case the music was too loud for talking, even for explaining that she needed to look for her mother. Her partner had grey sideburns and moles. She glanced around again for Bernice. When the bracket ended the pavement cleared a bit and she was able to catch her breath. 'Je cherche,' she said. 'Il faut que je trouve ma mère.' He was mildly bemused. Evelyn craned her neck. 'Victor,' he told her. 'Je m'appelle Victor.'

'There they are!' she cried.

Bernice was at the table with Victor's friend beside her. He wore an old teeshirt and a zip-up jacket and his paunch hung between his knees. 'I need to go back to the hotel,' Bernice said. 'Now.' She gave Evelyn her sharpest look. The men offered to take them: it was dark. 'Merci non, c'est trop loin. Nous prendrons un taxi.' Evelyn searched the street for a cab but there were none. 'L'autobus,' she said, pointing, and looked back rather sheepishly at Victor. They got on the first bus they saw and rode for a block. 'My God,' Evelyn laughed. 'All he wanted was a dance.'

'He wasn't my type,' Bernice said.

'I distinctly remember you telling me that there was good to be found in any man, as long as you were skilled enough to find it.'

'I'm getting a little choosier these days.'

'I've noticed. But you like the attention.'

Bernice shrugged. 'Not even that.'

They could hear the music throbbing in the square. Bernice was lying on the bed. Evelyn leaned on the windowsill. There was a strong smell of diesel but a slight breeze dried the sweat on her face, and the lights over on the dance floor seemed to sway. She focused on one of them, narrowing her eyes, watching it grow and recede and come back again, rhythmically, like a star.

'I can't help thinking of those kids,' she heard Bernice say, but the light had begun to hypnotise her and it took her a while to turn. Bernice was lying flat on the mattress, her feet wide apart, her arms hanging limp over the edges of the bed. 'The ones at the yeshiva.' She came up, somewhat red in the face, and rolled on her side. 'You were right not to have children.'

'Why? You did.'

'Yeah, and look at you. Fifty, and still counting dimes and nickels. No, seriously, honey, what could they look forward to? This world, it's no place for children. You couldn't stand the tension. And neither could I.'

Evelyn came away from the window. 'My kids wouldn't have gone to a yeshiva.'

Crudités

Surprisingly, the neighbourhood was short on cheap restaurants. There was a nice-looking one specialising in country cuisine near the shopping complex but Evelyn baulked when they saw the prices on the menu. Another one that seemed more reasonable had closed for the summer holidays. Bernice drew a line at the Croque Burger. They made do with ham sandwiches at the cafe and dim sims and other delicacies from the Cambodian grocer. They ate these on their beds watching movies on the television. But one night even Evelyn was bored with their economies, and agreed to go further afield. The cafes on the main boulevard were filled with Germans and Americans staying at some large new hotels: Hyatts, Hiltons, Sheratons. They avoided these and walked on. On a sidestreet they found an Italian restaurant that wasn't too crowded. A long open kitchen where the pizzas were made threw out blasts of hot air. They asked for a table near the window, where it wasn't much cooler. When they sat down Bernice fanned her cheeks with the menu. An old man with a gruff voice and a napkin over his shoulder jotted down their orders. Evelyn ordered pizza, Bernice scallopini, and he shuffled away to get their beers. He had grizzled hair brushed back from his forehead, hollow cheeks and, apart from the shuffle and the stoop, was not unattractive, a bit like a rake with everything gone but his depravity. Bernice held her head erect and asked that he bring the salad straightaway.

They waited. Bernice fanned herself and Evelyn pondered on the fact that to travel was to put oneself continually at other people's mercy. She wondered why Bernice did it – why she did for that matter – and it was too hot to come up with an answer, except the trite enough one that it was the curse of their blood. The old man brought the salad and Bernice peered into the wooden bowl before setting down the menu and picking up her fork. She glanced up at the man, and he swatted his neck with the napkin and shuffled away. And Evelyn thought of Sydney, every bit as dirty and congested as Paris, with fewer beautiful buildings that was true, but there was that harbour. So what was this thing about Paris?

Bernice was eating the salad with an expression of sombre patience on her face. She chewed slowly and appeared to be swallowing with difficulty.

'Any good?'

Bernice shrugged. 'It's okay.' But her voice was constricted. She took a few more tentative bites and pushed the bowl aside.

The waiter placed the pizza in front of Evelyn and stood beside Bernice with the scallopini. Bernice looked up with irritation. Evelyn felt a sudden sympathy for the waiter; she began to think of the paunchy workman at the dance.

'It's *swimming* in sauce,' Bernice snapped.

Evelyn cut into her pizza, trying hard to pretend that she wasn't there.

The waiter came back with Bernice's plate, emptied of most of the sauce. But there was a smear of it on the side where he had poured it off, and this was the side he presented to Bernice. 'Madame,' he said.

Bernice glared. Evelyn saw the faintest spark in his eye, as perceptible as the flick of a lizard's tail, as he sidled away.

'Italians are all right until they leave Italy,' Bernice shouted for him to hear.

'*Mom*,' Evelyn whispered.

'Don't tell me you've been waiting all your life for that pizza!'

How does an actor act upon the world?

It took at least a quarter of an hour for the waiter to take their orders for dessert, and when he did it took so long to come that Evelyn walked over to the red brick fence separating the ovens from the tables and asked the pizza cook what had happened. The cassata was delicious and could have been made on the premises, but the old man brought capuccino instead of espresso and by that time Bernice was so furious that he had to stifle a laugh. At this Bernice rose, her head high and shoulders back, and strode towards the door. Evelyn followed, grabbing their bags and stopping to ask the pizza cook for the bill. He was a man with pleasant, kindly features and fine dark hair limp from the heat. He came out of his brick enclosure and went up to the old man. The old man ripped a page off his pad and handed it to the pizza cook who, Evelyn saw, could well have been his son. She glanced at the old man again and a whole set of probabilities presented itself: the man owned the restaurant and these were his sons, the cook, the other waiters, and he waited on tables to keep his hand in, to feel useful, and young. Or perhaps he had lent them the money to buy the restaurant, or they had bought him out and he waited on the tables to keep his hand in; again, to feel useful, young, but also to make it a little difficult for them because he didn't like being in that position, didn't like the way the power had shifted to his sons.

She handed over the francs to the pizza cook and counted the change in her head as he gave it to her. But the calculations, as ever, depressed her, and she walked out of the restaurant with the same contradictory impulses and emotions that had dogged her throughout her stay in Paris. She looked for Bernice, and found her easily enough sitting on a low wall in front of the restaurant. It was just turning dark. The sky had paled and glowed a subtle orange in the west. The lights were shining on the boulevard and, despite herself, she felt her nerves quicken when she saw them. She helped Bernice up from the wall and the two of them began a quiet saunter back to the hotel.

'Madame!' they heard him call. And when they turned he was coming towards them, a long-stemmed yellow rosebud in his hand. He surprised Bernice so that she took it without thinking, blushing like an ingenue. And the old man, with a hank of hair flopping against the glossy sweat on his forehead and his dingy shirt agape and exposing the hairs on his chest, looked almost handsome as he bowed. He walked backwards for a while, smiling a lopsided smile, before waving his napkin at her and negotiating a turn on his heel. Bernice looked at her rose, wilting in the heat, the yellow head drooping on the stem and, on cue, started to laugh. Her laughter echoed in the street and Evelyn was sure that they could hear it on the boulevard, but she couldn't help adding her own. 'Oh, Evie,' Bernice gasped, clutching her daughter's arm. 'I think I'm going to wet myself.' Evelyn held her around the waist as she composed herself, wiping the dollopy tears that were streaking her mascara, and it struck Evelyn then how much she loved this woman, who in some unfathomed way had remained the triumphant virgin she must have been as a girl. And the laughter burst from Bernice's throat again, spurting through her lips until she had to clasp her mouth.